The Naval Cadet
A Story Of Adventures
On Land And Sea

by
Gordon Stables

The Naval Cadet
A Story Of Adventures On Land And Sea
by Gordon Stables

Copyright © 2024

All Rights reserved.

No part of this publication may be reproduced, stored in a retrieval system, or transmitted in any form or by any means, electronic, mechanical, photocopying or Otherwise, without the written permission of the publisher.
The author/editor asserts the moral right to be identified as the author/editor of this work.

ISBN: 978-93-62209-95-5

Published by

DOUBLE 9 BOOKS

2/13-B, Ansari Road
Daryaganj, New Delhi – 110002
info@double9books.com
www.double9books.com
Tel. 011-40042856

This book is under public domain

ABOUT THE AUTHOR

Gordon Stables turn out to be a prolific nineteenth-century Scottish author, physician, and naval officer, whose works regularly revolved spherical maritime and journey troubles. One of his exceptional creations, "Wild Adventures spherical the Pole," continues to seize the imaginations of readers. Published inside the late 19th century, this e-book is a thrilling and innovative story of polar exploration. "Wild Adventures round the Pole" takes readers on a charming adventure to the Arctic, where Stables weaves a story filled with daring exploits, breathtaking landscapes, and encounters with the cruel realities of the frozen frontier. Gordon Stables' writing is understood for its shiny descriptions and his deep knowledge of the seafaring lifestyles. His reviews as a naval officer lent authenticity to his maritime narratives, permitting readers to feel the loosen up of the polar winds and the push of excitement as explorers braved the unknown. Stables' works often convey strong moral undertones, emphasizing courage, camaraderie, and the indomitable human spirit in the face of adversity. "Wild Adventures round the Pole" is not any exception, as it encourages readers to undertaking into the uncharted territories of their very personal lives with a feel of marvel and resolution.

CONTENTS

CHAPTER I
    THE HERMIT OF KILMARA 9

CHAPTER II
    THE NIGHT CAME ON BEFORE ITS TIME 16

CHAPTER III
    THE STORM 22

CHAPTER IV
    STORY OF THE SKYE CLEARINGS 28

CHAPTER V
    A TERRIBLE ADVENTURE 34

CHAPTER VI
    IN SEARCH OF ADVENTURE 39

CHAPTER VII
    LOST IN A HIGHLAND MIST 46

CHAPTER VIII
    CREGGAN AND OSCAR 53

CHAPTER IX
    ON BOARD THE GUNBOAT *RATTLER* 58

CHAPTER X
    WAR AHEAD! 63

CHAPTER XI
    THE CITY OF BLOOD 71

CHAPTER XII
    CAPTURE OF THE CITY OF BENIN 79

CHAPTER XIII
    IN A WILD AND LOVELY MOUNTAIN-LAND 87
CHAPTER XIV
    A FEARFUL NIGHT 95
CHAPTER XV
    WELCOME BACK TO SKYE 104
CHAPTER XVI
    LIFE ON THE GOOD SHIP *OSPREY* 111
CHAPTER XVII
    MESS-ROOM FUN 117
CHAPTER XVIII
    ST. ELMO'S FIRE 125
CHAPTER XIX
    THE BURNING SHIP 133
CHAPTER XX
    GUN-ROOM FUN 140
CHAPTER XXI
    JACKO STEALS THE CAPTAIN'S PUDDING 147
CHAPTER XXII
    IN THE WILDS OF VENEZUELA 152
CHAPTER XXIII
    DOLCE FAR NIENTE 160
CHAPTER XXIV
    ON THE LONESOME LLANOS 167
CHAPTER XXV
    PROMOTION 170
CHAPTER XXVI
    ADVENTURE IN A PAPUAN LAKE-VILLAGE 177
CHAPTER XXVII
    A TERRIBLE TRAGEDY 183
CHAPTER XXVIII
    "THE BATTLE RAGES LOUD AND LONG" 189

CHAPTER XXIX
LIKE A BATTLE OF OLDEN TIMES 195
CHAPTER XXX
COURT-MARTIALED 199
CHAPTER XXXI
SAFELY HOME AT LAST 204

CHAPTER I
THE HERMIT OF KILMARA

There was something in the reply given by young Creggan M'Vayne to Elliott Nugent, Esq., that this gentleman did not altogether relish. He could not have complained of any want of respect in the boy's utterance or in his manner, but there was an air of independence about the lad that jarred against his feelings, and made him a trifle cross—for the time being, that is.

For Nugent was a great man,—in his own country at all events. He was an ex-secretary from one of the Colonies, and at home in Australia he had been like the centurion we read of in the New Testament, and had had many men under him to whom he could say "Do this" with the certainty of finding it done, for in his own great office his word had been law.

But here stood this kilted ghillie with his collie dog by his side—stay, though, till I present my young hero to you, reader. You will then know a little more of the merits of the case.

Than young Creggan M'Vayne, then, no boy was better known on land or at sea, all along the wild rocky shores that stretch from Loch Snizort to the very northernmost cape of Skye, well-named in the Gaelic "The Island of Wings". At any time of the day or by moonlight his little skiff of a boat might be met by sturdy fishermen speeding over the waves of the blue Minch, or lazily floating in some rock-guarded bay, while its solitary occupant lured from the dark, deep water many a silvery dancing fish. But inland, too, he was well-known, on lonely moor and on mountain brow.

And Creggan was welcome wherever he went. Welcome when he appeared at the doors of the rude huts that were huddled along the sea-shore, welcome in the shepherd's shieling far away on the hills, and welcome even at the firesides of gamekeepers themselves.

Up to the present time, at all events, Creggan's life had been a half-wild one, to say the least of it. Though tall for his years, which barely numbered fourteen, he was as strong and well-knit as the sinewy deer of the mountains. Good-looking he certainly was, with a depth of chin that pronounced him more English than Scotch; the bluest of eyes, a sun-kissed face, and fair, curly hair of so self-assertive a nature that Creggan's Highland bonnet never by any chance got within three inches of his brow.

From that same bonnet, then, down to his boots, or rather brogues, the lad looked every inch a gentleman. He was just a trifle shy in presence of his elders and those who moved in a superior walk of life to him; but every really good honest-hearted lad is so. Among the peasantry, however, he was always his own manly self.

There was one thing concerning Creggan's wild life that he did not care for anyone to know, not even his best friend, M'Ian the minister. And it was this: he was kind to the very poor. The fact is, that the lad was always either in pursuit of game, as he chose to call even rabbits, or fishing from his skiff or from the rocks, so that he had generally more than sufficed for his own needs and those of his guardian, whom I shall presently introduce to you. So when he appeared at the door of widow M'Donald, M'Leod, or M'Rae, as the case might be—for they were nearly all Macs thereabout,—you couldn't have guessed that he was carrying a beautiful string of codling or a "sonsy" rabbit, so carefully was it concealed in his well-worn and somewhat tattered plaid.

I am quite sure that Creggan's faithful collie, whose name was Oscar, quite approved of what his master did; he always looked so pleased, and sometimes even barked for joy, when Creggan presented those welcome gifts, and while the recipients called blessings down from heaven on the boy's curly head.

But not only did the poorest among the crofters, or squatters as they might have been called, love the winsome, happy-visaged boy, but many of them looked upon him with a strange mixture of superstition and awe. He was supposed to bear a kind of charmed life, because a mystery hung over his advent which might never, never be cleared up. For Creggan was an ocean-child in the truest sense of the word. When a mere infant he had been found in a small boat which was stranded on the rock-bound Isle of Kilmara, off the shores of Skye, one morning after a gale of wind. In this islet, which indeed is but little more than a sea-girt rock, he had dwelt for many years with the strange being who had picked him up half-frozen, and had wooed him back to life, and became not only a father to him but a tutor as well.

A strange being indeed was old Tomnahurich, the Hermit of Kilmara, the name by which he was generally known. Only old people could remember his coming to and taking possession of the island, which probably belonged to no one in particular, although in summer-time a few sheep used to be sent to crop the scanty herbage that grew thereon.

But one beautiful spring morning,—with snow-white cloudlets in the blue sky, and a light breeze rippling the Minch, till from the mainland of Skye it looked like some mighty river rolling onwards and north 'twixt the Outer and Inner Hebrides,—some fisher-lads on landing were confronted by a tall, brown-bearded stranger, dressed in seaman's clothes, and with a cast of countenance and bearing that showed he was every inch a sailor. He had come out from a cave, and into this, with smiles and nods and talking in the purest of Gaelic, he had invited the young fellows. They found a fire burning here, and fish boiling; there was a rude bench, several stools, and various articles of culinary utility, to say nothing of a row of brown stone bottles, the contents of one of which he begged them to taste.

But where the hermit had come from, or how or why he had come, nobody could tell, and he never even referred to his own history.

He had ceased to dwell in the cave after a time, and with wood from a shipwrecked barque he had built himself, in a sheltered corner, a most substantial though very uncouth kind of a dwelling-hut. As the time went on, silver threads had begun to appear in the brown of the hermit's beard; and now it was nearly white. He was apparently as strong and sturdy as ever, notwithstanding the wintryness of his hair, and the boy loved his strange guardian far more than any friend he had, and was never so happy anywhere as at the rude fireside of his island home.

We never think of what Fate may have in store for us, especially when we are young, nor at what particular date fortune's tide may be going to flow for us.

This morning, for instance, when Creggan came on shore with Oscar, he had no idea that anything particular was going to happen. He had first and foremost drawn up his little boat—the very skiff it was in which he had been cradled on the billowy ocean,—then gone straight away up to the manse. Here he was a great favourite, and M'Ian, the kind-hearted minister, had for years been his teacher, educating the boy with his own two children, Rory and Maggie, both his juniors.

I am not going to say that Creggan was more clever than children of his age usually are, but as the instruction he received was given gratuitously or for love, he felt it to be his bounden duty to learn all he could so as to gratify his teacher.

His English was therefore exceptionally good already, and he had made good progress in geography, history, arithmetic, and knew the first two books of Euclid; and he could even prattle in French, which he had learned from the hermit. It was usual for Creggan to spend an hour or two playing with Rory and little winsome Maggie, after lessons, but to-day they were going with their father to the distant town of Portree, so, after bidding them good-bye he shouldered his little gun, a gift from M'Ian, and, whistling for Oscar, went off to the cairns to find a rabbit or two.

The cairns where the rabbits dwelt were small rounded hills about a quarter of a mile inland from the wild cliffs that frowned over the deep, dark sea. These knolls were everywhere covered with stones, and hundreds of wild rabbits played about among these. But no sooner had Creggan shot just one than the rest disappeared into their burrows as if by magic. The boy had plenty of patience, however, so he simply lay down and began to read. Not to study, though. His school-books he had left in the graveyard on an old tombstone, and near to the last resting-place of the romantic Flora M'Donald, the lady who had saved the unfortunate Prince Charlie Stuart.

After half an hour he secured two more rabbits, and as the sun began to wester, he strolled slowly backwards towards the spot where he had beached his boat, with no intention, however, of putting out to sea for some little time.

With the exception of his school-books poor Creggan's library was wonderfully small, and his literature was nearly always borrowed or given to him. For instance, even in the most squalid huts he had often found books that gave him no end of pleasure. They were mostly in the grand old Gaelic; but Creggan could read the language well, and in the long dark forenights of winter he used to delight the old hermit by trotting out the mysterious and Homeric-like lines of Ossian's poems. Then tourists, to whom he acted in the capacity of guide in summer-time, sometimes gave him a book, and M'Ian's library was always at his service.

So to-day he had thrown himself on his face on the green cliff-top, and had commenced to read his Ossian.

What a glorious summer afternoon! There was the blue Minch asleep in the sunshine, and stretching away and away far over to the hazy hills of Harris and Lewis. White gulls were floating on its billows close inshore, or wheeling high in air around the stupendous cliffs, where their nests were,— their plaintive, melancholy notes mingling with the song of the lark, the mavis, and the merle, while the solemn boom of the breaking waves made a sweet but awful diapason.

The air all around was warm and balmy, and laden with the sweet breath of wild thyme.

And Creggan M'Vayne was just reading one of his favourite, because most romantic passages, when the dry and business-like tones of Elliott Nugent fell upon his ear. Beautiful, indeed, did the boy consider every line of that wild and weird poem *Carric-Thura*. The ghost scene therein made him shudder; but it was the death of the lovers on the field of battle—the death of Connal and Crimora that affected him most. She had given him his arms with sad and woesome foreboding, but at the same time had determined to follow him into the fight.

Here was the din of arms; here the groans of the dying. Bloody are the wars of Fingal, O Connal, and it was here thou didst fall! Thine arm was like a storm; thy sword a beam of the sky; thy height a rock upon the plain; thine eyes a furnace of fire. Warriors fell by thy sword as the thistles by the staff of a boy. Then Dargo the mighty came on, darkening in his wrath.

Bright rose their swords on each side; loud was the clang of their steel.

But Crimora was near, bright in the armour of man. Her yellow hair is loose behind, her bow is in her hand.

She drew the string on Dargo; but—erring—she pierced her Connal. He falls like an oak on the plain; like a rock from the shaggy hill. What now can she do, O hapless maiden? See how he bleeds, her Connal dies!

All night long she weeps and all the livelong day. O Connal, O Connal, my love and my friend!

But with grief the maiden dies, and in the same grave they sleep. Undisturbed they now sleep together; in the tomb on the mountain they rest alone, and the wind sighs through the long green grass that grows twixt the stones of the grave.

Autumn is dark on the mountains; gray mists rest on the hills. Dark rolls the river through the narrow plain. A tree stands alone on the hill and marks the slumbering Connal. The leaves whirl round in the wind and strew the grave of the dead. Soft be their rest, hapless children of streamy Loda.

Here Creggan had closed the book with a sigh.

"Boy, are you willing to earn an honest shilling? Keep back that dog, please!"

The boy had sprung to his feet and seized the all-too-impetuous Oscar by the collar.

Nugent's appearance was somewhat out of keeping with the grandeur of the scenery around him. Thin and wan he was, with close-trimmed whiskers turning to gray, a London coat, and a soft felt hat.

"Earn a shilling, sir?"

"I said earn a shilling, an honest shilling. But perhaps you are above that sort of thing. You Skye Highlanders are, as a rule, so lazy."

"Thank you, sir, but I am not a Skyeman, though I should not be ashamed to be. I was born on the high seas, and I have neither mother nor father."

Nugent's voice softened at once. His whole bearing was altered.

"Poor boy!" he said. "I fear I talked harshly. But come, we were directed here by an old man who told us you could guide us over the mountains inland. My wife is an artist, and wants to make a sketch or two. See, yonder she comes, and my little daughter, Matty. Come, you seem to be a superior sort of lad, you shall have half a crown."

"I don't want your money. I sha'n't touch it. But if you wait a few minutes I will guide you to a strange land far away among the hills. There will just be time to return before sunset."

"And you will take no reward?"

"Oh yes, sir, I will. I love books. I would have a book if you could lend it to me."

"That we will, with pleasure. I have a boy just about your age—sixteen, and he lives in books. You are a little over sixteen, perhaps?"

Creggan smiled.

"No, sir," he replied, taking off his bonnet now, for Mrs. Nugent and Matty had come up; "I want some months of fourteen."

"You are a very beautiful Highland boy," said Matty, gazing up at Creggan with innocent admiration; "and if you is good, mamma will paint you."

"Hush, dear, hush!" cried the stately mother.

Creggan looked at the child. He had never seen anyone so lovely before, not even in Portree. But there was a little green knoll high up in a glen that he knew of, on which, as the old people told him, fairies danced and played in the moonlight. He had never seen any of these, though many times and oft he had watched for them. But he thought now that Matty must just be like one.

I must confess that there was a small hole in each of the elbows of Creggan's tweed jacket, but nevertheless when he stepped right up, as if moved by some sudden impulse and shook Matty's tiny hand, his bearing was in keeping with the action, and even Nugent himself admitted afterwards that he looked a perfect little gentleman.

"I wish you were my sister."

That is all he said.

But for the next few minutes very busy was Creggan indeed.

First and foremost he made a flag of his handkerchief and hoisted it on the end of his gun. This he waved in the air, until presently an answering signal could be seen on the distant island.

Then to right and to left, alow and aloft, he made signals with the flag, much to the delight of little blue-eyed Matty, ending all by holding his gun perpendicularly and high in air, after which he turned to his new acquaintances.

"I'm quite ready," he said.

The march towards the mountains was now commenced. But the road led past the manse, and thither ran Creggan, returning almost immediately with a tiny Shetland pony. This consequential little fellow was fully caparisoned, with not only a child's saddle but saddle-bags. Into the latter Mrs. Nugent's sketching-gear was put, and then Creggan picked Matty up and placed her on the saddle. Oscar barked, and the child screamed with joy, as off they headed for the wild mountains.

High above the blue-gray hills of Harris lay streak on streak of carmine clouds, with saffron all between, as Creggan's skiff went dancing over the waves that evening, towards his little island home. But the boy saw them not, saw nothing in fact till his boat's keel rasped upon the beach, where his foster-father stood, ready to haul her up.

For Creggan's thoughts were all with his newly-found friends and the doings of this eventful day.

CHAPTER II
THE NIGHT CAME ON BEFORE ITS TIME

The home of Hermit M'Vayne, which was Creggan's foster-father's real name, was indeed a strange one. Situated under the south-western side of a rock, partly leaning against it, in fact, stood the strong and sturdy hut. The sides, and even the roof, were of timber, the latter thatched with heather and grass; though only one gable was of stone, and here was the chimney that conducted the smoke from the low hearth upwards and outwards to the sky.

And night and day around this log-house moaned the wind, for even when almost calm on the mainland a breeze was blowing here, and ever and aye on the dark cliff-foot beneath broke and boomed the waves of the restless Minch. But when the storm-king rose in his wrath and went shrieking across the bleak island, the spray from the breakers was dashed high and white, far over the hut, and would have found its way down the chimney itself had this not been protected by a moving cowl.

But I really think that the higher the wind blew, and the louder it howled, while the waves sullenly boomed and thundered on the rocks below, the cosier and happier did the hermit and his foster-child feel within.

Although, strangely enough, the hermit had never as yet told Creggan the story of his own past life, nor his reasons for settling down on this sea-girdled little morsel of rock and moorland, still he never seemed to tire of telling the boy about his adventures on many lands and many seas, nor did the lad ever weary of listening to these. And the wilder they were the better he liked them.

It was on stormy nights, especially in winter, that Creggan's strange foster-father became most communicative. But on such nights, before even the frugal supper was placed upon the board, the hermit felt he had a duty to perform, and he never neglected it. For high on a rock on the centre of the island he had erected a little hollow tower of stone. It was in reality a kind of slow-combustion stove filled with peats and chunks of wood, and with pieces of sea-weed over all. It was lit from below, and when the wind blew through the chinks and crannies, it sent forth a glare that could be seen far and high over the storm-tossed ocean. Many a brave brig or barque staggering up the Minch, and many a fisherman's boat also, on dark and windy nights had to thank the hermit's beacon-light that warned them off the Whaleback rocks.

Having set fire to his storm-signal, the old man's work was done for the day. Supper finished, a chapter from the Book of Books was read, then a prayer was prayed—not read from a printed book,—and after this the inmates of this rude but cosy hut drew their stools more closely to the fire. No light was lit if not needed, and indeed it was seldom necessary, the blazing peats and the crackling logs gave forth a glare that, though fitful, was far more pleasant to talk by than any lamp could have been.

Now, Mr. Nugent and his wife had promised to visit Creggan some evening on his lonely island, and not only Matty but her brother also were to accompany them. They did not say when the visit would be made. Their lives were as unlike Creggan's as one could possibly imagine. They were spending the summer here in Skye, living in a rough sort of a shanty, which, however, they had furnished themselves and made exceedingly comfortable; and every day brought them some new pleasure: boating parties, long journeys over the mountains, painting, botanizing, or collecting specimens and even fossils, for on no island in all our possessions, does nature display her stores on a more liberal scale than in this same wildly romantic Skye.

The afternoon's outing for which they were indebted to young Creggan Ogg M'Vayne had been pronounced delightful beyond compare. It was indeed a strange land they had reached at last, pastoral and poetic as well. Bonnie green valleys, watered by many a rippling burn, and little waterfalls that came trickling down from the rocks, and studded over with lazy, well-fed cattle and a few sheep. There were but two huts here, near-by the banks of a little stream, that went singing onwards till its brown waters were swallowed up in a small lake, the surface of which was everywhere wrinkled by sportive trout, leaping high to catch gnats or midges even in the air.

The Nugents were surprised, but charmed to find that the tiny encampment was inhabited only by sturdy bare-footed, bare-headed lassies, who were here to tend the cows, and to make butter and cheese, which would afterwards be sold at the distant market town of Portree.

Creggan had to be interpreter, for never a word of English had these girls to bless themselves in.

And Mrs. Nugent stayed long enough to make several delightful sketches in water-colours, over which the lassies went into raptures. The clouds in the blue sky, the distant peeps of ocean, with here and there a little sail, the darkling rocks, the mountain peaks, and nearer still in the foreground, the foaming linns, the green braes, and the beautiful cows, with their attendants, all came out on the paper by the magic touch of the artist's brush.

Long before they had once more reached the cliffs by the sea that night, Matty and Creggan seemed to have established a friendship as frank and free as if they had known each other for many and many a year. Then good-byes had been said, and the promise given by Mr. Nugent to come out to the island some afternoon, or to take it in their way home from the far-off island of Harris. But a fortnight passed by and they had not yet appeared. Nor, although he thought about them, and especially about Matty, times without number, had Creggan seen them even at a distance.

One afternoon, the boy in his skiff returned home much sooner than usual.

It is not in winter only that wild storms sweep up or down or across the Minch, for even in summer, and suddenly too, gales arise, and while, as far as eye can see, the Atlantic is one wide chaos of broken and foaming water, the cliffs and hills seem shaken to their rude foundations by wind and wave. Yet speedily as such tempests come, there are generally indications beforehand that tell the fishermen abroad in their open boats that they must run quickly for the nearest shelter, if dear life itself is to be saved.

"Right glad to see you, lad," said the hermit, as he helped Creggan to secure his boat high and dry behind a rock, where, blow as it might, nothing could damage her.

"You think it is going to blow, Daddy?"

"Aye, sonny, that it is. Night will come on, too, long hours before its time. Ah, boy, we'll have to pray for those at sea to-night! I hope your friends will not think of leaving Lewis."

"You have seen them, father?"

"Aye, boy, aye. They passed the island almost within hail of me, in a half-deck boat, which I think must have been hired at Portree."

"And was little Matty there?"

"Yes, lad, and her father and mother, and a boy older than you—though not so brave-looking."

The old hermit put his hand fondly on young Creggan's curly head as he spoke. No father could have been fonder of a son than was he of this motherless bairn.

"But, dear boy, you haven't come empty-handed, I see."

"No; I never had a better forenoon among the trout. Look!"

From under a thwart of the boat forward, Creggan lugged forth and held up for admiration, a string of crimson-spotted mountain trout that would have caused many a Cockney sportsman to bite his lips with envy.

The old man smiled, patted the boy once again, then hand in hand—such was their habit—they took their way along the winding path which led to the hut.

Oscar had been at home all day, but he now came bounding out with many a joyous bark, to welcome his master back. More quietly, too, though none the less sincerely did Gilbert, a huge, red tabby cat, bid the boy welcome, rubbing his great head against Creggan's stocking and purring loudly, while from the inner recesses of the hut a voice could be heard shouting:

"*Come in, Creggan! Come in, come in!*"

It was the voice of no human being, however, but that of a beautiful gray parrot, who had been the hermit's companion since ever he had taken up his residence on this little isle of the ocean.

The afternoon wore away quickly enough, as afternoons always do when one is busy. And Creggan had hooks to busk, and his foster-father was busy mending nets.

But the sun set at last, in lurid fiery clouds, over the hills of Harris, and soon after those very clouds, dark and threatening now, began to bank up and roll forward over the sea, on the wings of a moaning wind, shortening the twilight and obscuring the rising stars that had already begun to twinkle in the east.

The beacon had not been lit for many weeks, but to-night the hermit seemed to take extra pains with it, and as soon as the shadows of night fell over the sea its red glimmer shone far over the darkling waves, on which already white horses had begun to appear.

Bleak and cold blew the wind, too, for in these northern climes summer is not always the synonym for warmth of weather.

But supper and prayers over, the two Crusoes, as we well might term them, drew closer round the fire. Even Polly asserted her right to join the circle.

"*Poor Polly!*" she cried; "*poor dear old, old Polly! Polly wants to come!*"

Then Creggan carried her cage forward and placed it in a corner, where the firelight might dance and flicker on it. Collie curled up in front of the fire, and close beside him Gibbie the cat sat down. And before seating himself near to his foster-father's big easy-chair, the boy handed him his pipe, and not that alone, but a fine old fiddle that he took from a green baize bag which hung upon the wall.

"And now," said Creggan; "now, dear Daddy, I feel just very happy, but I'm not quite sure yet what I shall make you do. You shall sing, anyhow, over the fiddle, some fine old sea-song, father, that will bring right up before me all the romance of your early days, just as this little book of Ossian's poems makes me think I am living in the olden times, and can hear the clang and crash of battle, or the sweet notes of harps sounding low and sweet in halls by the stormy sea."

"Verily, boy, you are a poet yourself. Ah, lad, when you enter life all will be stern reality!"

"I never want to enter life, Daddy dear; I want always, always to be here with you on our own little island home. But listen, Daddy, was that not a scream? There again?"

"Nay, boy, nay, it is but the cry of some storm-frightened night-bird rising shrill and high over the wail of the wind and dash of the waves. Yet may Heaven in its mercy protect any craft on a lee shore to-night!"

But Creggan felt uneasy, and for quite a long time he sat in silence, while the hermit, gazing quietly into the blazing fire as he smoked, seemed to recall many a strange event in his former life.

Suddenly Creggan sprang up. He had keen ears. The dog ran towards the door at the same time, barking aloud.

For adown the wind, twice repeated, had floated the sharp sound of a rifle or gun.

"Oh, Daddy," cried Creggan, now pale with agitation, "some ship or boat is on the Whaleback rocks out yonder! That was a signal of distress."

"Then, boy, we must give all the assistance in our power, and if in doing so we die, we shall die doing our duty. Light the great hurricane-lamp. Keep calm, lad; while there is life there is hope."

Next minute both stood together on the edge of the cliff that pointed nor'ard and west, while behind them on a pole was fixed the hurricane-lamp.

What a wild turmoil of a sea was down below. As each white wave dashed against the beetling rocks, high upwards almost to their feet rose the singing seething water. But at present the sky was not wholly overcast. There were rifts among the scudding, hurrying clouds, and now and then the moon shone through.

"Look! look!" cried Creggan. "Can you see it, Daddy? High and dark on Lorna's rock! The boat, the boat, with the waves sweeping past and over it!"

The hermit passed his hand across his brow and eyes, and strained forward to gaze into the darkness.

Just then the moon cast a pale glimmer across the waves, and every line of the stranded boat stood darkling out against a background of white and stormy water.

The old man shuddered.

"Heaven be near to help us, boy," he cried, "but yonder is the Nugents' boat!"

CHAPTER III
THE STORM

Never would I dare to detract from the glory and honour that hangs, halo-like, around the memory of one of our nation's heroines—poor Grace Darling; but there are deeds done along the shores of this land of ours every winter, ay, and every summer too, that, although they shine not in story, are as bravely undertaken and as courageously carried out as that rescue at the Longstone lighthouse.

Though the hermit was white as to hair, though his beard flowed backwards now in the breeze like a silver stream as he stood in the glare of the hurricane-lamp, he was not an aged man. Every limb was straight, every muscle was strong, and his lowered brows nearly hid eyes that burned like living coals as he stood there on the cliff-top, pointing towards the doomed and stranded boat.

"Creggan, my lad," he cried, "we may not be able to save a single life, but our duty lies plain before us—we shall try!"

He unfastened the lamp and swung it to and fro for a spell, as if to give heart to those on board, then hastened with it down to the beach, closely followed by Creggan.

Not only was there here, in a little rock-bound cove, Creggan's own skiff, but one of far broader beam, one with a sturdy keel, and encircled as to its outside with a great and thick band of cork. The old man called it his lifeboat, and it had done duty more than once before, but never perhaps on so wild and stormy a night as this.

It was quickly launched now, and, being to the manner born, Creggan seized the tiller and the hermit took the oars.

Every rock around the islet was well-known to both. The lamp was hung aloft on a morsel of mast that was stepped near to the fore thwart, and cast its red glare on the seas ahead as well as on the faces of these daring heroes.

Once beyond the protection of the black jutting rocks, it was all that M'Vayne could do—strong though his arms were—to keep the boat from broaching-to, but soon he got weigh on her and then the rudder told.

But how the wind howled, and how the seething, angry waves dashed over them! Sometimes the bows were tossed clean out of the water, and it seemed for a second or two that she would go down stem first into the trough of the sea; and as that wave went racing past her, down dashed the bows again with a slapping sound that could be heard high over the roar of the wind.

CREGGAN KEPT THE BOAT HEAD-ON TO EACH THREATENING WAVE

CREGGAN KEPT THE BOAT HEAD-ON TO EACH THREATENING WAVE

Not a word was spoken. Not a word could have been heard in the turmoil, unless it were shrieked. Yet Creggan knew enough to keep her head on to each advancing, threatening wave. Neither the fury of the tempest nor the anger of the curling waves frightened him. He felt in that state of exultation which danger never fails to raise in the hearts of the truly brave, and beside which fear finds no place.

So sturdily did the hermit row, that in less than twenty minutes' time—and this did not seem long—the boat was well to windward of the stranded craft.

The danger now was great. To bear down on the wave-tops and get alongside seemed almost a hopeless task.

But although she shipped some water she came bravely round, and went heading inland now, like a bird adrift on the ocean tide.

The Skyemen on board the stranded craft saw her, and did not require to be told to throw a rope. Next minute it seemed—so quickly did the minutes fly—that the tiny lifeboat was alongside and fast.

"Quick now!" shouted the hermit. "Lower down the ladies and the boy. We can only manage three. Bear a hand, my lads. Bear a hand!"

It seemed in answer to the hermit's prayers that at this moment a lull in the storm took place, and the moon shone out bright and clear over the tempestuous sea.

Nevertheless, the labour of getting the trembling lady and frightened little Matty on board was most dangerous, and had to be undertaken with the greatest caution.

Nugent shouted to his son Willie to go next, but the brave boy positively refused to get over the side until the boat returned from the shore when his father had landed. His father must go first, he said.

She did return, and then took off young Nugent and two seamen, all she could stow away with safety. There was but one man left in the lugger now.

Alas, for his fate!

Just as M'Vayne's boat was once more leaving the beach, a heavier squall than any that yet had swept over the sea dashed her back and beached her. When the wind subsided somewhat she was once more launched, but had not proceeded far from the shore when she found herself surrounded by wreckage.

Just for one moment, in the side of a darkling wave and in a glimpse of moonlight, a white face could be seen and a raised arm.

That was all, and the unfortunate fisherman's body was never found.

Everything possible was done for the comfort of Matty and her mother and father. A bigger fire was made up, and from his cupboard, honest, kind-hearted Tomnahurich brought forth refreshments for them as they sat before the roaring fire to get dry and warm. The hermit even made tea for his guests, a luxury he seldom indulged in himself, or Creggan either. Then he said "Good-night", blessed them in his semi-patriarchal kind of way, and left with Willie Nugent. They reached the bottom of the cliff by the zigzag path safely enough, though the spray dashed over them in sheets of white and blinding foam. It was indeed a fearful night.

The boat had already been secured, and when they entered the cave they found that a good fire had already been lit by Creggan, and was roaring up the rude chimney that led into a cleft in the rocks.

For a long time the hermit, with the two seamen and Willie and Creggan, sat around the fire, talking low during a lull in the storm, or remaining silent and awe-struck when the huge waves boomed and crashed against the rocks, seeming to shake the very island to its foundations.

Sorrow induces sleep, and at last all turned in on beds of heather, and the events of this terrible night were forgotten.

Morning broke, bright and clear, but still the storm raged on.

Skyemen, like most Highlanders, are very superstitious, and one of these honest fishermen declared that he had slept but little, for every now and then he had heard poor Matheson—the drowned sailor—calling, calling, calling from the deep.

The hermit assured him that it was but the scream of the frightened sea-birds.

"Och and och no, Mr. Tomnahurich. Mind you, I'll no be sayin' it was Matheson himself—it was his wraith, sure and sure enough!"

Prayers were row said, and a hymn sung to that beautiful old melody called "Martyrdom", the hermit leading with his clear and manly voice, which many a night, when far at sea, had been heard high over the raging storm and the dash of angry seas:—

> "Take comfort, Christians, when your friends
>   In Jesus fall asleep;
> Their better being never ends:
>   Why then dejected weep?
>
> "Why inconsolable as those
>   To whom no hope is given?
> Death is the messenger of peace,
>   And calls the soul to heaven."

All seemed more cheerful after this, and breakfast was cooked and eaten with relish.

Then the hermit and the two boys, who were already great friends, ascended the cliff. They met Nugent, and were glad to hear that Matty and her mother were well and happy. They had been told nothing about the lost sailor.

"There will be no getting on shore to-day, I fear," said Mr Nugent.

The hermit shook his head and pointed to the seething sea, on which white horses[1] were riding.

[1] White horses=the spume on the breaking waves.

"No, sir, no," he said; "but we have plenty of food and plenty of fire. Heaven be praised!"

Tomnahurich all that day laid himself out to please his guests. He did all the cooking himself; and the food was by no means to be despised, for the old man was plentifully supplied with stores from shore, Creggan being the purchaser. Well, they had fish and bacon, and the eggs of sea-birds, so beautiful in colour and markings that Nugent said it was almost a sin to break them. The fish were of the best, for off the rocks mullet can be caught with rod and line. Rock pigs these delightful little seafarers are called.

They had potatoes, butter, and, last but not least, beautiful lobsters. What more could anyone expect on a hermit's isle?

When the sun went down the storm lulled somewhat, but it was thought advisable to remain one more night on the island.

After an early supper in the hut, and, the cave also, where the fishermen remained as troglodytes—if you don't know this word, dear young reader, take your dictionary and look it up;—after an early supper, I say, the hermit went down the cliff and returned soon.

"I'm going to bring up my wife," he said with a quiet smile.

"Your wife, Mr. M'Vayne!" cried Mrs. Nugent in astonishment. "Have you a wife, then? We will be delighted to see her."

"That you shall, and hear her too. Her voice is sweetness itself."

There was a roguish smile playing about his eyes as he departed.

Creggan was in a corner near the fire talking low to Matty, Pussy was curled up beside Collie (Oscar), and Polly was making droll remarks to all, when Tomnahurich entered with his "wife".

He carried her in a green baize bag. A strange place to stow away a wife in, it must be admitted.

"Have you brought Mrs. M'Vayne?"

"Yes," said the hermit, "and here she is!"

As he spoke he opened the green baize bag, and pulled out his Cremona fiddle.

He smiled, but he sighed as well. "Och hey!" he said; "this is the only wife I have now!"

But sweet was the music he brought from that old fiddle. Sweet and plaintive at first. Then he sang over it,—grand old sea-songs in which his listeners could fancy they heard the "coo" and the "moan" of the waves, as they dashed along the quarter of some gallant ship, far, far at sea.

Then looking up, and thinking he was making the young folks a trifle *triste* or sad, he burst into such a rattling cheery sailor's hornpipe, that the children laughed aloud in spite of themselves, while Polly danced for joy on her perch, uttering every now and then that real Irish "whoop!" which used to be heard at Donnybrook Fair.

That evening, as all sat in a wide circle around the fire-peats and wood, and after a momentary lull in the conversation, Mrs. Nugent addressed the hermit.

"Mr. M'Vayne," she said, "I noticed that you sighed deeply when you took your violin from its bag. Now, I know yours may be a sad story, but will you not tell it to us?"

"Oh, tell us a stoly!" cried bonnie Matty, clapping her tiny hands.

"I have never told my story to anyone hereabouts yet," said the hermit; "not even to my sonny, Creggan Ogg. But," he added, "when ladies ask, what can I do but obey."

"Well, light your pipe."

"May I?"

"Certainly."

The hermit smoked for a minute or two, looking into the fire, as if to renovate his memories of the past.

Then he began.

CHAPTER IV
STORY OF THE SKYE CLEARINGS

"I must be brief, madam," the hermit began, as he glanced at a little "wag-at-the-wa'",[1] "for night comes on apace."

[1] A small clock, with weights and pendulum exposed, that is hung against the wall.

"I was born, then, in Skye, and not fifty miles from the spot where I and Creggan here now live."

"You were born in Skye," interrupted Mrs. Nugent, "and yet you never go on shore!"

"Ah, madam! there is a reason for that, which I will presently tell you. But for just one day I shall go, I hope, before I die, and visit a green and lonesome grave close to the cliffs where the sea-birds scream, and where, for ever and for aye, one can hear the moan of the waves—the sweet, sad song of the sea.

"I was born in a beautiful glen, and down near to the beach was my father's cottage, only one of many that clustered here and there, forming a village without either street or lane, and more like the towns one sees in Madagascar than anything else. We were all poor enough, goodness knows, but still we were happy. Our farms were mere crofts, and we tilled only the tops of the ridge with the wooden plough, or what is called the crooked spade. We paid but little rent, it is true, but our wants were easily satisfied. We were called lazy by visitors who in summer passed through the glen. We were not. For well we knew that if we improved our land as some did, the grasping landlord would at once raise our rent.

"We were—and many Skyemen are to this day—in a condition of serfdom. The old feudal system still existed, and we had even to leave our own corn standing until we cut down and stooked that on the minister's large and beautiful glebe. For this we received nothing, and often before we were finished at the manse, a wild, wet storm would come on and our own little patches of grain would be spoiled.

"So far was feudalism carried, that the first and choicest of the fish we caught, whether mullet or saith or codling, had to be given to the minister, and the best of the crabs and lobsters also. In return for this the minister visited the sick, with medicine in his pocket—salts and senna or a nauseous pill. But he never brought food. And many an old man or woman, aye, and many an innocent child died, not of disease, but of sheer starvation, although the minister's barns and stackyards, and the landlord's also, were full to overflowing.

"It was not from choice that we dwelt in those windowless huts, with a raised stone in the centre, around which the fire was built, with simply a hole in the roof to let out the eye-racking smoke when it chose to go.

"But in dark, dreary winters those roof-holes not only permitted a little smoke to escape, but the snow to drift in. The soft, powdery snow also sifted in under the door, and through the apertures in the eaves which did duty as windows.

"It was no uncommon thing for some of these huts to be entirely buried in the snow. When one or two neighbours escaped they dug the rest out. For water we often had to melt the snow.

"Food? Well, madam, in summer we were not so badly off; we had oatmeal and fish and a herring harvest. But in some icy winters, when we couldn't launch a boat, and when fishing from the rocks was useless, as the mullet refused to bite, we lived principally on oatmeal—often bad at the best,—and limpets that we gathered from the great black rocks when the tide was back. They are poor eating, but we gathered dulse from the boulders, roasted it with a red-hot poker, and ate it with the limpets. At every door you would have seen a large pile of empty limpet-shells, that told of the poverty within.

"My father's hut was one of two rooms. Our two cows were turned into one at night and we occupied the other. There were many other huts with two rooms and a cow, or perhaps more than one. Often the dividing partition between the cow's room and the family apartment was but a few ragged old Highland plaids hung upon a rope.

"They used to say that the breath of the kine and the smoke were healthy, and kept us all strong and hardy. Well, as a boy I preferred the fresh air. I got plenty of this, because every day it was my duty to collect all the cattle in the village, after they had been milked, and, assisted by two honest collie dogs, drive them far away to the uplands for pasture. Would you believe it, madam, that even this privilege was finally taken from us, and there being but little herbage in the glen, many of us had to take our cows to Portree and sell them? Yes, our homes were miserable enough; but still they were homes, and we dearly loved them—loved the seas that swept the craggy shores, loved the green braes, the rocks and cliffs, and the grand old hills that frowned brown o'er all the scene. For home is home, be it ever so humble.

"Well, I grew up to manhood. Both father and mother were now dead, and when one day the neighbours saw me and some friends start building a better sort of hut, they smiled to each other, nodded and winked. They knew what was coming. True enough, for I loved sweet Mary Gray as I believe only Highlanders can love. I won't bother you with this part of my history. But I just went on building my house. You see it was like this, madam. Many of the lads of the glen went every year to the herring-fishery at Peterhead, and thus we saved a little money; why, I even got real glass windows from Portree, and had a real chimney in my hut, chairs, and a good bed. I built also a byre for my two cows, so that I was considered the richest man in the glen.

"Then one day Mary and I got married, and I'm sure that when we were settled in our home there was no more happy couple in all the glen, or in any other glen. I had no ambition then. I only wanted to live and die in our cottage by the sea. And I used to take down my fiddle, a gift from an Englishman whom I had saved from drowning, and sing over it such love ditties as this."

And the hermit played:

"O, whar was ye sae[2] late yestreen,
 My bonnie Jeannie Gray?
Your mither missed you late at e'en,
 And eke at break o' day."

"Dear sister, sit ye doon by me,
 And let nae body ken,
For I hae promised late yestreen
 To wed young Jamie Glen."

[2] To English boys. 'Sae' and 'hae' are pronounced 'say' and 'hay', and in all Scotch words ending in '-ae' the 'ae' sounds like 'ay'.

"Well, time wore on; a year and a half—Oh, what a happy time! Then a beautiful child saw the light of day, and our joy was trebled. But about three months after this came a bolt from the blue—an order that every man, woman, and child was to clear out of the glen.

"We would have a free passage to America, but the glen was wanted as a sheep-farm.

"What wailing and anguish there was now in every hut and hamlet!

"But the men were furious. They would take no notice of the cowardly edict. They could not, would not, leave their Highlands.

"Another month went past, and then half a dozen men from Portree arrived with summonses and delivered them. These long blue letters were torn from their hands, rent in pieces, and thrown fluttering on the breeze. The men tried to use their sticks. There was a battle, but a brief one. The minions of an unjust law were soundly thrashed, and two were thrown into a pond. They were glad to get away with their lives, I think.

"Police were sent next, and a more terrible fight ensued. Many of our brave glensmen were wounded, but eventually this enemy also had to beat a speedy retreat.

"Nothing more happened for three weeks, and we were beginning to think we should be left in the peaceful possession of our bonnie glen. But one day, much to our surprise, a small steamer cast anchor in the bay, and on her deck were redcoats. Alas! I knew now the grief had come. But still we determined to resist to the bitter end. Bitter it was bound to be, for it was a cold, bleak day in early winter.

"We speedily placed heaps of stones where they would be handiest.

"The fight lasted till nearly darkling. We kept well beyond reach of the fixed bayonets, and battered the soldiers severely with stones. Again and again the order was given to charge. But these fellows might as well have tried to follow Highland deer on foot as lithe and active Skyemen like us.

"At last the order was given to fire, and two of our poor fellows were stretched bleeding on the grass.

"The end had come. What is a stone-armed mob against soldiers with ball cartridge!

"So we gave in, and I myself advanced with a white rag tied to my stick as a flag of truce.

"But the officer in charge was furious. He must do his duty, he said. He had dallied too long. Out we must turn. He would give us an hour to save any small articles we valued, no more.

"Oh, madam, fancy the sadness of that night! The old, the young, and the infirm were turned forth into the bleak cold of a wind-swept glen. The sick were carried out in blankets, and put down on the bare green braes to die or to live.

"Then at midnight every hamlet was fired, and the glen was lit up by a blood-red blaze that tipped even the distant hills with carmine, while tongues of flame, mounting every moment higher and higher, seemed to lick up the rolling clouds of smoke, while showers of sparks, thick as flakes of snow in a winter's storm, were carried far away to leeward.

"I was dazed. I knew not what to do. I knelt beside my poor Mary, but she spoke not. How cold her hand was! And her face. 'Ah,' I shrieked, 'my wife, my wife is dead!'

"I remember nothing more. I had fainted, but in the dusk of the morning I recovered my senses. Not only was Mary dead, but poor baby had rolled over her on to the grass, and there lay stark and stiff."

Tears were trickling down the hermit's cheeks, and it was some time before he felt fit to continue his story.

"Ah, madam," he said, "that was a sad morning. The people of the glen, I could just see, were all loaded on to that steamer, which was to bear them away, far away across the broad Atlantic. I could hear their weeping and wailing, I could see the women wringing their hands and the men tearing their hair as they gazed on the land they should never see again. The soldiers, too, were on board, and steam up. Speedily she rounded the cape, and I was left alone with the dead.

"All that day I lay beside Mary and baby, and all the next bleak, cold night. The people that crowded in kindness to the deserted glen could not get me to move.

"But next day I consented to have my darlings buried.

"And there they lie, and my heart lies also in that shallow grave.

"Since then, madam, and until I came to this island, my life has been one of constant wandering by land and on the sea. I am a good sailor, but I have also been gold-miner, treasure-hunter, and pearl-fisher by turns. Anything that could give me excitement and help me to forget was new life to me, so my career has been a chequered one.

"I have made a little money, and that is safe. But at long last an indescribable longing to visit dear old Skye seized me, and I returned to Glasgow. Here I bought a boat, and having been offered a passage as far as Skye in a sailing ship, which, however, did not mean to put in there, I gladly accepted it, buying stores, &c., and feeling that if it were possible I should get a site for a house however humble, and live once more near to baby's and Mary's lonely grave.

"Well, my heart failed me at the last moment, and when the kindly skipper lowered my boat and stores and bade me farewell, instead of rowing to the glen I landed here with my parrot. And here I have been ever since, and here I may remain, madam, till God calls me. I am willing to live, but I am also ready to die.

"And my sonny here,"—he put an arm over Creggan's shoulder as he spoke,—"who came to me in so strange a way, and has been such comfort to me, he, I say, must go out into life soon and see the world.

"Hush, lad, hush! You must have a career—you must be a sailor!

"Why," he added, "you may yet clear up the mystery of your childhood. But come, children, I fear I have saddened you;" and once more this strange mortal put his fiddle under his chin, and dashed off into one of the maddest, merriest airs the Nugents had ever listened to.

Next morning all the hermits were landed, Matty being delighted because Creggan took her, and her only, in his skiff.

It was a lovely day now, blue sky above and rippling waves beneath and around, that broke in long white lisping lines on the beach where they landed.

M'Ian and Creggan's two playmates, Rory and Maggie, were delighted to see them all. Their anxiety had been very great, for pieces of wreckage had been washed up on the beach, and they believed that every soul on board the lugger had perished. They dined at the manse, and afterwards Nugent took Creggan aside.

"Come with me for a walk, my boy. I have something to say to you, but I must have you all alone."

So off they went, down along the cliffs, and at last seated themselves on the grass, high above the blue Minch, the summer sunshine sparkling on the sea, and the soft summer wind perfumed with the odour of wild thyme.

CHAPTER V
A TERRIBLE ADVENTURE

Mr. Nugent sat down among the wild thyme, and beckoned to Creggan to follow his example.

Then he lit a huge meerschaum, and smoked in silence for a time, gazing thoughtfully far over the Minch at the mountains of Harris, that lay like clouds of blue on the horizon.

"Now boy," he said at last, "I'm a plain-spoken man. You were instrumental in saving my life, my wife's, and dear Matty's. How can I reward you? Not with money, I know. You couldn't have lived so long in Skye without being proud."

He smiled as he spoke, afraid apparently of offending the brave and spirited lad.

"Well, sir, I don't want any reward at all, I only did my duty, and the hermit has often told me that when I clearly saw my duty, I was to go straight for it, through thick and thin. But, sir—"

He paused, looking shy.

"Well, lad?"

"You may lend me a book to read."

Mr. Nugent took his pipe out of his mouth to laugh aloud.

"A book, my boy! A book for saving all our lives! Ha, ha, ha! This is really too amusing.

"But, tell me," he added, "what you would like to be?"

"Nothing at all. Just live on the island with Daddy."

"Nonsense, that will never do."

"Well, sir, I suppose I must leave Daddy and Oscar, but if I do, I shall go to sea, before the mast."

"That will never do either. Now, your hermit Daddy told me that he had gold, and that all was yours. I have not very much gold, but, lad, I have influence, much influence, and it is into the Royal Navy you must go as a brave cadet, and if you keep up your self-respect and never give way to temptations, I feel certain your career will be a brilliant one. What do you say?"

There was a big lump in Creggan's throat, and as he gazed across the Minch he could see his dear island home only through a mist of tears.

But he turned bravely round and said to Nugent:

"Thank you, sir; I will go into the navy and try to do my duty."

"Well, that is spoken right manfully. Leave all the rest to me. All you have got to do is to continue your studies; but take plenty of open air exercise as well, for in the service they like strong hardy boys."

Then he shook hands with Creggan and rose to go.

"We will be three weeks longer in this wild and romantic island, and during that time you'll be our guide, won't you?"

"That I will, sir," said Creggan, his eyes all in a sparkle now. "I'll show you everything, and Matty can always ride on the Shetland pony. Can't she?"

"You young rascal," replied Mr. Nugent laughing. "I believe you have fallen in love with my little Matty!"

Creggan blushed, but spoke out straightforwardly.

"I don't know about love, sir. I love Oscar and Daddy, but I like Matty so very, very much. To be sure she is a child; but she is pretty, and talks just like a linnet."

"Well, well, boy, the sea will soon drive all that out of your noddle."

So they parted, and soon Creggan's little skiff was dancing over the wavelets, her prow turned towards Kilmara.

Dear boy readers, I hope that many of you will one day visit the Island of Wings—Skye. I've travelled the world around, but I have never yet landed on a wilder or more romantic island. I have no idea of describing the grandeur of its scenery. Walter Scott himself were he alive could not do that; but if I now close my eyes just for a moment, it rises before me, its mountains towering far into the blue of the skies; its thousand-feet-high cliffs; its bonnie bosky glens; its long stretches of heath-clad moorland; its streams; its torrents; its castles, mostly ruins, that carry the thoughts back and away into the long forgotten feudal past; and, last but not least, its dark tarns or lochs, and the awful desolation of some of its cañons.

But independent of the wildness of its scenery, Skye is not only a man's paradise as regards sport, but a boy's as well, if he is fond of fishing. The dark lakes abound in trout, and all around the island the sea is alive with fish.

It was not only for three weeks, but four, that the Nugents remained on the island, and happy weeks indeed they were to Creggan, and I'm sure to Matty also. The bracing sea breezes that blew across the hills and braes had heightened her colour, and she now looked more like a fairy than ever. Only, as a rule fairies don't ride on Shetland ponies through the bonnie crimson heather.

Many a dark night at sea while keeping the middle watch, when hardly a sound was to be heard, except now and then the nap of a great sail overhead, or the dreary cry of some belated sea-bird, did Creggan's thoughts revert to those days he had spent in the Island of Wings with the Nugents.

And when the stars were shining overhead, so big, so clear, and so close that it seemed as if the main-truck could touch them, the sailor-boy used to hope, aye, and pray, that he might be spared to go back to Skye, to see old Daddy, and to meet the Nugents—especially Matty—once again.

His adventures with the child were principally among the heather or at sea in the skiff. He was so strong a boy, and so tall and brave that neither Nugent himself nor his wife were afraid to trust him with the child. So, on fine days he used to row her right away out to the hermit's isle itself, and spend hours listening to the old man's yarns, but above all to his music.

Well, the two would sink baited lobster-traps in the deep water near the towering cliffs, on which stood the grand old castle of Duntulm. They used to go for those lobster creels next day, and always found plenty of shell-fish.

Or they would fish from the boat lent them by a fisherman, the saith leaping at times around them as thick as rain-drops in a thunderstorm.

But it was even more pleasant to sit on the rocks, and fish with a white fly for mullet or herring. The idea of angling for herring may seem a droll one to a South Briton, but it is done nevertheless, and many is the good haul I have made myself.

From the place where the children used to fish, to Nugent's little home was a good three miles' walk. They had to pass over a chain of boulders, where wild cats dwelt. One evening they had stayed longer fishing than usual, and it was quite gloaming ere they reached the stony chaos.

Matty was trembling with fear, so Creggan threw his plaid around her, placing her on his right hand, because that was nearest to the sea, and not to that cleft and precipitous mountain face where the danger lay. Matty crept as close to the boy as she could.

Now, Creggan usually carried a stout stick with a pointed iron-shod end. It was well, indeed, that he had it to-night. For they had hardly got half-way through the chaotic mass of boulders, when the boy saw something dark in the road ahead that made his heart beat quicker for Matty's sake.

The something dark sprang off the road as Creggan and Matty slowly advanced. Indeed the child had not seen it, for she had quite buried her head and face in the plaid. The boy was beginning to think that the danger was over, but he grasped his cudgel nevertheless. Lucky for him he did so, for they had advanced but fifty yards farther, when with an unearthly and eldritch yell that dark something sprang at Creggan's neck.

It was doubtless the scent of the fish that had excited the monster. But the lad's stout plaid saved him. Matty had disengaged herself and stood trembling by the roadside, while Creggan fought this miniature tiger.

Again and again it charged, its eyes gleaming like yellow diamonds. Again and again the lad drove it off.

Victory came at last, for with one well-aimed blow it was laid dead on the road.

"It's all right now, Matty," cried Creggan cheerfully. "Come on, a run will warm us."

So it did, and they soon got clear of the "Wild Cats Cairns", as the ugly place was called.

But they never permitted themselves to be belated again.

These wild cats are still common enough in Sutherlandshire, and the adventure I have just related is very similar to one a boy had in that county. The cat on this occasion sprang from a tree. The lad was severely wounded, and although he managed to beat the beast off he did not succeed in killing it.

In the soft and fleshy part of the middle finger of my left hand are still the marks of the bite of a wild cat, with whom I had a difference of opinion. The beast had the best of it, and I went about with my arm slung to my head for three weeks at least.

That ruined castle of Duntulm was a favourite resort with the children. The donjon-keep was still entire, and from a window, or the hole where a window had been, one could look down over the precipice into the deep but clear water; and Matty used to clap her hands with joy to witness the great medusæ or jellyfish swimming about. Very beautiful indeed they were; some as big as a small open parasol, and fringed with long soft legs that kicked about in the drollest fashion.

Creggan used to read Ossian in English to Matty, and she would listen with open eyes to the wild and wondrous stories, all so full of romance and war. He knew the history of the castle too. It was at one time, he told Matty, the head stronghold of one of the M'Donald clans, and here dwelt the warlike chief. But across the sea-loch was the M'Leod country, and in his strong castle of Dunvegan dwelt the head of the clan. This castle is still inhabitable. Between the M'Donalds and the M'Leods was a blood feud, and many a fearful fight was the result.

Once the M'Donalds surprised the M'Leods in church. They heaped up banks of peats and wood in front of doors and windows, and burned or smothered every man, woman, and child. But the M'Leods took a terrible revenge, and for a long time the M'Donalds were quiet. But a thirst for revenge still lay latent in the breast of the Highland chief, and one day, under the guise of friendship, he enticed M'Leod to Duntulm Castle. When M'Leod arrived with his followers the latter were immediately set upon and slain, and although M'Leod himself laid about him boldly with his broad claymore, he was eventually captured and thrust into the donjon-keep.

Here he was kept for nearly two days without food. Then a trencher of salt beef was handed into him, and a large flagon which M'Leod thought was sack—a kind of claret. He ate heartily, then turned to the flagon to allay his thirst.

Alas, it contained only sea-water!

So poor M'Leod perished miserably of thirst and delirium.

This is a strange story, reader, but I have every reason to believe it is a true one. It quite entranced little Matty, and when Creggan had finished she sighed, looked wistfully into his face with her bonnie blue eyes, and said:

"Do tell us some more!"

CHAPTER VI
IN SEARCH OF ADVENTURE

Willie Nugent was as far from being what we call a "snob" as anyone could well wish. Looks are nothing, so long as one is pleasant and affable, so long as the ready smile—not the artificial one—beginning at the lips spreads upwards over the face like morning sunrise, and so long as heart and soul speak through a pair of kindly sympathetic eyes.

Well, Willie Nugent was not extremely good-looking. For my own part I do not like to see what we called "pretty boys", because they are usually goody-goody, namby-pamby, and affected, sometimes even effeminate. But Willie was manly in appearance, and so kind-hearted that I am certain he would not have trampled on a beetle crossing his path.

Creggan Ogg[1] M'Vayne was at best, for the present at all events, only a peasant boy, and had not Willie been a bold, frank Colonial young gentleman he might have treated Creggan with some approach to hauteur. In his face at times, had he been a snob, there might have been a look that said plainly enough, "Not too near, please".

[1] Ogg is really a Gaelic word, and the "o" is pronounced long: thus "Oag". It signifies "young".

Instead of this he noted at a glance all the good in Creggan'a character, and, figuratively speaking, held out to him the right hand of fellowship and *camaraderie* from the first day they met.

Willie was like his little sister in many of his ways, and Creggan loved him all the more for this.

I think that nothing cements friendship between two boys more than a long tour on the road. Skye isn't much of a place for cycling, you must know. If you attempted to cross country your bike would be just as often on your back as beneath you, and there is a probability that a dive over a precipice might end your earthly career. But there is no grander country in which to travel that I know of, even if you do not climb the mountains, many of which, however, are all but inaccessible, even to members of Alpine clubs.

So one beautiful summer day, when a wavy transparency like molten glass or the clearest of water seemed rising from the ground, when the sky was ethereal-blue, with here and there just the ghost of a cloud, and a gentle breeze blowing from far over the wide Atlantic, Willie and Creggan, with their knapsacks on their backs and sticks in their hands, started to explore the land. Of course Matty had a good cry, and kissed both boys.

"Oh," she cried, in semi-Scriptural language, "don't let any naughty evil beast devour you!"

Away the lads went, their hearts as light and joyous as that of the laverock[2] yonder, who, hovering high in the brightness of the sky, so high that he could hardly be seen, trilled his jubilant morning song.

[2] Scottice="lark", but a much more musical word.

Creggan had on his very best Highland costume, the suit he wore every Sunday to kirk, and Willie was neatly clad in strong Scotch tweed, so neither were likely to suffer from the dews of night should they be belated.

They bent their steps first to the bonnie wee village of Uig that nestles close to the loch, an arm of the sea. And here they had an excellent second breakfast, and much enjoyed the well-cooked mullet, the delicious ham and eggs—the latter those of the seagulls,—and the butter and white crisp cakes.

They had tea.

The landlady was good-hearted evidently.

"And is it," she said, "is it that you won't be taken just a thistleful[3] of mountain-dew to make your meal digest?"

[3] A glass shaped like a thistle.

But the boys only laughed and shook their heads.

The sea out yonder was very blue and still to-day, but while Willie was gazing away across it, somewhat pensively perhaps, suddenly first one then another and a third great fountain of snow-white spray was thrown about twenty feet into the air.

"Oh, look, look, Creggan! What can it be?"

"Only the blowing whales," our young hero replied. "They are always about. And there are always plenty of seals about the low rocks, but I never shoot them, because they are so beautiful, and have eyes that look through and through you."

In their march across a long heathy moorland on their way to Quiraing, for the first time in his life Willie Nugent had the pleasure of seeing a real Scottish eagle. He was wheeling round and round in circles, but ever upwards, as if he would seek to reach the sun itself, and ever and anon his wild whistling scream made hills and rocks resound.

"There now," cried Creggan, pointing skywards, "that isn't a lark this time. And that isn't a lark's song."

"No," said Willie, gazing wonderingly up at the huge bird.

He added:

"I think I should like to be an eagle. Is it true they take babies to their nests?"

"They build," said Creggan, "on shelves of rock, that in some parts here rise sheer up from the sea a thousand feet or more. Their nests are huge bundles of sticks, built as a wild pigeon arranges her nest, and in the centre is often moss, hay, and feathers. These are called eeries. Men or big boys have sometimes been let down by ropes to rob these of their yellow, fluffy, red-throated gaping fledglings; but Mr M'Ian says it is very cruel, and highly dangerous. Once, when a man went down like this and stood on the eerie, where whole skeletons of lambs lay bleaching in the sun, and many other strange bones as well, the she-eagle with a deafening scream dashed at him. He managed to beat her off, and the fight for a time was fearful. He signalled soon to be hauled up, but hardly was he in the air before the eagle swooped down again. This time she tore at the rope, and—oh! wasn't it awful, Willie?—it snapped, and the man was hurled down, down eight hundred feet into the sea."

"Terrible!"

"Yes. But though his body was found it was a headless trunk, for in his descent, you know, and when about half-way down, a piece of sharp rock cut the head clean off; and they do say that when well out to sea you can see the bleached skull, if you have a good glass, grinning on that shelf of rock."[4]

> [4] The same kind of accident occurred to a shepherd in Skye, who had fallen over a precipice while trying to save a lamb.

They went on now.

Not only was the moorland covered with moss and green heather, but many charming wild flowers were scattered about, with here and there patches of sweetly-scented bog-myrtle and white downy toad's-tail, and the whole place was musical with the song of tit-larks and linnets.

They climbed that day high up into the crater of the extinct volcano Quiraing. Right in the centre is a round raised green plot, big enough to drill a company of soldiers on. At one side the wall of rock is black, wet, and solid, but at the other it is split up into needles, higher far than Cleopatra's on the Thames embankment, and between these, to-day, the boy-adventurers could catch glimpses of a sea of Italian blue, dotted here and there with many a sail, snow-white or brown.

To gaze on such a scene as this, in a silence so dread that you could hear the water dropping from the rocks, is very impressive; but like everything solemn and beautiful in nature, I think it brings one into closer union with God.

Having slid down about five hundred feet through a chaos of shingle, the boys completed the descent on firm ground, and then bent their footsteps back to Uig. They were tired enough to sleep soundly after a capital supper, and next day they crossed the loch to visit the land of the M'Leods, and the grand old feudal castle of Dunvegan.

And so, on and on and on for many days, by moor and mount and fell, and by many a brown and lonesome tarn, the boys wandered. They cared not either to fish or to collect specimens. Amidst such scenery and surroundings, in the glad sunshine and bracing air, to live was sufficient happiness.

I cannot say they had any wild adventures worth the name. They saw many huge heather snakes curled up in the sunshine asleep, but passed them by.

Once when on a moorland, they felt very hungry and there was no house near. But after walking a mile or two farther, a shepherd's hut hove in sight There was no one inside except the comely wife of the shepherd, who was away on the hills with his flocks.

But this woman was as kindly as comely, and regaled the lads with pea-meal bannocks and creamy milk. Willie averred it was the best meal ever he sat down to. Nor would the good lady accept even sixpence for her hospitality.

They bade her good-bye.

"The nearest road," she said in Gaelic, "is across that grassy moor. It would save three miles, but it is swarming with adders. I advise you to go round."

But the saving of those three miles tempted the lads, and they took to the grassy moor. The patch altogether was barely two hundred yards across. The grass was longish, withered and dry, and they soon found to their dismay that it literally swarmed with vipers. It was the home of the viper, and the viper was at home. They heard them in their hundreds rustling about, and they saw them too. But the lads would not show the white feather. To walk across, however, would have increased the danger. So they took to their heels and ran, as barefooted boys do when passing across a field of low white clover, with bees in thousands on it. The bees haven't time to sting, and in this case the vipers hadn't time to bite even if trampled on.

"That's a sweater!" said Willie, when they landed safe on bare ground.

"I'll go round by the road next time," said Creggan laughing.

However, all is well that ends well, so they went on their way rejoicing.

It wasn't the first time that Creggan, young though he was, had made a walking tour in Skye, so he made an excellent guide for his friend.

Near to the wildest scenery of Scavaig, Coruisk, and the Cuchullin mountains, they lived for a day or two at a hotel that was palatial. Almost too much so, indeed, for simple Creggan's taste. He was not accustomed to carpeted rooms and silver forks, so he told Willie. He was at home in a moorland, he said, but not among lords and ladies dressed in silk and satin.

But Willie only laughed, and did all he could to put him to rights, and to teach him the manners and customs of polite society, both at table and in the drawing-room.

However, Creggan sighed like a steam-engine—a sigh of relief, however,—when he found himself once more in the cosy parlour of an old-fashioned glen inn.

"This is true pleasure, Willie," he said.

"Well," answered Willie, "I'm not shy, you know. I am as much at home in an old farmer's house as in a nobleman's drawing-room. Always keep cool, Creggan. Don't imagine people are staring at you in particular, and if ladies in society say pretty things to you or praise you up, don't get hysterical, for they never mean it."

Creggan laughed.

"Sometimes," continued Willie, "I am asked to sing or recite. By people who don't know me, I mean. They say, 'Now, Master Nugent, I'm sure you can favour us with a song, or a recitation'. 'Most certainly', I reply, and do both; but as I sing like a crow and recite like a hen that has just dropped an egg, they never ask me twice."

There were just one or two little things that marred the pleasure of this wild and delightful tour. They were indeed little, but very wicked. First there were the midges. Among the bushes or in a garden in the glens, there is no going out of doors of an evening without muslin over one's face. If one neglects this, the face will be bitten all over, till it resembles badly pickled cabbage.

Then the gnats or mosquitoes are very venomous. Centipeds abound in some parts, great healthy greenish-brown brutes, and if they bite you in a tender part, it is nearly as bad as a snap from an adder. In the dark you may see these fellows hurrying through the short grass like miniature railway-trains, all aglow with a phosphorescence that streams out from both sides of them. Centipeds are nasty persons and have more legs than they know what to do with.

Away up on the moorlands, however, you don't find these things; only daddy-long-legs in millions in August. They are so tame that they are troublesome. Their favourite seat is a-straddle of one's nose.

"Give us a ride old chap," they seem to say. "I'm going the same way as you."

I believe myself that the best plan is to leave the duddy on your nose, though I confess it looks funny; but, as certain as sunrise, if you knock one off another gets on. So what are you to do?

Well, at long last the two young tourists, somewhat dusty and tired, and sadly in need of clean collars, bore round to Portree.

Here they rested one night.

Portree is a nice little town, and the people are kind and obliging. But there is a herring there, and you can scent him, either in boats or reclining in a frying-pan, wherever you go.

I forget how many miles it is from Portree round the northern portion of the island to Duntulm Castle. Perhaps thirty. The boys hired a boat to take them round, and a more delightful row or grander rock-and-mountain scenery it would indeed be difficult to conceive.

Willie wondered to see the tartan rocks, but he wondered still more to see a waterfall shoot right over a cliff many hundreds of feet in height, so that you could have sailed a boat between the rock and the linn, and hardly get wet even with the spray.

There are no such sunsets anywhere in Britain as there are in Skye. This evening the sun went down in a glory of crimson, gray, and orange, which it is impossible to describe.

Matty could not have been more rejoiced to see Creggan had he been away for a year.

"Oh, I is glad you've comed!" she cried, jumping on his knee with childish abandon.

Then in the starlight, Creggan launched his skiff and rowed swiftly away across a heaving waveless sea, to where the beacon burned afar on his own little island home of Kilmara.

CHAPTER VII
LOST IN A HIGHLAND MIST

Soon now the scene must change, and we shall find ourselves afloat on the dark blue sea, and taking part in adventures far more thrilling than any that could possibly be met with even in the wild Island of Wings itself. I have said that, when not fishing or boating with Matty, Creggan used to be guide to Mr. Nugent and show him all the sights. In these devious wanderings both rode, when the ground permitted it, Nugent on a pretty bay mare, Creggan on a daft little Shetland pony, who sometimes pitched him off and then rolled on him. Only play certainly, but play may be a trifle rough at times.

For example, I was walking—in full uniform—one day in a lonely part of the city of Zanzibar. Well, just as I entered one end of a rather narrow lane a camel entered the other. There wasn't a soul in the street but our two selves.

"There is plenty of room to pass," I said to myself. So on I went, and on came the camel, with his head half a mile in the air (more or less). When we met about the centre, instead of nodding to me in a friendly way and saying "*Yambo sana*" (good luck to you), he snuffed the air, grinned, uttered a little scream and made straight for me. I thought my hour had come. He didn't bite, however—he did worse. He crunched me against the wall and turned me right round. Oh, how I ached! For the next hour or two I felt as flat as a pancake. I have never trusted camel or dromedary since.

But just one little adventure before we leave dear old romantic Skye—for a time, at all events.

It was early morning.

Creggan had just finished a homely but delicious breakfast of mullet, crisp oat-cakes with butter, and sea-gulls' eggs, and after bidding Daddy good-bye, had launched his skiff, and with faithful Oscar in the bows might have been seen speeding shorewards over a blue but somewhat uncertain sea.

"Might have been seen," I said. Yes, and was seen. For look yonder, a tiny tottie of a child high on the cliff-top waving a white handkerchief to him.

Creggan replies, and at once Matty disappears. She is making a somewhat perilous descent a-down the high cliff, which here is of grass and rock commingled. She is there on the beach to meet Creggan and his collie doggie nevertheless. And now after the usual affectionate greetings she scrambles into the skiff, and, with reason or none, the lad has to take her for a little row.

They are soon on shore again, for Creggan has promised to guide Mr. Nugent far over the mountains, in order that he may make some additions to his collection of Skye flora.

"Ah, welcome, Creggan lad!" he cried, as the latter, hand in hand with Matty, came up the little path that led to the bungalow. "What do you think of the weather, my child of the ocean wave?" he added merrily. For despite the severe style of his whiskers he could be right merry when he liked.

"I don't quite like it," answered Creggan dubiously.

"And why, lad?"

"Well, sir, you see it is nine now, and the hills haven't taken their night-caps[1] off yet. That is one thing. Then the sea is a bit lumpy, and every now and then comes a puff, making big cat's-paws on it."

[1] The morning mist on the mountain-tops is so called.

"Well, lad, I start in two days' time for the tame, domestic south of England, so if you are willing I'll venture."

"Oh," answered Creggan flushing a little, "I'm ready, sir, aye ready!"

"Bravo!"

Willie and his mother were off to Portree, so poor Matty would have a lonesome day with only the servants to amuse her. The journey would have been too much for Matty at any rate. After a second breakfast at eleven o'clock they started. One, by the by, can always eat two breakfasts in Skye, just as I do while travelling in my caravan, "The Wanderer".

Oscar went with them of course. Oscar went everywhere. And so much did Creggan love the dog, that his heart beat high and the tears sprang to his eyes when he thought that in about six months' time they would have to part.

And who can blame one for loving a dog?

Right happy were Mr. Nugent and Creggan as they set out over the moor towards the mountains that forenoon, while Oscar ran on in front barking for joy, sometimes starting a bird, and actually pretending to jump after it into the sky.

"If I only had bits of wings," he appeared to say, "I'd soon catch that quack-quacking old duck."

The hills had by this time thrown off their nightcaps and were fully awake, but the wind seemed on the increase, blowing in uncertain squalls, then dying away again into a calm. This is always an ugly sign. Besides, there was a nasty bank of "sugar-loaf clouds", as Creggan called them, rising slowly in the west. Nor did Creggan like the appearance of them, and said so to Mr. Nugent.

"Never meet troubles half-way, my lad," was the answer. "For troubles, you know, are never quite so bad when they do come as we imagined they would be. The cloud approaching the moon is black and dark, but lo! when it gets in front the light shines through."

"Well, sir," said Creggan, "I shall always try to think of that, but I myself do not mind storms. I was thinking of lonely Matty's father if we get lost."

Creggan had a botanical case slung over his shoulder and Nugent a much larger one. This latter contained the luncheon.

They collected a large number of specimens on an upland moor they reached about one o'clock. Many of these were well-known to the boy, but he could only give Gaelic and English names to them.

Now, in a mountainous or Alpine region like that of Skye, however high you climb it seems there are still higher hills ahead of you. By three o'clock Creggan suggested that they should not go farther.

It was good advice, for the sea-damp wind from the west was increasing every minute, while away to the east the moisture had already condensed against the cold sides of the lofty hills, and here the wind was blowing high, sweeping before it a genuine Scotch mist.

Very few people in England have any idea what a real Scotch mist means. Some think it is a fog, some a drizzle. It is neither. It is rain broken up into mist by the violence of the wind, and driven along the sides of the hills or valleys in intermittent clouds. It is searching, bitter, miserable, and will not only wet an Englishman to the skin in five minutes, but will penetrate even the plaid of a Scot.

They now sat down to luncheon. It was a very sumptuous one, for Nugent was nothing if not a good and generous eater. As he discussed his meal he talked away right merrily, and told Creggan scores of humorous and other anecdotes of colonial life and adventure. So delightful were these that Creggan said he longed to be there.

"If," he continued, "I could only take poor Oscar."

"Look here, my boy; Oscar is young, isn't he?"

"Only two, sir."

"And you love him?"

"Very, very much."

"Well, I have a deal more influence than I care to boast about. So, after you have passed through the *Britannia*, if you are appointed to a small ship, as you most likely will be, I'll see to it that Oscar and you shall not be parted."

Creggan's joy was so great that for a few moments he dared not trust himself to speak.

"Oh, thank you, thank you, sir!" he said at last; and then Oscar had an extra hug, for a load had been lifted off his master's mind.

While talking thus they did not observe a bank of rolling fog creeping gradually up the hillside.

Creggan saw the danger first and sprung to his feet.

"We must hurry, sir; it is a fearful thing to be lost in the mist all among the lonely mountains.

"If we hurry, though," he added, "I think we can reach old Donald Clearach's cottage before the mist gets near us."

All sail was now made downwards and homewards. But this meant meeting the mist!

In less than an hour, and while only a mile from the shepherd's hut, they were enveloped in so dense a fog that even Oscar was puzzled. Donald's hut stood on a bit of moorland, that, though far above the level of the sea, afforded excellent pasture for the sheep he tended.

Well, it is far more confusing to walk in a fog like this than in the dark of the darkest night, for one speedily loses his bearings, and owing to the muscles of the right side of the body being stronger than those of the left, the person who is lost usually walks round in a circle.

"What's to be done, boy?" said Nugent uneasily.

"Nothing, sir, but wrap our plaids about us and wait. Even Oscar could not guide us now."

Mr. Nugent smiled faintly, lit his pipe, and sat down.

The wind now began to get higher and higher, but it had no visible effect upon the fog.

The time went on and on, oh! so slowly, although Nugent continued to talk and tell of far-off lands beyond the seas.

Six o'clock, seven, eight o'clock, came and passed. But still no change. Creggan had a splendid plaid, and his companion a stout coat of frieze, but the wet, cold mist that went curling round their necks made them shiver and shudder.

"Is it not possible to proceed, lad?"

"No sir; we are on level ground now, you see, and we should only go round and round and further astray. We might fall into a wild-duck pond and get drowned. Even if we were on a hillside, though we could descend, we might go astray and tumble over a precipice."

"You speak like an old man—wisely," said Mr. Nugent. "Well, anyhow we can have supper. That will warm us."

By the time they had finished it was dark.

The darkness soon grew dismal. Not a star would shine to-night, except far away beyond the clouds. It was pleasant, though, to think and know that the stars and moon were there.

Both now remained silent for a very long time. Their faculties were quite benumbed with the cold.

Then Nugent lay back.

"Are you going to sleep, sir?"

"Yes, just forty winks."

"No, no, no! I cannot let you, for many and many a man lost on the moors as we now are has been found stark and stiff when the mist cleared away, just because of falling asleep."

His companion, now thoroughly aroused to a true sense of his danger, tried to pull himself together. He even tried to tell more stories, but his teeth were chattering in his head, and his lips were all but frozen. He could not.

Soon after there was a wild blood-curdling eldritch yell heard, that startled both.

"Heavens! what is it?" cried Nugent.

Something dark rushed past next moment at their very feet. It was a wild cat, and Oscar jumped up to pursue it, but Creggan quickly caught him by the collar.

"No, Oscar, no. I might never see you more, and you're going to sea with me, you know."

Another long dreary hour passed, perhaps two. Both were now resigned to their fate. They must spend the night on the moor.

Even Creggan himself began to nod.

Suddenly Oscar sprang up and uttered a short defiant or challenging bark.

And lo! not far off, a light appeared glimmering hazily through the dismal fog, and a spectre-like figure, so magnified by the mist that it seemed to reach from earth to heaven, slowly approached.

"Is it that there is any-pody here at all at all whatefer?"

Once more Oscar barked, but it was with a ring of joy and pleasure.

"Oh, Donald, is that yourself?"

"To be surely, boy, to be surely; and is it you, my dear lad Creggan?"

"Oh, I am so glad you've come! This is my friend Mr. Nugent, and we're lost, you know."

"Well, well, well, but it isn't long lost you'll be whatefer. Sure I know the sheepies' tracks, and can guide you safely to my hut.

"Ay," he continued, "and it's as dead as braxie you'd have been 'fore mornin' if I hadn't been out lookin' for a sheepie."

How gladly they followed him need not be told, and how delighted they were to find themselves seated once more in front of a fire of wood and peats.

Donald hastened to make supper—oatmeal porridge and milk. Though eaten from caups[2] and with horn spoons, Nugent told the old shepherd that he had never supped more sumptuously in his life.

[2] Round, strong, wooden bowls.

Then Donald himself sat down, and while the two collies fraternized in a corner, the men folks had a long and enjoyable conversation.

Donald next made "shake-downs", or heather beds, for both, and they slept as sound as babies.

Early astir they were, however, and after more porridge and milk Nugent thanked the shepherd—solidly, and away they went down the hill with poor Donald's blessing ringing in their ears.

It was a bright and beautiful morning, with ne'er a cloud in all the sky.

What a relief for poor Mrs. Nugent when they entered the bungalow! And innocent wee Matty must jump up into Creggan's arms and cry for joy.

CHAPTER VIII
CREGGAN AND OSCAR

"Boy, you've been crying," said the hermit one forenoon, as Creggan jumped on shore with Oscar from his little skiff.

He had been rowing more slowly to-day towards his little island home. Usually he made the skiff dance over the water, singing as he rowed, but his arms seemed to be lead this morning.

"Well, Daddy," said Creggan, with an apology for a smile, "I—I—I'm afraid that I did let a tear or two fall.

"I've been parting from the Nugents, you know, and Matty would hang about my neck and cry—and so I really couldn't help joining in for a moment. Oh, only for a moment, Daddy! But partings are such nasty things, aren't they?"

The hermit put his hand on the boy's head, and looked kindly in his sunburnt face.

"Boy," he said, "never be ashamed to shed an honest tear. It is nature's way of showing that the heart is in the right place. As to partings, they are always sad, and one of the joys of heaven will rest on the fact that there won't be any more partings. You mind what the hymn says:[1]

> "'A few short years of evil past,
> We reach the happy shore,
> Where death-divided friends at last
> Shall meet to part no more'.

[1] *1 Thessalonians*, iv. 13 to the end.

"But come on, Creggan, and have dinner, I've something very nice, and then I'll tell you stories. Ah, we'll all be happy yet!"

But Creggan had another sad grief to face that evening.

It will be remembered that Nugent had not only promised to get him a cadetship for the Royal Navy—if he could pass the examinations,—but, if appointed to a small ship, work the oracle so that he might take poor Oscar with him.

Well, as the boy and his foster-father sat by the fire with the collie between:

"I'm so pleased you're going to the service, lad," the hermit said. "Oh, there's nothing like a life on the ocean wave, and I've sailed the seas so long that dearly do I love it. I'm gladder still to think that from the pile I made at the gold-diggings and pearl fisheries, I can make you a comfortable allowance. Bah! what is the dross to me, and it will be all yours when I am gone."

"Oh, don't talk of death, Daddy; though you are gray you are not old."

"Well, no, I cannot as yet give myself airs about my age, but I'm wearing on. But to business, lad. The examination is a stiff one."

"Yes, Daddy. But won't I study just; and I'm sure I'll pass even in history, though I hate it. I'll read up like fun."

"There won't be much fun in it. But I'll coach you in French anyhow. You are right as to age for eight months to come. Well, of course your old Daddy will get your outfit. And as they give no pay to cadets in the *Britannia*, but demand £75 a year, I'll make it £85."

"Oh, thanks, dear Daddy!"

"Fain would I go south with you, but I shall not leave my island for some time yet. Don't imagine I am going to be downright unhappy,—because I sha'n't be. Your friend Archie M'Laren will bring me all I want off from the shore. Fishermen will often visit me, and your minister M'Ian. Then I shall have my fiddle, and, last but not least, our dear doggie here. We'll both miss you, but I shall think of you every time I gaze into his loving eyes."

If a bomb-shell had suddenly burst over the hut it would have had a far less stunning effect upon poor Creggan than the hermit's last words. Would he, after all, have to go away without his doggie? Had he looked at Oscar for even a moment, he would have burst out crying like a girl.

He just gazed into the fire for a few minutes in silence, then rose.

"I'll be back in a very short time, Daddy," he said. "And shall I light the beacon?"

"Do, like a good lad."

Creggan went out into the clear and starry summer's night.

A great round moon had just arisen, and was casting a broad triangular light across the sea, the apex down there close to the island, its base on the far-off horizon. How calmly it shone! It seemed a holy light. But neither moon nor the bright silvery stars could soothe our young hero then.

He lit the beacon almost automatically and afterwards paced up and down for five minutes or over, then stood by the beacon resolved and firm.

A brave boy now—a hero, indeed!

"I'll do it," he said half-aloud. "Oh, how I should like to take my Oscar with me, but I shall not, cannot! I'll suffer myself rather than let dear kind Daddy suffer."

He felt easier now and happier, and returned smiling to the hut; and the hermit played and sang for an hour at least.

There was a kind of incubus at Creggan's heart when he awoke next morning, and for a time he could not quite make out what it meant. Then all at once he remembered his doggie. The recollection came so suddenly back to him that at first he was nearly crying. But he jumped out of bed, and lightly dressing went down the cliffs with Oscar to enjoy his morning swim.

Then back to breakfast.

Well, you know, reader, "sorrow may endure for a night but joy cometh in the morning".

It did. For that very forenoon a humble friend of Creggan's—Archie— came off in a shore-boat, bringing a long letter for the hermit, and a childish but loving scrawl from Matty to Creggan. He put that carefully away, and determined to take it to sea with him.

He certainly was a romantic boy, and this is not to be wondered at seeing the wild life he led, the wild scenery around him, and the voice of the sounding sea ever changing and ever telling him something new.

As soon as the hermit had read the letter he jumped up and took Creggan's hand.

"This is from Nugent, dear sonny, and he is going to get leave to let you have Oscar with you."

"No, no, no, no!" cried the boy. "He must stay with you and make you happy."

"And I say 'no, no, no!'" replied the hermit, laughing now. "Go he shall; I have my bird, my cat, and my violin. Oh, believe me, boy, I shall be happy enough till you come back to see me."

And so it was decided.

Archie was but a crofter's son, but he was a particular friend of Creggan's, and they used to be constantly together before the Nugents came, fishing, shooting, or wandering over the hills and far away.

Archie thought that Creggan was very clever, and laughed inordinately at all the stories he made up and told him while they lay together on the cliff-top, where the wild thyme grew. It was here they used to meet, and Archie always brought his dambrod (draughts) with him. He had made it himself, and together in the sunshine they used to play for hours and hours. They had no real men, only bits of carrots and parsnips to represent the black and the white, and as Archie was a far better player than Creggan, he always removed a few men from his own side before the game began.

But Archie could play chess as well, and always solved the problems given in the weekly papers, which the minister kindly lent him. Creggan had no patience with so deep a game. Life, he appeared to think, was too short for chess. Well, so far I believe he was right, for in studying for an exam. one wastes brain power by playing so difficult a game.

Poor Archie was just a year or two older than Creggan, but over and over again, as they used to lie together on the wild-thyme cliff, he would say with all the ingenuousness and frankness of youth:

"Oh, Creggan, you don't know how much I love you, and I'll just cry my heart out when you go away."

Ay, and there wouldn't be a hut in which there would be no sorrow, when our young hero went to sea.

By the way, I may mention just one thing to prove the genuineness of the old hermit's kindness.

Archie had a brother called Rory, a tall yellow-haired sturdy young fellow, but somewhat of a doll. The father was dead, the two boys tilled the small croft and tended the cows; but somehow Rory took it into his head to enlist. Some recruiters came marching through the parish with kilts and plumes and ribbons fluttering in the wind, and they marched off with Rory and some other young fellows too.

Well, that same evening Archie met Creggan near the manse.

His eyelashes were wet with tears.

"Oh, man!" he cried, "what will we do? Rory has gone off with the soldiers. Oh, come and see poor mother!"

Creggan went at once, and entered the hut. Such grief he had never witnessed before. Among the ashes by the fireside, with little on save a petticoat, sat Rory's distracted mother, her gray hair hanging dishevelled over her shoulders, and her body swaying to and fro constantly in the agony of her sorrow. She was mourning in the Gaelic.

"Oh, my son, my son! Oh, Rory, Rory, love of my heart, my Rory! Oh, heaven look down and help me! Rory, Rory, will I never never see you more!"

Her face was wet with tears and covered with ashes.

She was still sitting there when Creggan left at eight o'clock, still swaying her body, still mourning, mourning, and mourning.

And when Creggan returned early next day there was no change.

There she sat, as she had sat all night long, among the ashes, still swaying to and fro, still plaintively calling for Rory.

"Love of my heart, my Rory, will you never, never come again?"

Ah, but Creggan had glorious news for her. "Cheer up, dear mother," he said, showing her shining gold, "I am going to Portree to bring your Rory back."

And Creggan, with the hermit's money, did buy the foolish lad off, and Rory never left his mother more until she was laid in the quiet churchyard beside the blue and rolling Minch.

CHAPTER IX
ON BOARD THE GUNBOAT *RATTLER*

Creggan Ogg M'Vayne worked very hard indeed to make sure of passing. I am quite certain of one thing, that did any lad study so hard in a city, burning perhaps the midnight oil and sitting in a badly-ventilated, stuffy room, although at the examination he might make quite a good show, still "his face would be sicklied o'er with the pale cast of thought". He could not be in good health; and I have known many a boy who, bright in intellect, was too weakly to "pass the doctor", as it is called.

But it was all so very different with Creggan.

There is no more bracing or healthy island in the world than Skye, and during the summer, and all throughout the autumn till the "fa' o' the year", his study was out of doors.

On fine days it was always on that green-topped cliff where the wild thyme grew. I verily believe, and Creggan himself used to think so, that the song of the sea as the waves broke lazily on the brown weed-covered boulders, far beneath the cliff, making a solemn bass to the musical cry of the gulls, the kittiwakes, and skuas, helped the lad along. It lulled him, soothed him, so that his head was always clear and his mind never too exalted.

City students often need a wet towel to tie around their brows when at work. Creggan needed none of that; his bonnet lay near him, on Oscar's ear, and the cool and gentle breezes fanned his brow, so that hard though his "grind" undoubtedly was his face remained hard and brown, with a tint of carmine on his cheeks.

On stormy days even, he did not go indoors, for M'Ian the minister knew the value of fresh air, and had a kind of summer-house study built in his garden for his son and daughter, Rory and Maggie, and Creggan.

Both were very fond of Creggan. In fact, being brought up together, they were like brother and sister to him, in a manner of speaking, and well he loved them in return.

But the winter itself wore away at last. And a wild tempestuous winter it had been. There were weeks at a time when Creggan could not leave his little island home, for the seas that tumbled and heaved around, and surged in foaming cataracts high up the sides of the black and beetling cliffs, would have sunk the stoutest boat that was ever built.

But Creggan had not been idle for all that. There had come a six weeks' spell of calm, clear, frosty weather, with seldom a breath of wind or cat's-paw to ruffle the glassy surface of the smooth Atlantic rollers. So high were these "doldrums" at times, that when Creggan's skiff was down in the trough of the seas as he rowed manfully shorewards, there were long seconds during which Rory and Maggie, watching his progress eagerly, could not see him.

Then, when he mounted a house-high wave, they would rejoicingly wave their handkerchiefs to him, and he his bonnet to them.

Yes, winter flew far away back to the icy Arctic regions on snow-white wings, and soft gentle spring returned, laden with bird and bud and green bourgeon to scatter over hill and brae and moorland.

And next came Creggan's time to start for the far south to face his examiners. I shall not linger over the leave-takings. He departed with many blessings, and many prayers would be prayed for his success. M'Ian kindly accompanied him to Portree and saw the steamer off. Then the boy was all alone in the world, because for the time being he had left even poor sad-eyed Oscar with Daddy the hermit.

Yes, Creggan was bold enough to take the journey all by himself—by steamer to Glasgow, by train to Leith, and by steamer again to London. He had been recommended to a small but comfortable hotel, and here he took up his abode till the exam. days came round. Of course everything in London streets was strangely foreign to Creggan, and very confusing. He didn't like it. The twangy jargon of the guttersnipe boys grated harshly on his ear; the streets were thick in greasy mud; all aloft was gloom and fog, and never a green thing about.

"I'll do my best to pass well," he said to himself as he left one day to be present at the examination; "I'll do my best to pass, but I sha'n't be sorry if I don't."

There were other boys trying to enter the Navy creditably, and though many were bold, handsome English lads, most were pale, nervous, and frightened.

About a week afterwards Archie M'Laren's boat might have been seen driving over the Minch towards the island.

The hermit knew from his face that he was the bearer of good tidings.

"Hurrah, sir!" he cried, waving a letter aloft. "I've had one myself. Creggan has passed with more marks than anybody. Aren't you joyful, sir?"

The hermit, as he rapidly read Creggan's schoolboyish caligraphy, was indeed too joyful to speak, and I'm not sure but that his eyes were moist with tears.

Before going to sea, of course, Creggan had to put in time on board the *Britannia*, and after that to be further examined. He was a great favourite with the other cadets, and a noisy, joyous lot they were, brimful of fun, commingled with a modicum of mischief.

At long last he was appointed to a small ship, and this was an ironclad too. He didn't like her. This wasn't his idea of a ship. She lay at Sheerness; and he didn't like Sheerness either, and I never knew anyone who did.

But the *Rattler* was only a gunboat, and bound for the African shores.

Now Creggan was a brave lad, so he took a step that few boys would have dared to take. He went to visit Captain, or rather Commander Jeffries at his hotel. He found that gallant gentleman lingering over dessert. A very tall and handsome man, with a jolly, smiling face, but exceedingly stout.

"Well, my lad," he said, "come in and bring yourself to anchor. You're one of the *Rattler's* middies, aren't you?"

"WELL, MY LAD, YOU'RE ONE OF THE 'RATTLER'S' MIDDIES, AREN'T YOU?"

"Yes, sir."

"Have a glass of wine, my lad. No? Better without. But what can I do for you?"

"If you please, Captain Jeffries, I have a lovely gentle collie dog. Can I take him to sea?"

"I love dogs, my lad, and would gladly have your collie. But," he paused and laughed till the glasses rung, "a curious thing has happened. I cannot go to sea in the *Rattler*, and another officer must be appointed in my place."

"May I ask, sir—"

"Yes, I'll tell you the 'why', and it is just here where the smile comes in. I am too big to get below, through the companion, and I couldn't remain on deck all the cruise, you know. I've had a deal of correspondence and red-tapery already about it. 'You must take up your appointment', said their lordships. I wrote a few days ago saying plainly 'I sha'n't', adding, 'What's the use of a commander taking a ship if he can't get more than just his legs below'."

"Yes, sir," said Creggan smiling.

"Well, at last they are going to appoint another officer, and I'm sorry to tell you, my lad, that Captain Flint, who is what we call a kind of sea-lawyer, and pretends to know everything, hates both dogs and music. I'm sorry for you, boy, but keep up your spirits. Your ship won't be more than two years out, and when you return, owing to the splendid show I hear you made at your examinations, you'll be entitled to apply for any ship you like, and if I'm in England call on me and I'll put you up to the ropes. There, good-bye. Keep up your heart, my lad, and you'll do well."

Creggan walked briskly and quickly towards the pier; he was determined he would not give way for anything.

Just two years after this we still find the *Rattler* cruising about the west coast of Africa, and despite its unhealthiness there was no extra sickness on board and no fever.

Captain Flint was really a good sailor, but snappish and ill-natured. He bullied everyone around him, and often punished his men and boys severely.

Under such a commander it is almost needless to say that Creggan's life was not altogether a happy one. However, he did his duty, and did it with method and precision. He was so strong and healthy that there was no one on board that ship who could make him nervous. But he used to pity some of his messmates who, though a year or two older, were smaller and less bold than he. Both the first and second lieutenants were real good fellows, but this little fiery-haired, ferret-eyed commander, or skipper, as all hands plainly called him when out of hearing, cowed even these.

I do not suppose that Flint could help himself, and it is always best, I think, to say all one can for even bad men. Now, whisper—the commander's wine-cellar was far too big for him. I do not think anybody ever saw the little man intoxicated, on deck at all events, but that curse of our nation—alcohol—made him crabbed and peevish, and he did not care then whom he insulted.

One or two instances of how Flint carried on may serve to show my readers what a tyrant even the commander of a Royal Navy screw gunboat may make himself, on a lonely coast like that of the western shores of Africa.

Please remember that I am not depending on my imagination for my facts, the experiences were my own.

The surgeon of the *Rattler*—and there was but one—for the craft was only 800 tons, was a sturdy Scot, who did his duty, and did not care a pin-head for anyone. His very independence annoyed Flint.

"I'll bring that saucy Scot to his senses," he said one night to his first lieutenant, who was dining with him.

The first luff, laughing, told the doctor next morning that he was to be brought down a peg, and asked him how he would like it.

The surgeon—Grant, let us call him—merely laughed and said quietly:

"It won't be that little skin-Flint that will do it. Why, Lacy, I could take him up with one hand and hold him overboard while I shook his teeth out into the sea. I could mop up the quarter-deck with him, then stand him on his head on the top of the capstan."

Everyone laughed, because everyone liked the surgeon.

But as the commander had said he would make the surgeon haul down his flag, he determined to act, and went to bed grinning to himself.

The persecution began next morning.

CHAPTER X
WAR AHEAD!

The skipper was on the bridge near the quarter-deck next morning, when the surgeon tripped up the ladder, saluted, and handed him the sick-list book.

"What!" shouted Flint. "Fifteen on the sick-list, sir, out of a small crew like this?"

"Yes, sir."

"What's the meaning of it, sir? What's the meaning of it? I've been in a line-of-battle ship with no more on the list than this."

"The cases, Captain Flint, are chiefly coast ulcer. I do my duty, sir, and it will go hard with anyone who denies it. And it is also my duty, sir, to inform you, that if you continue to get into red-faced rages, like that from which you are now suffering, you will before long have a fit of apoplexy."

"When I want your valuable advice, Dr. Grant, I will send for you."

"Thank you, Captain Flint. Delighted, I'm sure!"

The captain took a turn up and down the bridge.

Then returning to the charge:

"Is there any hygienic measure you could suggest for the removal of this ulcer plague?" he roared.

"Oh, yes, the place where the sick lie is as hot and stuffy as the stoke-hole. I'd like screen-berths on deck."

"Well, well, have my quarter-deck by all means!"

The commander was talking sarcastically now, of course.

But the surgeon's chance had come.

"Thank you, sir," he cried, laughing in spite of himself. Then he wheeled, and was down below before Flint had time to utter another word.

Now, the little man dearly loved his quarter-deck. He was king there; a sea-king and monarch of all he surveyed. Well, he was in the habit of taking a sleep-siesta every afternoon, as soon as luncheon was over. And this was the surgeon's time. He got the carpenter and his mate to remove their shoes, and put up the screen-berths and hang the hammocks as silently as moles work. Then the worst cases were got up and put to bed.

It was really very nice for them, because they could look at the blue sparkling sea, get fresh air, and watch everything that went on around them. When the skipper came on deck, he was fain to catch hold of a stay to prevent himself from falling. So at least the quarter-master said. But he himself had given the order, and as the surgeon had obeyed it, nothing could now be done.

Two days after was the Sabbath, and before divisions the commander and first lieutenant, accompanied by Surgeon Grant, walked round the ship and down below to inspect. As usual, those of the sick who could stand were drawn up in single file. Now, the skipper ought to have asked the surgeon, not the men, about their complaints, only Flint was still intent on bringing the doctor low.

"What's the matter with you, my man? And what is the surgeon giving you?"

"It is my business to answer that question, sir," said the surgeon angrily.

"I'm not talking to you, doctor."

Grant said nothing. He simply lifted his cap, wheeled about and walked on deck.

His flag wasn't down yet.

The war went on.

Next morning a boy was, by the captain's orders, introduced to the gunner's daughter for some trifling offence. This means that without being undressed, a boy is tied breast-downwards to a gun, and in this position receives a rope's-ending.

The doctor was walking the quarter-deck laughing and chatting with a messmate, when the commander advanced.

"Surgeon Grant," he said, "attend to that boy's flogging."

Now, if a real flogging[1] or "flaying match" had to be played, and a man—guilty of some great crime—was stripped to the waist and tied to the rigging to receive four dozen with the cat, not only the doctor, in cocked hat and lashed to his sword, but all the officers and crew as well would have to be piped up to witness this fearful punishment. But it was no part of the surgeon's duty to attend a boy's birching. That indeed would have been *infra dig*. So, on this occasion the surgeon simply gave Flint a haughty stare, then continued his conversation.

[1] Flogging is now done away with in our Navy.

"Why, this is insubordination, sir! I've a good mind to put you under arrest."

Then, as the bo's'n's mate expressed it, "the doctor's dander riz". But he kept his temper.

"Captain Flint," he said, "you can put me under arrest if you please, but I shall not lower the dignity of a profession which is as honourable as yours by attending a boy's rope's-ending."

The commander stamped and paused.

"I'll—I'll—" he began.

"Now, now, now," cried the surgeon, "you'll have a fit! I warn you, sir. You're short-necked, sir, and excitable, and if—"

He got no further.

"Confound you, sir, I'll pay you out for this!"

Then he rushed below.

But there was nothing done about it. Flint simply nursed his wrath to keep it warm.

One day, some time after this, the ship grounded on a sand-bank. Luckily it was at low tide, so when the tide began to rise, all hands, even the officers, had orders from the commander to arm themselves each with a 56-lb. shot, and rush fore and aft, and aft and fore, in a body to help to swing the ship off.

But Grant stood quietly by the binnacle.

"Did you hear the order, sir?" roared the commander. "Get your shot and join the crew."

"Na, na, na," answered Grant, in his native Doric. "Man, I've gotten a laddie's back to see till, and a poultice to mak. Jist tak' a shot yoursel', man."

On this occasion the captain had to smile.

But the war culminated about a month after this, and on that occasion, it must be confessed, the doctor did lose his temper, and had the captain been able to get witnesses he could have tried the surgeon by court-martial, for Grant's conduct amounted almost to mutiny, albeit the provocation he received was very great.

You cannot insult a Scot more than by attempting to throw mud at his country.

Well, while anchored near a village the officers generally went on shore in mufti, and Grant was in the habit of wearing a Scotch Glengarry bonnet (called a cap by the English).

Now it occurred to the commander that he might give the surgeon a knock-down over this. So he called the assistant paymaster, and ordered him to write what is called "a memo.", which is really a tyrannical edict, which all the officers, however, must sign.

Flint dictated the memo., and when presented to him for inspection, it read as follows:—

MEMO.

It is my directions that the officers of this ship shall go on shore dressed as gentlemen.

This would have been insult enough to poor Grant, but the skipper added to it greatly, for between the words *as* and *gentlemen* he wrote the word *English*, making the memo, read as *English gentlemen*.

The doctor was writing in his cabin, between which and the commander's saloon there was only a single bulkhead. He was the last officer to be asked to sign the memo.

When he read it, then indeed his "dander riz".

His fury was fearful to behold, and the commander could hear all that was said.

Grant sprang to his feet.

"This from Flint!" he roared; "and he dares ask me to sign it! Is not a Scotch gentleman as good as an English gentleman any day? See here, Maxwell, I tear it in pieces, and fling them on the deck. Take it back to him thus if you choose, but he shall not insult my native land!"

At this moment the commander was heard shouting:

"Quartermaster!"

"Ay, ay, sir."

"Send Dr. Grant to my cabin at once."

Grant required no two biddings. He rushed up the ward-room companion and thundered down the captain's stair, while officers, quartermaster, and all rushed forward, determined not to be witnesses to anything that might happen.

Perhaps never on board a man-o'-war before did such a scene take place in a commander's cabin.

Grant had picked up a handful of the torn-up memo., and quickly now drawing back Flint's curtain he stood like an angry bull in the doorway.

The skipper started to his feet. He had been sitting in his easy-chair.

"Sir—" he began.

But he got no further.

"You sent this memo. to me? There! I fling it at your feet. I ought to fling it into your white and frightened face. How dare you insult my country, sir? You little tippling whipper-snapper!"

"This is rank mutiny!" cried the skipper. "I'll call the first lieutenant and quartermaster."

"You may call till you are hoarse, and they will not come to witness against me. Even your boy has fled, and now I'll speak my mind."

Here the commander attempted to run the blockade and force his way out.

"Stand back, sir," cried Grant, "or worse will happen!"

"Now, sir, listen to me. I have stood your tyranny long enough and as calmly as I could, and now it is my turn, and I tell you plainly that whenever and wherever I find you on shore in plain clothes, I'll give you such a thrashing that you won't forget it the longest day you live. Good-morning."

This ended the scene.

Some captains would have shot Grant where he stood. But Flint was terror-stricken and silent.

He was on deck again half an hour afterwards, looking as if nothing had happened.

Next evening the steward came in to say, with Captain Flint's compliments, that he wished Dr. Grant to come and share a bottle of wine with him.

"Tell the captain, with my compliments, that I refuse."

That was the answer.

The steward returned in three minutes' time.

"The captain wants to see you, sir."

"Oh, certainly; that is an order."

And off he marched to obey it.

When he entered Flint stood up, smiling.

"I'm afraid, doctor," he said, "I've been too hard. Are you willing to let bygones be bygones?"

Who could have resisted an appeal like this? It was as nearly an apology as any captain could make to a junior officer. And he held out his hand as he spoke.

"Willing," cried Grant with Scotch enthusiasm, "ay, and delighted! You know, sir, I'm only a wild Highlander, so I lost my balance when—but there, never mind. 'Tis past and gone for ever and for aye."

Then there was a hearty handshake and both sat down.

"There is the wine," said the commander, "and there is the whisky."

"I'll have the whisky," said Grant, "though not much. But it is the wine of my country, sir."

The commander smiled, and Grant drew the cruet towards him, quoting as he did so and while he tapped the bottle, the words of Burns:

> "When neebors anger at a plea,
> And just as wud[2] as wud can be,
> How easy can the barley-bree
> Cement the quarrel!
> It's aye the cheapest lawyer's fee
> To taste the barrel."

[2] Wud=angry.

Some time after this the commander fell ill, and so kind was Grant to him, and so constant in his attentions, that all animosity fled for ever, and Flint really got fond of Grant, whom he delighted when visiting on shore to call "my surgeon".

Well, whatever ill-feeling officers or men may exhibit toward each other if penned up in a small mess, when war comes it is all forgotten, and the British sailors and marines, when sent on shore to fight, stand shoulder to shoulder, and woe be to the foe who faces them.

One day, while lying off Loanda, startling intelligence came to the commander of the *Rattler* from a steam launch that had been despatched in all haste to hurry her up to the mouth of the Benin river. A party of European traders, many British as well as foreign, had been surrounded and massacred to a man. The steam launch belonged to H.M.S. *Centiped*, a cruiser far larger than the *Rattler*. The officer in charge could hardly stop to eat or drink, but food was handed over the side, and in ten minutes' time she was once more under weigh and steering rapidly north.

A glance at a map of Africa will show you that Loanda lies well to the south of the Bight of Benin, and show you, too, where the great river Niger or Quorra empties itself into the Gulf of Guinea.

All was now bustle and stir on board the *Rattler*. Steam was ordered to be got up at once. There used to be disputes between the engineer and captain, but these were all forgotten now.

Would you believe it, reader, that all hands, from the commander to the dark-skinned Kroomen from Sierra Leone, were as merry and happy as if they were going to a fancy ball instead of to battle and to carnage. Such is your British sailor.

Dinner was ordered half an hour sooner, so that the men should have plenty of time to get their arms and accoutrements into perfect fighting trim before the sun went down at four bells in the first dog-watch.

The captain felt in fine form; for whatever faults he had, he certainly was no coward.

He liked his middies well, too, when he had not those nasty little fits of bad temper on. To-day he walked up and down the quarter-deck holding our hero Creggan by the arm, and not only talking to him but encouraging the boy himself to talk.

Creggan was nothing loath. But from some words he let fall, Commander Flint found he had a romantic early history.

"You must come and dine with me to-night," he said, "and tell me all your story. You and Dr. Grant."

"Oh, thank you, sir.

"And now," added Creggan, "may I take the liberty of asking you just one question?"

"Certainly, Mr. M'Vayne, certainly."

"Well, sir, do you think we shall have a real battle with the savages?"

"Sure to, and perhaps half a dozen. The case seems very grave, you know."

"Well, I'll be glad to see some fighting."

"Bravo! And now you can go and tell the steward I want him."

Off went Creggan, and next minute up popped the steward.

"Sir?" he said.

"Splice the main brace," said the commander.

(This means, reader, an extra glass of rum to all hands.)

By this time the *Rattler* was ploughing her way through the bright blue sea, and heading for the north.

Exciting adventures were before them.

CHAPTER XI
THE CITY OF BLOOD

"In the city of Benin," said the commander, that night at dinner, "and all around it, westward to Dahomey, Abomey, and Ashantee, they are a bad lot, an accursed lot, treacherous and cruel to a degree."

"I've heard it said," Creggan ventured to remark, "that the men of Benin are not brave, Captain Flint."

The captain shook his head and smiled.

"We must not believe all we hear. Remarks like these are generally made by gentlemen journalists who live at home at ease. But I've been there, lad, and found it altogether different."

The dinner passed off very comfortably indeed. Dr. Grant would not touch wine, but when dessert had been removed, and the commander ordered the steward to bring in the tumblers, he helped himself somewhat liberally to the wine of his native land.

"Well, Captain Flint," he said, "I haven't really been a dog's watch[1] in the service, as you might say, and with the exception of a brush with the Arabs on the East Coast of Africa, and north of the Equator, I've never seen what we in Scotland term 'solid fighting'."

> [1] The dog-watches are from four to six and six to eight every evening, and therefore only two hours long, while all the others are four hours.

"I think you will have a chance now, doctor."

"Ay, sir; and I won't begrudge flailing around with the claymore a bit, and seeing my patients afterwards."

"Tell us something about Benin, sir, if you please," said Creggan.

"Well, lad, I've told you that the people are fearful savages when aroused, although seemingly quiet enough at all other times. Benin, you know, is really a country extending to Ashantee. Once exceedingly powerful, and densely populated still, it is now divided into many half-independent states.

"The city itself lies nearly eighty miles up the river Niger, from the Atlantic Ocean or Gulf of Guinea. It is about twenty miles inland. This river is miles wide where it joins the sea, and if you once get over the bar, it may be cautiously navigated by boats and launches nearly all the way up. But there is the dreaded bar to cross. What are those lines, lad, about Greenland's icy mountains?"

"Oh, I know," said Creggan, holding up one arm as if he were a schoolboy.

"'From Greenland's icy mountains,
From India's coral strand;
Where Afric's sunny fountains
Roll down their golden sand.'

"Is there a lot of golden sand, sir?"

"There is a lot of constantly shifting black-brown mud, but if you expect to find gold or see it, you'll be sadly disappointed.

"The city itself contains from twelve to twenty thousand natives, as well as I could guess.

"The king is a savage emperor of the deepest and blackest dye. His reign is a reign of terror. He rules his unhappy subjects with rods of iron and knives of steel. I hope you'll never see what I have seen there. The sight of those human sacrifices, boy, would return to your dreams for years afterwards. They do to mine, whenever I am ill or troubled."

"You saw them, sir?"

"I was despatched on a mission of peace, one might say. I had a bodyguard of fifty armed men, and blue-jackets and marines, and had need been, we could have fought our way to our boats through all the king's fanatics.

"The mission was this. You must know that all the coast-line is British, and the people at home were constantly being shocked to hear of the terrible human sacrifices occurring in Benin, while it was nothing uncommon to find a mutilated and headless corpse, that the sharks had spared, cast up with outspread arms on the beach."

"Terrible!" said Dr. Grant.

"Yes. And my mission was not to take revenge, but to endeavour pacifically to get the king to give up those massacres of men, women, and helpless children, for whom he had no more pity than the self-named sportsmen who follow the Queen's hounds have for the innocent and hunted stag.

"The king was amply supplied with bad rum or arrack, the worst and most fiery of all spirits. He got this stuff from the palm-oil traders of Gato, men who came from Portugal and even Britain itself.

"He was three sheets in the wind when we arrived on a beautiful afternoon. He told us, through our interpreter, how delighted he was to see us, and how he would give us a grand show next morning.

"We occupied portions of his grass-hut palace, keeping well together after lying down on grass mats, with our arms by our sides; for as the king had got drunker and drunker, and was now yelling and whooping like a madman, we feared he would make an attempt to murder us all before morning.

"You see, Creggan, that cutting throats was a fancy or fad of this brutal monarch's, just as collecting foreign stamps is with most English boys.

"All around the back part of the palace lay bleaching skulls and skeletons, that the blue-bottle flies and ants had polished, and recent corpses also, from which so fearful a stench arose and poisoned the air that we could scarcely sleep.

"But I fell off at last, and the sun was shining over the dense forests of the East before I awoke. Something was going on behind. Something dreadful, I felt sure. There was a low and pitiful moaning, but no cries. Yet every now and then came a dull thud, similar to that which a butcher makes in splitting a pig in two.

"I peeped through the back wattled wall. Oh, lad, may you never see such a sight!

"Over fifty poor creatures were huddled together mournfully awaiting their doom. Every half-minute one was dragged out, and stood with his or her hands between the knees and head bent down, till the cruel blow fell that severed that head from the body.

"But three or four were crucified in another corner.

"My remonstrances were in vain. The king only laughed, and told me that it was all got up in my honour.

"As no more could be done, we left almost immediately. We regaled ourselves on fruits as we passed on through the jungle to our sailor-guarded boat, and glad enough were we all when we found ourselves rowing once more down the beautiful river, on each bank of which—alive with beautiful birds—the foliage and trees were like the forests and woodlands of fairyland.

"But," continued the commander, "to change the subject to one more pleasant, tell us the story of your young life, my lad."

Nothing loath, Creggan told the doctor and him all he knew from his babyhood, and all about the hermit also.

"Why, it is a perfect romance, Creggan," said Flint.

"Indeed it is," said Grant. "I'll take more interest in the lad now than ever."

Arrived at the mouth of the Niger, they found the *Centiped* anchored outside the bar.

She was not going to venture across, being too large.

On the bar itself the breakers were dashing and curling house-high. There was just one gap in the centre, and through this the saucy *Rattler* must force her way.

Before proceeding she was lightened as much as possible, that is, all men not required were sent on board the cruiser.

Then "Go ahead at full speed", was the order.

The *Rattler's* full speed was nothing very extraordinary, but when she reached the gap at last and entered it, poor Creggan felt appalled. The roar of a seeming Niagara at each side was so terrible, that even through the speaking-trumpet scarcely could the skipper's voice be heard.

The roar was mingled with a seething, hissing sound, which was even more deafening than the thunder of the breakers itself.

She bumped her keel several times on the bottom, which here was hard, so violently that the men were thrown down, and Creggan began to say his prayers, thinking the ship must undoubtedly become a wreck. Nevertheless, in a minute or two they were into the deep smooth water inside the bar. Here she was anchored for a time, until all the marines and blue-jackets of both ships were got on board the *Rattler*. The boats and steam launch would accompany the expedition, and after all were loaded up with armed men, the advance was made up stream.

It was now about two bells in the forenoon watch, and they expected to get up as high as it was possible before night.

This it was found impossible to do, so she was anchored, and next day succeeded in reaching a station some forty miles from the sea, called Sapelé.

This in launches, the gun-boat being left further down. Here to their joy they found a fort or barracks, containing in all about two hundred and fifty officers and men (soldiers).

The expeditionary force from the *Rattler* was soon landed and hailed with delight. Together they were now quite a strong little army.

The commanding officer told Captain[2] Flint a sickening story of the massacre of the traders.

> [2] A Commander in the Royal Navy is not in reality a captain, but is usually addressed so by courtesy.

"The king, in fact," he said, "is jealous of the approach of the Protectorate."

After the murders he, the officer, had sent a sergeant with a flag of truce and several Kroomen, to ask for an interview with the tyrant.

Two days afterwards the white sergeant dragged himself, wounded and half-dead, into barracks. Before he expired, poor fellow, he had only time to report that every Krooman was murdered, and that Benin was in a state of terrible ferment, like a hive of hornets.

"And so, Captain Flint," he added, "between your force and mine, I think we can give this murderous assassin such a drubbing that he will not forget it for years."

"We'll do our best," said Flint; "and I suppose the sooner we start the better."

"Certainly; it is always wiser to attack than wait to be attacked."

So it was determined to give the little army a hearty supper, let them turn in early, and ready to start by three, inland now through the jungle, towards Benin. The real distance from Sapelé to Benin is, I believe, about twenty-five miles, but the road, if road it could be called, was bad enough in all conscience.

Nevertheless, it was determined to drag along two guns, with a good supply of shell. The bugle sounded prettily over woods and dells and river, shortly after two, and on finishing their hurried breakfast the force fell in.

Very proud indeed was Creggan to be allowed to go along with it, armed not only with a good cutlass, instead of the almost useless dirk, but with a revolver.

This was indeed a forced march, for before four o'clock next day they had got within twelve miles of the dismal city, with only one halt to partake of food, although much wood had to be cut down. They immediately hewed trees and bushes and went into laager, expecting an attack at any moment. When as safe as could be, fires were lit and supper cooked. Under other circumstances they would have remained silent and in the dark, but the commanding officer well knew that long before this time the blood-stained king would have heard of their advance. So, no attempt at concealment was necessary.

But the men were tired, so soon after supper fires were banked, and in an hour's time there was hardly a sound to be heard in the laager.

Dr. Grant and Creggan were the last to stretch themselves on their pallets of grass. Grant in his own wild Highland home had been used to roughing it, and Creggan, as we know, led a very active life on the Island of Wings. So neither felt tired.

The night was balmy with the odour of many gorgeous wild flowers, and it was even cool. The moon shone like a disc of gold, high up near the zenith, dimming even the effulgence of the brightest stars, and casting a strange, dreamy, phosphorescent light over the shapeless masses of cloud-like trees, and a brighter glimmer on the tall feathery cocoa-nut palms. Now and then away in the woods, there arose the mournful cry of some bird of prey, a cry that would make the marvellously beautiful king-fishers crouch lower to the perches on which they sat, and thrill their hearts with terror.

Now and then a fleecy, snow-white cloudlet would sail gently over the moon's disc, making the light scenery momentarily dimmer, but soon all was brightness once more. From an adjacent creek at times would come the sound of a heavy plunge, but whether from ghastly crocodile or hippopotamus they could not tell.

"It is indeed a goodly night," said Grant.

"Oh, it is heavenly!" cried Creggan; "but will we all be alive this time to-morrow?"

"Who can tell, my lad? No one dies till his day comes."

"But," he added with some hesitation, "you're not afraid, are you?"

"Oh, no indeed, doctor; just a little anxious, that is all. This will be my first fight, you know. But I am seventeen now—"

"Yes, and hard and strong, Creggan."

"So, doctor, if I get a chance to hit a nigger, I mean to hit him just as hard as I know how to."

"Very good. So shall I; but let me give you a word of good advice, because I'm older than you. Don't get carried away by excitement. He fights best who fights as calmly as possible. Keep to the fighting line or square, as the case may be, and you'll do well.

"And now I think I'll turn in, and may God in his mercy preserve us both to-morrow, and our Captain Flint as well."

"Amen!" said Creggan.

In less than half an hour after this Creggan was fast asleep, and dreaming that he was bounding over the smooth waves of the blue Minch in his skiff, with poor honest Oscar in the bows, and bonnie wee fair-haired Matty in the stern-sheets all smiles and dimples, her eyes twinkling with fun and merriment.

The dream seemed a very short one.

"Surely," he said, when the bugle sounded, "I cannot have slept an hour."

Yet it was already half-past one, and the moon had westered and was slowly sinking towards the horizon.

Before two breakfast was finished, a ration of rum served out, and the march resumed.

They must walk silently now.

The road was better, so that under the light of the stars only, for the moon had sunk, they had reached the wide straggling city by five o'clock.

Here the forces separated, the marines and blue-jackets lying in wait in a piece of jungle in the east; the soldiers making a silent detour to the back of the city, where was a dense primeval forest.

The guns were a long way behind, but just as the sun was tipping the glorious clouds of palms with its crimson rays, they were dragged in.

The sound of one gun and a bursting shell was to give notice to the soldiers hidden in the forest that the battle had indeed begun.

Just as the sun cast his bright beams across the darkling forest a buzz of awakening life began to arise from the city.

A spy had informed the naval commander where the king's forces, to the number of five thousand at least, were concentrated.

He now pointed out the very spot, a kind of fort and eminence in the centre of the town, and not far from the awful blood-stained palace.

"Now, gunner," cried Captain Flint cheerily, "give us the best shot ever you fired in your life."

"I'll do my level best," was the reply.

There was no quaver in the man's voice, no quiver in his hand.

The gun rang out in the morning air, echoed and re-echoed from forest and brae, and the shell was planted right in the centre of that heathen fort, bursting, and evidently doing tremendous damage. The battle had begun.

CHAPTER XII
CAPTURE OF THE CITY OF BENIN

There is nothing that African savages dread more than shells and war-rockets, and Arabs themselves are equally demoralized by these dread missiles.

They care but little—I am talking from my own experience—for ordinary round shot, if they are any distance off, in their dhows. From the cruiser's black side they can see arise a white cloud of smoke, with a spiteful tongue of fire in the centre; in a few seconds they hear the roar of the gun, and see the shot itself.

Well, they but utter a word of prayer to Allah, and ten to one the shot goes hurtling past high overhead, or it doesn't reach, but goes ricochetting past, half a mile astern perhaps, taking leaps of fifty yards at a time, throwing a cloud of foam up from every wave it strikes, till at last it sinks down to the slime of the fathomless sea.

If a cannon ball comes near enough to dash the sea-spray inboard, the Arab captain curses the British as heartily as he prays for himself, though he keeps cracking on.

But the shells, ah! the shells, that hiss and hurtle and fly into splinters in the air above the dhow, scattering death and destruction along its decks and poop; they will not yield to prayer, and I never yet saw an Arab captain who would or could stand the brunt of three or four well-aimed ones.

If one of these shells hit a mast, even if you are unwounded, the fall of that spar is something terrorizing to look upon, with its tangled rigging as well.

It does not come down quickly; it quivers and reels uncertainly for a time, while you gaze upwards and probably utter involuntarily a helpless moan.

It is coming down on you, and how can you escape death? More quickly, more and more quickly now, it descends. Then there is a crash, smashed bulwarks, and splinters flying in all directions. But, you are safe after all!

Captain Flint and his men had a good supply of shells, and it was lucky that the guns got up in time and were not damaged, for during the march there had been many small streams to cross, in which it was difficult at times to find a ford.

What wild yelling and shouting comes from the city now! Were it a large, compact town, with high houses and towers, Flint would shell it. But it were a pity to expend a shell in knocking a few grass huts to pieces, and scaring, killing, or wounding, perhaps, only helpless women and children.

"Just one other startler, sir, — shall I?"

The tall, dark young gunner was as good a shot as ever drew lanyard, and he told a messmate before he addressed the commander that he was spoiling for a shot or two that would astonish the weak nerves of the niggers.

"Well, Mr. Gill," said Flint smiling, "just one other; but I want to spare the ammunition till we see the foe."

"*Br—br—brang!*" went the gun a few seconds after, and the great shell went shrieking away on its mission of death.

Louder yelling than before followed the bursting of this shell.

Still the enemy did not appear.

Some men would have stormed the town, and attempted after a rifle volley or two to take it at the bayonet's point.

But this Ju-Ju king, with his naked feet caked with the blood of the victims that he had walked among, had a force of fiendish soldiers at least ten times greater in number than Flint's sailors and the soldiers behind. With these the king over-awed the the neighbouring states, and carried fire and spear and sword into their midst if they owned not his superiority and greatness.

Two hours passed away and still they did not show face, though the blue-jackets were stamping on the ground, and itching to get at them. Waiting for a tight makes the bravest sailor or soldier nervous.

The cause of the delay was that Benin, being completely under the dominion of a set of bloodthirsty scoundrels of priests, there were fetishes or oracles to be consulted, and all kinds of mumbo-jumbo business to be gone through, before the Ju-Ju king's army could come forth. Oh, as for the king himself, his person was far too sacred to risk. The priests told him so, and he was by no means loath to believe it. Besides, he was so covered with beads from chin to ankle, that he had some difficulty in walking much.

Far better to stay in his harem, and listen to the yelling of his soldiers, the rattling of the musketry, and roar of the guns, until, as the priests assured him would be the case, the British prisoners—all that were not slain—should be brought in.

Ah! then, he said to himself, the fun would begin. He would roast some alive. "Man meat", as these cannibals call human flesh, which, by the way, is sold openly in the market-place, is ever so much more tender and juicy when cooked alive. Well, the king made up his mind to roast a few; he would torture and crucify others on trees, with widely-extended arms and legs, and wooden pegs nailed through the flesh of feet, legs, and arms to hold them up. Others, again, he would tie to stakes, where he could see them starve to death in the broiling sunshine, half-eaten alive at night by loathsome beetles and other fearful insects. All the rest he would either behead, or hand over to the women to be tied down and slowly disembowelled alive!

That was the programme.

And now it was to be carried out. So the king believed. The British tars and marines were well stationed on slightly rising ground, half-sheltered by straggling bush, and were all ready when the enemy appeared in his thousands.

Mercy on us, how they yelled, and waved aloft shield and spear or guns, as they came on like a black and awful avalanche!

They fired first, and a few of our fellows fell, but only wounded.

"Reserve your fire, lads, till they get nearer!" cried Flint, for the blood of the sailors was getting hot.

Still on came that yelling avalanche. The sailors could see their red mouths, flashing teeth, and fearful eyes, when the captain shouted:

"Aim low, lads. Fire!"

That was a splendid volley!

Its effects were startling. The enemy was packed together, and some of the British bullets must have killed or wounded two at a time. It was followed up by others quite as good, and the dark skins, kicking and squirming like wounded rats, blackened the ground as their comrades sprang past or over them.

Nor did the hissing, spluttering war-rockets, tearing through their centre, repel their determined advance.

It seemed for a time that win the battle they must, by mere force of numbers.

Their terrible yelling now increased. All savages make these sounds, which they believe paralyses the enemy. Our brave Jacks and Joes, however, don't paralyse worth a groat. They were now formed into squares for a time, which the Ju-Ju's devils could not break.

Revolvers did lovely work!

Again and again the black savages advanced, only to be hurled back.

Then they threw their spears.

This was nasty, and wounded many of the man-o'-war's men.

"Fix bayonets!" cried Flint.

The bayonets were really cutlasses, and our fellows know how to use them too.

"Charge!"

How our men cheered, as they dashed on to the work of death! A true British cheer. The king heard it and trembled.

For a time it was a hand-to-hand tussle. But look yonder, in a more open space the captain himself has fallen, and three armed savages are on him instantly; two have spears—one is about to dash Flint's brains out with the butt-end of a beggarly Brummagen gun, when in the nick of time Creggan, who is near at hand, fires, and the fellow, with arms aloft, falls dead. Then, cutlass in hand, our hero rushes at the other two, as did the wild cat at his neck on that starlit night long ago, when he was returning home with dear Matty by his side. He has cut one across the neck with terrible effect, but the very strength and impulse of the blow, somehow, makes poor Creggan stumble and fall.

Next moment savage No. 3 has a spear very near to his chest indeed.

Yes; but the captain has now sprung up,—he was merely stunned,—the spear is splintered with the first blow, the second cleaves the savage's skull through to the eyes.

"God bless you, boy," cried Flint, "for your timely aid! I'll not forget it."

And blood-dripping hands are shaken there and then.

But how goes the battle?

Ah! right bravely. You can tell that by the royal cheers of Jack and Joe.

The foe reels backwards, wavers, flies. No use for blue-jacket or marine to follow. These fiends run swift as deer!

But shells and war-rockets do dread work now, and sadly thin the ranks of those shrieking fiends.

Nor is it all over yet. For look, right in front of the defeated and fleeing army there suddenly springs, as if from the earth itself, a thin red line of British soldiers.

Rip—rip—rip go the crackling rifles all along this line. As pretty platoon firing as one could wish to see or hear.

And the effect is deadly. The black army bids fair to be wiped out. They attempt to fly to the right—to the left. But Flint has divided his little army and outflanks them on both sides. Then, cowed and appalled, those among them who are still intact throw away their arms, throw themselves on the ground, throw themselves even across the bleeding bodies of the slain, and shriek aloud for mercy. Mercy? It is never refused by British soldiers to beseeching foemen.

The carnage has been dreadful, but silence reigns now, except for the pitiful moaning of the wounded. No sound of rifle, no slash of cutlass, or hiss of flying spear!

A blue sky above, and bright sunshine, in which the woods around seem to swelter and steam. The blue above—the blood below!

Yes, readers, war may be glorious, but it is after the battle has ceased to rage that one sees Bellona[1] in all her dreadful deshabille, her blood-stained arms, her soaking hair, and cruel and fiercely flaming eyes. May heaven in its mercy keep war and famine far away from our own sweet island home!

[1] The goddess of war.

The arms were now taken from the prisoners, and they were left huddled together like an immense herd of seals, for all were lying down exhausted. Only fifty men were left to keep them together. The main little army then marched into the city.

Will it be believed that women and children rushed to meet our heroes, kneeling in the dust and weeping, embracing our blue-jackets' knees, till more than one tar was heard to remark: "I'm blessed, Bill" (or Jim as the case might be), "I'm blessed if I don't feel like blubbering my blooming self."

For the British sailor, though the bravest of the brave in battle, has ever a tender heart to a child or woman.

But there was one particular cry that rang all through this poor forlorn mob. When translated it was found to mean:

"Kill the devil—Oh, kill the devil-king!"

The awful odour of this blood-stained city cannot be described. Nor can the sights that were seen in the market-place and around the palace. The skulls set on sticks, the skeletons, the putrid bodies; the crucified men still rotting on the trees, their heads fallen down till the chins touched the breast-bone; the "man-meat" in joints left on the now deserted stalls, the joints not unlike those of black pig. But the most disgusting sight of all, perhaps, was to see naked black children squatting on the murdered dead or drumming on their chests with the bones of the skeletons. And there was, as Burns says, in his inimitable *Tam o' Shanter*,

> "Mair o' horrible and awfu',
> Which ev'n to name wad be unlawfu'".

What a surprise his sable Majesty got when our blue-jackets, to the number of twenty, stormed his harem!

He had expected his own warriors, with British heads to set on poles, with British joints to roast for dinner, and British men to torture and burn.

Tom Sinclair, of the *Rattler*, a beau-ideal seaman, led the rest. His white "bags", as he called them, were red and brown with blood, and his shirt besprinkled too. But his sun-tanned face looked as jolly as if he had only just come from a ball instead of a field of carnage.

"*Yambo sana!*" (a Swahili salute).

"*Yambo sana!*" he said to the king, who was stretched on a raised, mat-covered couch. "W'y, what a luxurious old cockalorum you are, to be sure!"

Tom hitched up his trousers as he spoke, and looked pleasant.

But like fire from flint the Ju-Ju king sprang up, and attempted to knife poor Tom. And Tom with a single twist disarmed him, and next moment the king in his beads was lying on his back, the blood flowing from his nasal organ.

Tom was as calm as a judge.

"'Xcuse me, old chap," he said, "for making your morsel of a nose bleed. Would have preferred giving ye a pair of black eyes, only they wouldn't show like, your skin's so dark.

"Seems to me," he added, "yer soul's as black as yer blooming skin. Wouldn't I like to trice yer Majesty up and give ye four dozen.

"Here, interpreter," continued this tormenting Tom, "'terpret wot I says to this ere himage o' Satan. Are ye ready?"

"Tell him that we've wiped out his sodgers, and ask if he could oblige us by turning out a new army. We were only just a-settlin' down to serious fightin' when the beggars bolted.

"Told him?"

"Yes, sah. And now he groan and shake his big head plenty mooch, for true!"

"Tell him not to be afeard, that we won't scupper him (kill him) for a day or two, but that we means only to put a hook through his nose and 'ang him to a branch. Have you got a grip o' that, 'terpreter?"

"Yes, sah. And see, he shake his big head once more. Hoo, hoo! How he make me laugh!"

"Tell him that we may also build a fire under him just to keep his toes warm, 'cause it would be a terrible thing if a monarch like he was to catch his death o' cold."

The interpreter had barely finished telling the trembling king all this, when a stir in the after part of the room announced the arrival of the commanding officer, Fraser, and Captain Flint.

The sailors fixed bayonets, and drew silently up.

Then Colonel Fraser, through the interpreter, sternly ordered the king to stand up, and just as sternly addressed him. Pointing out to the assassin the enormity of all his fearful crimes, and what his punishment might be, if he, the commanding officer, cared to go to extremes. He told him much else that need not be mentioned here. But the palaver thus begun did not end for days.

The soldiers and sailors meanwhile commanded a large body of niggers to go everywhere over the town and bury every human carcase, and even every bone. The market stalls were heaped around the crucifixion trees and fired. The trees themselves burned fiercely.

The king's special murder-yard was also seen to. Then a grass and bamboo house was run up for the king in a different part of the town. To this he was escorted, laughed at and jeered by women and children, while his old blood-stained palace and everything in it was burned to the ground. Many of the adjoining huts caught fire, but the conflagration, though at night it looked very alarming, did not extend far, and was soon got under by the natives themselves throwing earth over it.

In another week's time the brave little army was once more on the march back to the river at Sapelé.

But the king had almost emptied his treasures of gold-dust to pay the demanded indemnity; he agreed also to send to New Benin much ivory, copal, nutmegs, and spices and palm-oil. A treaty was signed (it has not been kept, by the way) which bound his Majesty down to discontinue the awful human sacrifices, and to rule his subjects peacefully, on pain of another invasion by British forces, who next time, the commanding officer informed him, would hang him on the nearest tree and annex his country.

Just before the sailors and soldiers commenced their march to the river a strange and curious thing occurred.

There came emissaries from the hill tribes of the Wild West seeking an interview with Colonel Fraser.

The men, who were as wild-looking as any savages ever seen, and armed with spears and strong shields, looked nevertheless far from unpleasant.

The colonel was found after a little delay, and then the interpreter.

The first thing these strange men did was to lay their spears and their shields at the colonel's feet, then they grovelled, head down, in the dust, which, as they muttered some strange words, they mingled with their bushy heads of hair.

"Tell them to rise," said Colonel Fraser. "I cannot spare long time in ceremony."

The savage emissaries arose at once and stood before him.

"What can I do for you, my men?" said the commandant.

Their answer was so voluble that even the interpreter could not for a time understand it.

CHAPTER XIII
IN A WILD AND LOVELY MOUNTAIN-LAND

I believe, reader, that human nature is pretty much the same all the world over. The motto, "Don't sit on a man when he is down", is strictly adhered to, only the word "don't" is always deleted. And when a man is down, physically, morally, or financially, people, even old "friends", do sit on him, just as a cabby sits on his fallen horse's head to keep him down.

There is hardly any such thing as extending a kindly hand to a fallen man to help him up again, or even giving him a word of encouragement which might save his life itself. He is simply ostracized.

But in very truth there was considerable excuse for those hillmen from the Wild West. That blood-stained Ju-Ju king had ruled them with a rod of steel, ravaged their country, killed the men who could not escape, and carried off their women and children.

And now their time had come. The trampled worm had turned, and their proposal was simplicity in itself. It may best be expressed in the interpreter's own words.

"Dese gentlemans," he began, as he pointed to the niggers, and Creggan and some other officers smiled aloud; "dese gentlemans come from de far-away mountain. Plenty cold sometimes up dere. Dey want to bringee down five, ten tousand warrior to help we. Dey kill all, all dey men-men, take away de women-men and de little chillen. All de men-men dey eat plenty quick, and dey will nail de debil-king to a tree, all spread out, and roast he alive, for true. De king, when all nice and plopah, dey give to you to gobble up."

Colonel Fraser had a hearty laugh over this, then he made a short speech, in which he said he did not see his way at present to accede to their request, but if they would promise not to attack the king till he, Colonel Fraser, returned to punish him again, he would accept their proposal, but was not quite certain that he would eat the king, even if he were done to a turn.

Then with his own hands he returned to them their spears and shields, and, bowing and salaaming, thanked them.

Those emissaries of a poor oppressed race went back to their mountains rejoicing, and the march to the river was at once commenced.

They carried the wounded and even the dead in hammocks. Had they buried the latter anywhere near Benin they would, Colonel Fraser thought, be speedily disinterred and eaten.

In the woods, ten miles from the City of Blood, they buried their fallen comrades, after Colonel Fraser himself had said a prayer—not a printed one, but an earnest prayer from his honest, kindly heart.

Many a tear trickled down the cheeks of the blue-jackets and marines as comrade after comrade was laid side by side in the deeply-dug trench, while such expressions as the following were heard on every side:

"Good-bye, Bill, we'll never see you more!"

"Ah, Joe, you and I 'as spent many a 'appy day together. Farewell, old man, farewell!"

"Jim, if I thought a pipe 'ud comfort ye, I'd put all my 'baccy beside ye in the grave. Blest if I wouldn't, messmates!"

Rough but kindly words, and not without a certain degree of pathos.

There was no need to hurry back; so, after crossing a creek about ten miles from the river they bivouacked at Siri, a wretched village, for the night. But the inhabitants had heard of the battle, and the downfall of the assassin king, and brought them presents of fruit and cassava, besides nutmegs and spices, for all of which they were substantially thanked with gifts of coloured beads, which made the sable ladies chuckle and coo with delight.

Next day the expedition reached the river and crossed to Sapelé, and soon after the sailors reached their ship.

But they had not quite done with Benin yet. The wounded soldiers had been safely seen to at Sapelé, but the colonel and a Lieutenant Aswood boarded the *Rattler* to dine with Flint and his officers, and considering everything, a very jolly evening was spent. The doctor had reported that the wounded would all do well, so Commander Flint gave a dinner-party, and orders to splice the main brace, from the gun-room aft right away forward to the cook's galley.

There was jollity, therefore, forward. Yarns were told, songs were sung, and every now and then the sweet music of guitar and fiddle floated aft.

It was for all the world like an old-fashioned Saturday-night at sea.

And those in the saloon or commander's cabin, including the soldiers, the ship's doctor, first lieutenant, and Creggan, felt very happy indeed. The chief talk naturally centred on the recent fight, and the terrible condition of the City of Blood.

"Now, Flint, as far as niggers go I'm not a bad prophet." This from the colonel. "And I'll tell you what will happen."

"Well, Fraser," said Flint, "heave round and give us your ideas."

"Well, then, I'm half-sorry now that I didn't hang that blood-drunkard of a king to begin with. But the king that the priests would have then placed on the stool called a throne might have been quite as bad, if not worse."

"True, Fraser, true."

"Do you think he will be influenced by that treaty?"

"About a week, perhaps."

"Just so."

"On the other hand," said the colonel, "I am half-sorry I didn't allow the mountain-men to wipe the savages out.

"But," he continued, "that Ju-Ju monarch is no more to be restrained from sacrificing his subjects than a cat could be from catching sparrows. Now he'll go on till he gets hold of some whites and massacres these. Then there will be another war. If we do not kill the king, he'll be sent down to the coast and imprisoned for life."

"I follow you," said Flint. "What next?"

"Oh, annexation of course, and the whole of this rich and lovely country will become ours.

"What do you think of its healthiness?" he added, turning to Dr. Grant.

"Give a dog a bad name," replied Grant, "and you may kill him as soon as you like. When we annex this land of Benin, the niggers under our kindly sway—and they swarm in millions, you know—will till it and drain it for us; cut down useless jungles, fell valuable timber, which will help to dry up the creeks and bogs. All unhealthiness will then vanish, sir, like the morning mist from the mountain tops; land will be cheap and good, and colonists will come from Scotland by the shipload. As for sickness, we shall have splendid sanatoriums far away among those lofty mountains, where the climate must be temperate, and even bracing."

"Capital, Dr. Grant! Capital! Just my own ideas," said the colonel, "only expressed in far prettier language than any I could use. And now, Flint, what say you to stay for a week here, while we explore the country as Moses did the Holy Land?"

"Oh, Colonel Fraser," cried Creggan laughing, "it wasn't Moses, but Caleb and Joshua. Poor Moses only had a bird's-eye view of it from a hill-head, you remember."

"Quite right, boy, and thank you. Well, Flint, suppose you and I on this occasion go and spy out the land, which must eventually be ours, you know."

"Good!" said the commander. "We shall go in peace, and with peace-offerings for the people."

"Beads and bonnie things," said Grant, with a broad Scotch smile.

"That's it, doctor," said the colonel. "Beads and bonnie things. But an escort as well, eh?"

"Yes, fifty marines and blue-jackets."

"And start to-morrow?"

"Capital!"

"And now, Grant, I know you sing and play. Yonder is the piano; sit down and delight us."

Grant required no second bidding.

After a most charming prelude he said smiling:

"I'm going to sing you songs of the triune nation—Scotland, England, and Ireland."

And so he did.

After a beautiful, sad, and plaintive Scotch song, he rattled off into a strathspey and reel. After singing *"Good-bye, Sweetheart, Good-bye"*, he played a waltz, and on concluding *"The Harp that once through Tara's Halls"*, he dashed off into such a soul-inspiring, maddening, droll old jig, that everybody all round the table clapped their hands and shouted "Encore!"

Well, on the whole, the evening passed away most delightfully, but by eight bells or the end of the first watch, all on board save those on duty were sound asleep in hammock or cot.

The exploration of the country was commenced next day. Tents were not taken, but tins of potted meats, and potted vegetables. They would sleep beneath the stars in open ground. Rum was also taken, but it was mixed with quinine.

The explorers were fifty-and-six all told, including Creggan and Dr. Grant. Creggan, being a mountaineer, proved himself invaluable. He was so light to run, too, and went on ahead here, there, and everywhere, even shinning up trees to find out the best roads.

The people they encountered were none too gentle. They even looked askance at the presents. So Colonel Fraser decided not to make use of any as guides, for fear of being led into an ambush.

When they came at last to—altering Scott somewhat—a

> Land of green heath and shaggy wood,
> Land of mountain and of flood,

the forests grew denser, darker, and deeper. The roar of wild beasts, too, was heard by day as well as by night, so that caution had to be used. And here were many lakes, though there were streams instead of creeks. And these lakes were literally alive with fish.

"Beautiful! Beautiful! What a happy hunting-ground!" exclaimed Fraser, as two strange deer went past like the wind.

"It is indeed a land flowing with milk and honey," said the doctor.

"And all to be ours. All to be British!"

They passed the forests safely enough, and now got fairly into the mountain-land. Here were glens, as bonnie and bosky as any in Scotland. They entered one particularly beautiful dell.

They had paused to admire and wonder, when the distant sound of war-drums or tom-toms fell upon their ears, and presently a huge band of savage warriors appeared, as if by magic, on the opposite brae. So suddenly did they spring up, that the brave lines of the poet came back with a rush to Creggan's mind. Yonder, of course, were no waving tartans or plumes. Yet that dark army rose from the bush in the same startling way. It is in Roderick Dhu's interview with the Saxon Fitz-James on the Highland hills. Roderick cries:

> "'Have, then, thy wish!' He whistled shrill
> And he was answered from the hill;
> Wild as the scream of the curlew,
> From crag to crag the signal flew.
> Instant, through copse and heath, arose
> Bonnets and spears and bended bows;
> On right, on left, above, below,
> Sprang up at once the lurking foe;
> From shingles gray their lances start,

The bracken bush sends forth the dart;
The rushes and the willow-wand
Are bristling into axe and brand,
And every tuft of broom gives life
To plaided warrior armed for strife.
That whistle garrisoned the glen
At once with full five hundred men,
As if the yawning hill, to heaven
A subterranean host had given."

"Why," said Colonel Fraser, pointing to the hillside, "just look yonder, Flint. We don't want to fight these poor hill-men. They are doubtless the same from whom the emissaries came."

"Well, anyhow," said Flint, "they look as vicious as vipers. Let us send our interpreter over at once. He will explain things."

"Good!"

So this was done.

But it was evident that the hill-men were not open to reason, for the poor fellow was immediately seized and bound.

"Now," cried the colonel, "we must and shall advance. If there were twice five hundred we should not submit to that indignity."

So the little brave band proceeded at once to descend the hill and ford the stream. Bayonets were fixed, and all were climbing slowly up the steep brae on the other side, but a long way to the right, in order to get higher than the threatening savages and thus have all the advantage, when wild whooping and yells arose above them.

They could not understand this, until down rushed the guide and interpreter—a free man.

"All right, sah, all right! De men who come to Benin, dey am dere now, and all de oder sabages am plopah fliends now.

"Come on! Come on!" he added.

And on they went.

They were received by the hill-men with shouts of joy, and one tall, very black savage, much ornamented with feathers and beads, insisted on taking Colonel Fraser's hand, and bending low over it touched it with his brow. He repeated the same ceremony with all the officers, then waved his dark hand in quite a dignified way to the blue-jackets and marines.

Strange to say, he could even talk a little English.

"I am please, I am mooch delight," he said. "At Gwato I meet plenty goot trader, ah! and plenty vely bad. Ha, ha!"

The officers laughed.

"Well, chief, we have thrashed the cruel king of Benin, and now we want to see your dear mountain-land, because one day we shall kill the Ju-Ju king, and then the kind-hearted Great White Queen shall reign over you, and you will be all very happy."

"I guide you, I guide! Be delight,—plenty mooch delight!"

So, high up into the mountains marched the sailor-band, with the chief and twenty savages as guides.

It was getting late now, but before sunset they arrived at a mountain village, the huts of which seemed to be perched upon the shelves of the rock, like eagles' eyries.

They found the village clean and sweet.

The chief took the officers into the largest hut, which he had caused to be rebedded with withered ferns, while the couches all round were made of beautiful heaths, intermingled with wild flowers.

Then Creggan and the gunner went out to see to the men's supper, and found them all contented and jolly.

When he returned, lo! a banquet of fried fish, sweet potatoes, roast yams, capsicums, and fruit of many kinds, was spread on boards or pieces of bark before his shipmates.

"Take seat, take seat!" cried the chief, "and eatee plenty mooch foh true!"

"Why," said Creggan, as he squatted on the ferns, "this is indeed a land flowing with milk and honey."

It was, and behind each officer knelt a little girl with a palm-leaf fan to keep the guests cool.

A modicum of rum was served out, and the chief, Gabo, was asked to drink.

He drew back in horror.

"No, soldiers, no!" he cried. "Dat am de debil foh true. Sometime we hab plenty from the oil-traders at Gwato. Den we all go mad, and mooch kill eberybody. Now we nebber look at he."

A band of girls came in afterwards, and danced while they sang. A strange wild dance it was, with many wonderful swayings of arms and bodies.

An hour after this the British were sleeping soundly.

All hands were called just a little before sunrise, and what a gorgeous sight they beheld! Only a Turner could have done justice to that sky of orange gray and gold, and to the splendid landscape of forest and water that lay between. Lake on lake, stream or creek everywhere, and the purple mist of distance over all, save where a lake caught the crimson glare of the sun and was turned into blood.

And down beneath them the nearest braes were clad in a wealth of wild heaths and geraniums, and many a charming flower hugging the barer patches. The officers were silent as they gazed on all this loveliness.

"No beauty such as this," said Grant at last, "can be seen even in Scotland."

But every bush seemed to be alive with bird-song, every leaf appeared to hide some feathered songster; and when any of these flitted from tree to tree, it was found that they were quite as beautiful in colour as the flowers themselves.

The air, too, was cool and delightful.

Creggan and Grant went for a little walk farther up the hill, where they found a great basin of rock filled with clear limpid water, and here they bathed, so that the appetite both had for the excellent breakfast, roast wild game, birds, and mountain trout, with, as before, yams and sweet potatoes, was quite striking—striking down, I may say.

They all went hunting that day. But up in the hills there were few wild animals of any sort, yet they enjoyed the tramp nevertheless.

They stayed with this wild tribe for over a week, and every day brought them something fresh in adventure or pleasure.

Colonel Fraser made sketches, and took many observations of this beautiful land of wild bird, tree, flower, and fruit, which at no distant date will become the possession of the enterprising British colonist, and give riches to men now starving perhaps in the overcrowded cities of our island home.

Soon may this day come!

There is nothing impossible in Africa.

CHAPTER XIV
A FEARFUL NIGHT

But the scene changes, and will change still more as this story runs on.

Our heroes are back once more in the *Rattler*, that only last night bumped out over the bar, and is now lying alongside the *Centiped*.

Colonel Fraser, of course, has returned to his own barracks, and the officers of the expedition, including Creggan, are at dinner on board the larger ship, telling and talking of all their wild adventures.

"Now, gentlemen," said the captain, "I have news for you, which I would not tell you before, lest it should spoil your appetites."

They all waited to hear it.

"The *Wasp*, outward bound for the slave-coast of Eastern Africa, lay-to here three days ago and sent a boat with letters for you all."

"How delightful!" cried Creggan excitedly.

"And, Captain Flint,—the *Rattler* is ordered home."

"Hurrah!" cried Grant, and there was a general clapping of hands all round the table, and I'm not sure but that Creggan's eyes filled with tears. He was little more than a boy, remember.

Well, the sackful of letters was duly put in the *Rattler's* boat when she was hauled up, and that night everybody on board that saucy gun-boat got good news—or bad.

Creggan had quite a bunch of letters, which he read in the gun-room, and again by daylight next day.

That old song keeps running through my head as I write—

> "Good news from home, good news for me,
> Has come across the dark blue sea,
> From friends that I had left in tears,
> From friends I have not seen for years.
>
> "And since we parted long ago,
> My life has been a scene of woe;

But now a joyful hour has come,
For I have got good news from home."

The second line of the second verse is, however, hardly correct as far Creggan was concerned. On the whole he had passed his time very pleasantly indeed, with some little griefs, of course. Many a storm had the *Rattler* weathered, and many a strange sight had he seen.

He would be entitled to a good long spell of leave when the gun-boat was paid off, and what tales he would have to tell the old hermit (his Daddy) and Archie, and last, though not least, dear wee Matty! But stay, she would be eleven years old, for Creggan was eighteen or almost.

But here were the letters from home, one each, and long ones too, from Daddy, Mr. M'Ian, Rory and Maggie, Nugent and Matty.

He kept the latter to the last. What a dear, innocent little epistle it was, and though no praise could be given to the caligraphy, which was a trifle scrawly, childish, innocent love breathed from every line.

It was a bright and beautiful morning when the *Rattler* weighed anchor, left the Bight of Benin, and steered west and away, homeward bound for Merrie England.

As the gun-boat passed the *Centiped*, which would now take her place on this station, there was many a shout of *"bon voyage"* from the quarter-deck; the rigging was crowded with sailors like bees on a bush, and after three cheers were given, the little band of the *Centiped* struck up *Home, Sweet Home*.

The notes came quavering sweetly, sadly over the water, but soon they died away, and in an hour's time the ship they had left behind them could hardly be seen against the greenery of the trees that lined the Afric foreshore.

They made a good run that day, and when, after the ward-room dinner and gun-room supper, Grant and Creggan met upon the quarter-deck, steam had been turned off and the fires banked, for there was just enough wind to send the *Rattler* on. She ran before it, for it blew off the land, with stunsails set alow and aloft.

It was a delightful night, though not bright, but the clouds that covered the sky were very high and gauzy. They had many a rift of blue, however, and whenever she had a chance while the clouds went scudding on, the moon shone down on the sea with a radiance brighter than diamonds.

Now and then a shoal of playful dolphins would go leaping and dancing past. It was evident that they enjoyed the beauty of the night as well, if not better, than even Grant or Creggan could.

The *Rattler's* record till she reached the Bay of Biscay, which she skirted only, was really a good one for a ship of such small horse-power. Though an iron-clad, remember, she had sails and rigging as well as steam. But now the scene changed! The glass went down like falling over a cliff, banks of sugarloaf clouds rose one evening threateningly in the east, and it was evident to every seafarer on board that it was to be a dirty night. So sails were got in, and the ship made snug, while the engineer speedily got up steam.

Creggan was in the first mate's watch, and they had the middle watch to keep to-night.

A man had come down below to shake his hammock and call him. That hammock required a good deal of shaking before Creggan was thoroughly aroused. But he turned out at once.

"Better put on your oil-skins, sir," said the seaman.

"Is it blowing, then?"

"Hark, don't you hear it roar, sir? It's blowing real big guns, Dahlgrens and Armstrongs, all in a heap. Hurry up, sir! It's gone eight bells minutes ago."

Creggan was not long in getting on deck. He tied the flaps of his oil-skin over his ears and under his chin. A good thing, too, for the wind was wild enough to have torn one's hair off. Creggan could scarcely stand or stagger against it. Nor could the gun-boat make much headway either. Hardly, perhaps, a knot an hour.

The lad got aft to look at the compass. Yes, her head was north and a trifle westerly. She was boldly holding her course at all events.

It was very dark indeed, for all round the vessel the horizon was close on board of her, and the inky clouds must have been miles deep. The ship's masts seemed to cut through them when high on the top of a storm-tormented wave, and when down in the deep trough between two seas these waves thundered over the bows and came rushing aft in white foam, a rolling cataract, which, had the ship not been battened down, would have flooded the engine-room and probably drowned out the fires.

Creggan was perfectly alive to the extreme danger, for if the ship from any accident broached to, in all probability she would turn turtle and be heard of nevermore, until the sea gave up its dead.

Yet Creggan managed to get forward a few yards to the spot where the first lieutenant stood clinging to a stay, and they managed to carry on a conversation for a while.

But a kind of drowsiness stole over both, and presently they became silent.

Creggan was awakened from his lethargy by the crashing of wood forward. A mighty wave had splintered the bulwarks, and for just about half a minute the vessel fell off her course.

It was found necessary to put an extra hand to the wheel.

The storm was now at its worst. Ever and anon the waves, more than houses high, made a clean breach over her, the spray dashing as high as the fore-top, and even down the funnel.

To add to the terror, peal after peal of thunder appeared to shake the ship to her very keel. Louder far than the roar of the savage waves was this thunder, and the lightning lit up the slippery decks, and showed the men crouching and shivering aft, their faces like the faces of the dead, while over the ocean it shot and glimmered till the sea itself looked an ocean of fire.

Indeed, indeed a dreadful night!

Neither the first lieutenant nor Creggan was sorry when they were relieved.

The former beckoned the lad into the ward-room. Then he produced the beef and "fixings", as he called bread, butter, and the cruets. Both were hungry, and between them they made the joint look small.

Then Creggan went off to his hammock, commending himself as he lay down to that God who can hold the sea in the hollow of His hand.

Four hours of sweetest dreamless slumber, and when our hero went on deck after breakfast, though the wind had gone down and gone round, the seas were still high and darkling blue.

But it was now a beam wind, so fires were banked, and she went dancing on her course, as if she well knew that after all her trials and buffetings she would soon be safe in Plymouth Sound.

The evening before the *Rattler* sighted the chalk-cliffs of Old England Creggan had kept the first watch, from eight to twelve, therefore he would have what sailors call "all night in". That is, he turned in at twelve, and did not have to leave his hammock till about half-past seven.

On board a ship in harbour, the time youngsters turn out is five bells. I slept in a hammock myself when I first joined, and I assure the reader I didn't like to be called at five bells, or half-past six; but the quartermaster was inexorable, he used to pass along the orlop deck, where all our hammocks hung, and strike each a dig with his thumb underneath.

"Five bells, sir, please! Five bells, sir, please!"

This resounded all along the deck, and if we had not turned out in five minutes, then he took the number of the hammock and reported it to the commander. The owner of that hammock was planked. That is, he was brought on the quarter-deck and severely reprimanded.

Our sea-chests stood all round the deck, and as soon as we got up, our servants folded the bed-clothes, lashed up the hammocks, and trundled them away to the upper deck to be neatly stowed in the topgallant bulwarks.

But though we got up, we didn't always, if ever, begin to dress immediately. No, we used to mount to the top of our sea-chests, and with our night-shirts drawn down to cover the toes, and our knees up to our chins, squat there for perhaps a quarter of an hour, looking for all the world like a row of fan-tail pigeons.

Then we grew lively, opened our sea-chests, which, you know, contain a complete toilet service at the top, washed and towelled, skylarked, stole each others socks, and pelted each other with wet sponges. I dare say our marine servants were to be pitied in their almost fruitless endeavours to maintain order.

Ah! those dear old days are past and gone, and they will never come again!

However, although he had all night in, somehow it was quite an hour before Creggan dosed off. He was reviewing in his mind the events of the cruise, and thinking of home at the same time, anxiously too. It must have been months and months since the last batch of letters received were written, and some of his dear friends may have died since then. This thought made his heart beat uneasily.

Then he remembered that he had hurried into his hammock without saying his prayers.

But he did so now, and so felt more contented and happy.

All the scenes of the past three years then presented themselves in single file before his mind's eye. Had he done all he could for the service?

He really thought he had.

Poor old Daddy the hermit had given Creggan three maxims before he left his little island home, and the lad had always borne these in mind. They are not sentimental or namby-pamby, or I would not repeat them. They are just good, honest rules, that would help any sailor-boy to get his foot well on to the first rung of the ladder that leads to fame and fortune.

"My dear sonny," said the hermit, "mind you this, and mind it all your life:—

"First—If a thing is worth doing at all, it is worth doing well.

"Second—'Work while it is called to-day, for the night cometh when no man can work'.

"Third—Try to see your duty and make sure of it, and when you see it, go straight for it."

But Creggan dosed off at last, and soon slept soundly enough.

When he got into the gun-room next morning, he was saluted by his merry messmates in the following fashion.

"Creggan Ogg, hillo!"

"Hillo—o—o, old Creggan!"

"Creggan, ain't you just too awfully glad for anything?"

Our hero looked from one to the other in a kind of puzzled way.

"Are you all mad?" he said.

"No, no, no, but we're nearly home, man alive!"

"He isn't half-alive! He isn't awake yet!"

Then it began to dawn upon Creggan.

He jumped up on the locker, and had a peep out through the tiny port, or scuttle-hole.

Why, it was like looking through a mirror into fairyland. The picture was very limited, it is true, but yonder, high up on a green brae, was a long, white-washed cottage with a woman at a tub washing clothes in front of it, and a brindled cow quietly chewing her cud and looking on.

And this was home at last! A little picture from dear old England!

Creggan stopped longer upon the locker than there was any need for, because the tears had sprung to his eyes, and he cared not that his chaffing messmates should witness such weakness.

Well, soon after this they got past the breakwater and well into the beautiful Sound.

Boats in swarms begin to surround her, but not a soul, woman or man, can get on board till the medical officer comes and they get pratique, a clean bill of health.

But the men are allowed to talk from the gun-ports to their friends and relatives beneath. All are anxious all are either sad or joyful.

How the wife beams when she sees her Jack's brown face peeping smilingly down.

But oh! the grief and sorrow of some poor women when they ask some other sailor about their Tom or Bill.

"Where is Bill?"

"Where is my Tom?"

It is hard, hard to answer such questions, but it must be done.

"Ah, missus," says Jack at the port, "we've been a-fightin' hard wi' bloomin' niggers, and poor Tom got scuppered!"

Some women faint. Some turn pale, dazed, and sink down stunned in the stern-sheets.

But see, yonder comes the medical officer, and in a very short time the ship is free.

Then up swarm friends and relations, and meetings and greetings are very joyful indeed. There is a rattling fire of questions and answers all over the ship, and many a jolly laugh rings shoreward over the sea.

Creggan is on the quarter-deck. He expects no one, but suddenly he is hailed.

"Creggan, old man! How you have grown!"

"Why, is it you, Willie Nugent? And you've grown too, a little paler though."

"Oh, I wish I was as brown as you, Creggan, but I'm being dragged up for a political career, you know. And I do hate it. I wish I'd been a sailor."

"And how is your father?"

"Jolly."

"And Matty?"

"Your wee sweetheart is beautiful, and we are all well. My father has a better and larger bungalow now in Skye, and we often go out to see the hermit. He looks no older. Fact, I think he is getting young again."

"Oscar?"

"Oh, he did miss you at first. But Tomnahurich has another dog now, because he thinks on your next cruise you are bound to get Oscar with you. So Kooran, and he is a beauty, will then be his companion."

"Well, you're making me so happy, Willie; but just one more question. Ever see Archie?"

Willie laughed right merrily and mischievously.

"Why, he is here, Creggan; I was keeping this bit of news to astound you."

"Archie here!"

"Yes; I'll call him up now."

Next minute, with kindly hand extended, there walked, smiling but with eyes glistening with tears of joy, a fashionably-dressed young gentleman with a budding moustache.

"Man, is it your very, very self?"

"It is no other, dear old friend."

"I'd hardly have known you, Creggan."

"Nor I you. But explain, my boy. Why all this extensive rig-out—the top hat, the morning coat, the trousers instead of the kilt? Why all this thusness? Anybody left you a fortune, Archie?"

"No, no! I've lots of money, though," laughed Archie. "I've taken a small farm for mother and Kory, and they live in a red stone house, and have horses, cows, and sheep."

"But—"

"I'll tell you in a minute. You'll mind our games of draughts with the bits of carrot and parsnip for men?"

"Indeed I do."

"Well, a draught-player in Edinburgh challenged all Scotland for £20 to play with him. After you left I often played wi' Tomnahurich. He plays well, but though I took off men of my own, I very soon whipped off all his.

"'You'll go down to Edinburgh,' he said, 'and beat this boasting fellow. I'll lend you the money.'

"'But,' says I, 'suppose I lose it?'

"'Never mind,' says he. 'Off you go.'

"And off I went, Creggan, just the kilted ghillie I was when you left us. Well, there must have been a hundred great ladies and gentlemen to watch our ten games. They gave me a little cheer, but my opponent looked at me in proud disdain. I didn't like it, and determined to win. You know the old Cameronian motto—*Whate'er a man dares he can do*,—and by St. Kilda, Creggan, I soon lowered that toff's play. I won the first four games, getting his last crowned head in a fix every time.

"The room was stuffy and hot, and my head swam a bit, so he licked me in the fifth. Ah! playing in a hot room isn't like playing on the breezy cliffs, or among the wild thyme.

"Well, they opened a window, and our table was drawn near to it—and, Creggan boy, that toff never won another game.

"What cheering! what rejoicing! Why, a duchess took me in her arms and kissed me, and a tall swell caught me by the hand.

"'You dear little Highlander! You've got to come to my house to-morrow. I backed you for two thou., and I'll make you share it.'

"And now, Creggan, I'm champion player of Britain; but I've been challenged out to the States, and I hope I'll win there too."

Next day the three friends dined together at the chief hotel. Oh, such a happy night! Then, as soon as leave was obtained—the ship being paid off,—they all started for Glasgow by boat, and thence, again by boat, to the beautiful Island of Wings.

CHAPTER XV
WELCOME BACK TO SKYE

Creggan Ogg M'Vayne might well sing of

"A life on the ocean wave,
A home on the rolling deep".

Well, any man who is worth the noble name of sailor loves his ship, and looks upon her as "home" in the real sense of the word. Nor does he long for any other while the commission lasts. But oh! when the order to return comes on board, then there is something within him that, though it may have been slumbering for years, awakes at once, and he is eager, even to excitement, to see once more the woods and flowery fields of England, or the wild straths and glens of green Caledonia.

When the boat discharged Willie and Creggan at Portree, the latter felt that he was indeed at home.

"No, Willie, we won't walk. I'm too impatient far for that."

"I'll do whatever you do, old man."

So they hired a fast horse and dogcart; the driver a man who could hold the ribbons well, the nag as sure-footed as a mule.

The day was bright and bracing, so that Creggan's spirits rose with every milestone passed.

Perhaps in no country in all the wide world is the early autumn more lovely than in our own dear Scottish Highlands. The fierce heat of summer that erst was reflected from the lofty crags and mountain brows to the straths below, is mitigated now. The grass is still green in the bonnie bosky dells, through which streamlets meander over their pebbly beds and go singing to the sea. Though the winds are whispering now among the birchen foliage, and the tall needled pine-trees, with a harsher voice than that of sweet spring-time, the tall ferns in many a quiet and sylvan nook wave wild and bonnie, their fronds of green and brown making a charming background to the crimson nodding bells of the foxglove. And the hills above are purple and crimson with heather and heath, with many a rugged crag or gray rock peeping through, which only serve to enhance their beauty.

But here in the north of Skye are no trees, though the heather is a sight to see, and so you hardly miss the dark waving pines.

"I'm just so happy," said Creggan, "that I believe I could sing."

"My dear boy," said Willie, "I already know enough about politics to be able to assure you that no act of parliament has yet been passed against singing. Heave round, as you sailors say, and give us a ditty."

"Give us a bass then, Willie."

"That I will, and the horse himself will beat time to your melody."

"Well, I'll sing you a song our bo's'n used to troll at the fo'castle head in starlight evenings, when our ship was far at sea. But I have not his voice. It is called —

THE SAILOR'S RETURN.

Bleak was the morn when William left his Nancy,
    The fleecy snow frown'd on the whitened shore,
Cold as the fears that chilled her dreary fancy,
    While she her sailor from her bosom tore.
To his fill'd heart a little Nancy pressing,
    While a young tar the ample trousers eyed,
In need of firmness, in this state distressing,
    Will checked the rising sigh, and fondly cried:
        'Ne'er fear the perils of the fickle ocean,
        Sorrow's all a notion,
            Grief all in vain;
        Sweet love, take heart,
        For we but part
            In joy to meet again.'

Loud blew the wind, when, leaning on that willow
    Where the dear name of William printed stood,
Poor Nancy saw, tossed by a faithless billow,
    A ship dash'd 'gainst a rock that topped the flood.
Her tender heart, with frantic sorrow thrilling,
    Wild as the storm that howl'd along the shore,
No longer could resist a stroke so killing:
    "'Tis he,' she cried, 'nor shall I see him more!
        Why did he ever trust the fickle ocean?
        Sorrow's my portion,
           Misery and pain!
        Break, my poor heart,

> For now we part,
>   Never to meet again.'
>
> Mild was the eye, all nature was smiling,
>   Four tedious years had Nancy passed in grief,
> When, with her children, the sad hours beguiling,
>   She saw her William fly to her relief!
> Sunk in his arms with bliss he quickly found her,
>   But soon return'd to life, to love, and joy;
> While her grown young ones anxiously surround her,
>   And now Will clasps his girl, and now his boy.
>   'Did I not say, though 'tis a fickle ocean,
>   Sorrow's all a notion,
>   Grief all in vain?
>   My joy how sweet!
>   For now we meet,
>   Never to part again.'

As the horse went merrily trotting along the road, and the voices of those happy boys raised in song was echoed from rock and brae, little kilted lads and kirtled lassies ran out from cottage doors—for joy is infectious—to shout and wave their bonnets as long as they could see the trap.

And now, here is Uig once more. The landlady just as buxom and jolly as before, though at first she did not know Creggan.

Here a good luncheon was made, and the horse fed. Then on again for many a mile, till the gray ruins of the warlike old castle of Duntulm hove in sight, the swift rolling Minch, and, far beyond, the blue hills of Harris. And yonder, too, was the hermit's isle of Kilmara.

Some distance from the sea was Nugent's bungalow, but all were at the door to meet Willie and Creggan, the sailor-boy.

Matty could talk better English now, though still a child, and just as innocent as ever. While Creggan rested on a chair under the pretty verandah, trying to answer about a hundred questions at the same time, wee Matty climbed his knee, and with one soft arm around his neck, claimed her sailor all to herself.

Then there was the visit to the manse. More welcomes there from Rory, Maggie, and Mr. M'Ian.

Oh, it is really worth going to sea for a few years, if only to receive a welcome home like this!

The sea to-day was blue and smooth, so Willie had his skiff taken down from the manse, and with Matty in the stern-sheets—-just in the dear old way—he paddled out to visit his Daddy.

That was indeed a delightful meeting, but I cannot describe it. The new dog came furious, barking at Creggan, but poor Oscar knew him at a glance, and simply went wild with joy.

Let no one ever tell me that a dog forgets a kind master. When I myself first went to sea—in the Royal Navy—I left my beautiful collie with my mother. Not only did he know me when I returned after several years, but on the day my arrival was announced mother said to him: "Tyro, doggie, your master is coming to-day". He never left the window after that. Never ceased to watch till, afar off, he could see me. Then his impatience was unbounded till the door was opened, and he came rushing down the road to meet me.

Creggan spent the night with Daddy, who had not altered a bit, but he rowed Matty home first.

That evening a strange but true tale of the sea was related to Creggan, and the mystery that surrounded his childhood was cleared up once and for ever.

It was thought best by the minister, and by Nugent also, that the hermit should break the news to the lad.

Know then, that not more than a month ago, a lady in black, still beautiful, though she must have been verging on forty, was travelling in a dog-cart through Skye, with her own maid and coachman.

Calling at the manse, M'Ian happened among other things to tell her of the strange story of the finding of Creggan in the skiff on the beach of Kilmara isle.

She seemed strangely agitated.

"Is the skiff still to the fore, and might I see it?"

"Certainly, my dear lady."

She had hardly looked at it before she almost fainted, and would have fallen had not M'Ian's strong arms supported her.

"Oh, sir, that was our boat! Is the boy still alive?"

"Yes, and at sea. We expect him back in a month. He was brought up by the hermit of Kilmara out yonder."

"Do row me over there, will you?"

"With pleasure, madam."

And the minister's own boat was launched and soon reached the island.

The hermit was mystified at first, but soon recovering, told her all the reader already knows.

Then she told her sad story.

The *Sea-Swallow*—her husband's ship—was lying at Harris in a little bay. He, her husband, had been, alas! drinking hard some weeks before this, but seemed quite recovered, and one day she received an invitation from the minister of the parish to go on a picnic excursion with his children to see the beauties of the island. She would be back before ten. It was autumn, and the nights were long, with bright starlight and a little frost. Her husband would not go on shore, but appeared delighted to be left in charge of the child. The mother had not been gone over two hours, and night had fallen, when he told the first to call away the skiff, a light kind of dinghy. He told him he was going on shore to the manse, and would take the child with him. He was in no way excited, but quiet and calm, and singing low to the child as he went down the gangway ladder.

The mate watched him rowing himself towards the shore, then went below.

The captain was never seen again.

His name was Mearns, and the *Sea-Swallow* was as much a yacht as a trader, though she did bring cargoes of fruit from Italy.

Mrs. Mearns was prostrated with grief, and for many a long week never left her bed. The most Christian conclusion she could come to was that the boat had been swamped and sunk, and both the husband and child drowned.

But the *Sea-Swallow* was sold, and ever since poor Mrs. Mearns had lived alone with her grief, in her beautiful home down near to Torquay.

"And this lady is—my—mother, Daddy?"

"Yes, my lad; and you will see her to-morrow."

And next day he was early on shore with Oscar, and went straight to the manse.

The lady in black came slowly up the garden path about mid-day.

Something seemed to whisper to Creggan, telling him that this was indeed his mother. He ran to meet her.

She held him at arm's-length for a few seconds, while she turned white and red by turns.

"It is indeed my long-lost son!" she cried. "Oh, heaven be praised for the dawn of this day!"

Then woman-like she relieved her feelings by weeping.

Mrs. Mearns took up her abode at the manse for two months, all the time, in fact, that Creggan spent in Skye. But she seemed quite a changed woman, and looked ten years younger at least.

She no longer wore mourning, but light-coloured, beautiful dresses. She played and sang too, in a manner that quite fascinated the minister, and she took part in all the rambles about this wild romantic island.

Well, partings came again, and with them tears and blessings. Oh, that sad word "Farewell"!

In a week after this Creggan and his mother were at Torquay. But a delightful old-fashioned wooden paddle frigate was commissioned at Plymouth. She was going on Special Service, to carry despatches here, there, and everywhere. Creggan went on purpose to see her, and though the carpenters, or wood-peckers as we used to call them, were still on board, the lad—who, by the way, had been promoted to sub-lieutenant, wore a stripe and carried a sword—liked her so much, that he made an application to be appointed to her.

His appointment came in a few days.

Then Creggan once more took the bold step of calling on the captain, and with him went Oscar.

Captain Leeward opened the door, and when the young sub-lieutenant introduced himself—

"Oh, come in, my good fellow. No, no, don't shut the door in the dear doggie's face."

So in went Creggan and in went Oscar.

"I say," said Captain Leeward, a most pleasant-faced man, "I must ask you to bring this beautiful animal with you. I have a lovely black Newfoundland, and they will be excellent companions."

Had anyone handed Creggan a cheque for £10,000, he could not have been more delighted than he was at this moment.

Then in stalked the very dog the captain had mentioned. Creggan had never seen so noble a fellow before.

He appeared a little surprised at seeing another dog in the room, but as soon as Oscar went up and licked his ear—a dog's kiss—he took to him at once, and before Creggan left they both lay asleep together before the fire.

"I've heard all about you from Captain Flint himself—rather a tartar sometimes, but possessed of a right good heart. You must stay to supper, and we'll swap yarns, you know.

"By the way," he added, "do you know that your bold messmate, Dr. Grant, has been appointed to this ship?"

"I didn't know, but I feel so pleased!"

A very delightful evening Creggan spent, till nine o'clock, then he begged leave to go.

The last thing that Captain Leeward said as he shook Creggan's hand was this:

"You saved your captain's life, lad. Your courage in presence of the enemy was conspicuous, and although the Admiralty is slow—it won't forget you!

"Good-night. Join your ship in a week's time."

"Good-night, sir. You have made me very happy."

CHAPTER XVI
LIFE ON THE GOOD SHIP OSPREY

It was a stormy day in the end of October when the good frigate *Osprey* got up steam and put out to sea.

Signals had been exchanged for an hour before this between the admiral's office and the ship. The admiral thought it most imprudent to sail on such a day.

Captain Leeward was persistent, however, and at last, like any other wilful man, he had his way.

The wind was from the east-south-east, cold and bitter and high. The air, too, was filled with sleet or snow.

When they passed the breakwater it caught her bows smartly, and slued her for a few moments out of her course. But the helmsman quickly put her up, and the strong paddles fought the water fiercely, and successfully too.

Balked in its design of driving the *Osprey* against the breakwater, the wind did all sorts of ill-natured things. It cut the smoke of the funnel clean off, and drove its dark wreaths to leeward; it rattled the braces, it shook the rigging; it slammed the companion doorways, swayed the hanging boats about, and dashed the spray inboard with sometimes a green sea, till everybody who had to be on deck and hadn't an oilskin on was drenched to the skin. A nasty, disagreeable old wind!

The *Osprey* didn't seem to mind it a bit. She had a broad beam of her own, a strong bowsprit and jibboom, and she lifted her bows slowly, and with a sturdy disdain that showed she cared for neither wind nor sea.

Nor did the men either—every one of whom had been picked and chosen by Captain Leeward himself, every one of whom was as hardy as the vikings of old.

Before the ship was two miles from the Sound, and while standing amidships talking to Grant,—the *Osprey's* head being now turned to west-and-south, so that spray no longer flew inboard,—Creggan said:

"Listen, doctor; what a grand singer!"

For up from the forehatch rose high above the roar of the wind a manly voice, singing one of Dibdin's most favourite songs:—

> "Blow high, blow low, let tempests tear
> The mainmast by the board,
> My heart with thoughts of thee, my dear,
> And love well stor'd,
> Shall brave all danger, scorn all fear;
> The roaring winds, the raging sea;
> In hopes on shore
> To be once more
> Safe moor'd with thee."

"Yes, he sings well. And do you know, that with the kindliest heart that ever was in sailor's breast, Captain Leeward has his peculiarities."

"Yes?"

"Yes. I've known him before, and sailed with him, always in a wooden ship. He hates an iron-clad, and he must see canvas bellying out aloft if there be a bit of wind at all. He is really an independent man, and wouldn't take a ship at all unless he had all his own way. So every man-jack is a jolly tar of the good old school, and his officers too, are, I have always found, genuine fellows. He must have somebody to dine with him every night, and it is just as often a middie as a ward-room officer. As for myself, I have always a knife and fork laid for me, and if I don't dine with Leeward I look in after dessert, and many a yarn he spins me."

"So different from Flint."

"Oh, yes; but we must never say a word against the absent."

"No."

"Hark!" cried Grant; "didn't I tell you?"

The ship's head was kept away a point or two.

Next minute the bo's'n's shrill pipe was heard. "*Eep—eep—peep—peep—ee—ee—ee!* All hands make sail!"

Up rattle the watches below, and aloft they went right cheerily.

Creggan had never seen a ship's sails cast loose so speedily, nor so quickly braced up.

"They are indeed good sailors, Dr. Grant."

"Yes, I told you. But look here, old fellow, just call me 'Grant', and 'douse' the 'Dr.'."

"All right, Grant," said Creggan, laughing.

The fires were now let down and the paddles thrown out of gear, and presently that old *Osprey* was doing ten knots an hour on a beam wind.

I suppose that Captain Leeward had some inkling of where he was going to, else he would not have held this course.

But the sealed orders were opened next morning, and he found that the *Osprey* was on particular service, her first destination being Venezuela.

He told his officers this, and that they might then look in at Rio and open further orders there—probably.

If, reader mine, you knew the Service as well as I do, you would remark that it was very good of the gallant Captain Leeward to be thus explicit with his officers. Many men that I know, or have known, would have shrouded themselves in their cold dignity, and to any inquiry made by an officer as to their destination, would simply have replied—

"Venezuela."

If asked, "And where next, sir?" such men would reply, "I really can't tell you at present".

Well, lads who mean to join the glorious British Navy, and serve either as young officers or boys under—

> "'The flag that braved a thousand years
> The battle and the breeze',

must not expect their lives to be all sunshine, any more than they need expect the sea around to be always blue, rippled by balmy winds, and domed over with an azure sky, flecked with fleecy cloudlets, and at night studded with silver-shining stars.

In some ships they will find that fighting the waves is not fun by any means, because many of the best of our navy ships are sent to sea defective. Machinery—and it is marvellously intricate nowadays—may break down at an untimely moment, even in the midst of a terrible storm, and having no serviceable sail, even the largest iron-clad will then be at the mercy of the waves. Oh, how she rolls and yaws and plunges and careens at such a time!

The best sailors on board cannot keep their feet, their heads swim with the awful motion. Things break loose and play pitch-and-toss about the deck, the ward-room furniture may be all one chaotic heap, and all the while the seas are making a plaything of her, dashing over her, high as the conning tower, and rushing in cataracts fore to aft, or even vice versa. At such a time it seems as if the ocean wished to show those poor wave-beleaguered sailors how small the strongest works of man are, compared to those of God.

But independently of storms without or the breaking down of machinery, the ship may not be a happy one as far as officers and men are concerned. The crew, all told, may be a badly assorted one, and I have been in ships, only for a short spell, thank goodness, that were known on the station as "floating hells".

Much depends upon one's captain. If he is a kind-hearted, genuine fellow he can do everything to keep things smooth fore and aft. The ward-room officers take their cue from him, the gun-room follows the example which the ward-room sets them on deck or below, the midshipmen influence the warrant officers, and these in their turn the able and ordinary seamen and the first and second class boys themselves.

But I must heave ahead with my story, instead of hauling my fore-yard aback or lying-to, in order to ruminate and preach. Oh, I know my own faults, my lads; I have so much to say about sea and a life on the ocean wave, that, with a pen in my hand, I want to say it or write it all at once.

Well, Creggan hadn't been a day at sea before he found out that the *Osprey* was going to be a real happy ship.

They soon lost sight of land in the haze of the storm, though all day long the beautiful gulls kept sailing around the ship, tack and half-tack in the air. For these sea-gulls look upon ships as their own, because from them they receive their main supply of food; so they always follow them afar, trying, as it were, by their plaintive calls, to get them to return.

It was dark enough at eight o'clock to-night, and the gulls had all returned shorewards. The gale still raged, but the *Osprey* was under easy sail, and the motion was by no means disagreeable to a sailor.

Creggan had been keeping the second dog-watch, but now went below. There was first the fighting deck to pass through, where the great port-holes were, and the black, shining guns, each with its snow-white lanyard prettily coiled and lying on the breach. A fine open breezy deck, the shot and shell neatly arranged in racks around the hatchways, and the sick-bay far away forward yonder. Abaft here was the captain's quarters or saloon, with a red-coated, armed sentry walking near it, slowly fore and aft.

Then Creggan dived below. Aft again on this deck and right under the captain's quarters, only coming more forward, was the well-lighted ward-room, from which issued the sound of merry voices and laughing. Turning forward and on the port side there was first a cabin or two, and then the gun-room.

Below this was the orlop deck, where many hammocks were hung, and which was lined with two rows of dingy, dark, though white-washed cabins, lighted by day only by the round scuttle-hole, and at night by a candle hung in jimbles. These cabins were told off to warrant officers, bo's'n, carpenter, &c., &c., and to senior officers of the gun-room. But really most of these preferred a hammock just outside, for the sake of fresher air.

To-night, Creggan, to whom one of these cabins, and a good one too, was allotted, had occasion to go below. He heard a sad moaning proceeding from a hammock, and a white, white melancholy face hanging half over the side.

"I say!"

"Yes, my lad."

"Are you the surgeon? I'm very dickey. I'm a a clerk, and I wish I had never, never left the land."

"Well, I'm sub, and the second senior member of your mess. Don't give way. I'll go and get the surgeon."

And so he did.

Kind-hearted Grant first gave him a doze of something, which I know well but must not mention, then a tumblerful of good champagne, and in five minutes' time poor little Mr. Todd was wrapt in dreamless slumber.

There were two more of Neptune's young children who wanted seeing to. Having done so, Grant went aloft again.

Then Creggan went to his quarters.

"Come along, sir," cried one of three bold middies who sat around the gun-room table when Creggan drew back the curtain; "come along, and have a hand at whist."

"Thank you, messmates, but I must feed first."

"Steward!"

"Ay ay, sorr," said an unmistakably Irish voice. "That's me, myself, sorr;" and a tallish, smart fellow, with black buttons on his short jacket, and a blue ground to his beardless face, entered the mess.

"Bring in the beef, and all kinds of fixings."

"Any dhrink, sorr?"

"No drink, thanks. What's your name?"

"M'Carthy, sorr, sure enough."

"Well, Mac, heave round."

"Be back afore ye could say knife, sorr."

Creggan made a capital supper. Then he had just one game to please the youngsters.

"I'm dying with sleep, boys," he said, "so I'll turn in. Ta-ta, see you all in the morning."

He departed, leaving them singing, and, turning in, was soon sound and fast. And thus he slept till called to keep the morning watch.

It was a little cold, but Creggan had bent on his thickest pilot jacket, and the second lieutenant soon came stumping up, and he also had on his foul-weather gear.

But the wind had gone down considerably, and with it the sea. She had lost way, too. So Mellor sent men aloft to loosen and shake out sails. The effect was magical, and with the wind well abaft the beam the *Osprey* pulled herself together, threw off dull sloth and went through the water like a thing of life. All along the top-gallant bulwarks forward, the spray was sprinkled as the good ship spurned the billows, but nothing came aft.

Mr. Mellor, the lieutenant, a round-faced, fair-haired young Cornishman, strode up and down the deck talking, and smoking a short clay. Creggan and he were swapping yarns—humorous yarns mostly—and exchanging experiences, and were soon as well acquainted as if they had known each other for years.

Soon after five bells, a light was seen gradually spreading over the eastern horizon, getting higher and higher momentarily. It looked at first like the reflection of a far-off city on a dark night.

But the light grew whiter and brighter.

It was gray dawn now. Then high up in the west a streak of a cloud began to glow with orange and crimson beauty. Rolling clouds on the horizon astern were lit up with a fringe of gold and carmine. Then all the east became a glory of colour that was almost dazzling, but very beautiful. The god of day was rising, and this dazzlingly-painted orient formed the curtains of his couch.

Soon now, red and fiery, his beams spread in a path of blood across the sea, and lo! it was day.

Both Creggan and Mellor spent that watch very pleasantly, and before going below the latter held out his hand, and Creggan gladly grasped it.

"Good-bye," said Mellor. "We're going to be friends, you know."

CHAPTER XVII
MESS-ROOM FUN

The gun-room mess of H.M.S. *Osprey* was by no means an overcrowded one—three middies, an assistant-paymaster, a clerk, another sub-lieutenant, Mr. Wickens,[1] and Creggan himself.

> [1] My prototype for this young officer was Sydney Dickens, the son of the great novelist, with whom I was shipmate, the dearest little fellow I ever knew.—G.S.

One middie did not really belong to the mess. He was a supernumerary, going out to join the flag-ship on the South American coast.

Midshipman Robertson was a funny little fellow. Not bad-looking, but choke-full of merriment and ideas for practical jokes, and when he talked to his messmates down below, he always screwed his face into puckers and dimples with the laughter he tried in vain to conceal. He was an Edinburgh boy, while young O'Callaghan, the supernumerary, came from Killarney, and was just as Irish as the steward.

Many a droll logomachy used to take place at dinner-time between little Scottie and this Killarney lad. All in fun, of course.

Young Bobbie, as he was called, delighted to tease Paddy O'Callaghan.

"Oh, don't give Paddy another morsel!" cried Bobbie one day at dinner, as the Irish boy passed his plate to sub-lieutenant Sidney Wickens for another slice of beef.

"And why not, you Dougal Crayture?"[2] cried O'Callaghan.

> [2] The red-haired Highlander in Scott's tale of "Rob Roy".

"For your own sweet sake, Paddy. I really must look after you. Coming from a land of potatoes and buttermilk and—want and woe, over-indulgence in the roast beef of Old England might have serious consequences. Indeed, indeed it might."

"Want yourself! I hurl the insinuation back. Sure, it wasn't for want that I came here."

"No, Paddy, no,—because you had too much of that at home, you know."

And the laugh was all against poor Paddy this time.

When the plum-pudding came on that day, again Bobbie held up a warning finger.

"Mind what I told you, Paddy," he said solemnly, "or I'll have to write to your mother, and she'll take you back home to look after the pigs."

"Sure it's yourself that should go home," retorted O'Callaghan. "If all reports be true, you'd make more money in bonnie Scotland than here."

"But how, Paddy darlint?"

"How? Is it yourself that asks? Didn't the Duke of Argyle—God bless him—put up rubbing-stones in every field? Well, you'd make a dacint living if you just stood beside one and sold butter and brimstone. That's for you this time!"

After the first storm the weather became glorious. A splendid breeze, that filled every sail, blew over the sparkling sea—a breeze that made every sailor's heart beat with joy, a breeze that made every man-Jack lithe and active, ay, and happy, bringing merry laughter to the lips and song from the very heart.

Captain Leeward was very proud of his ship.

"She isn't much of a fighter perhaps, you know," he said, "and I dare say a shell or two from a big gun would speedily rip her up, but she is comfortable and dry and nice, and for all the world like a yacht, and so I love her."

"You wouldn't be a sailor if you didn't, sir," said Grant, whom he was addressing. "But I never saw a ship before so prettily finished, both on the upper and fighting decks. The Lords Commissioners have been good to you."

"Ha, ha!" laughed the captain. "It is little indeed you can get out of them. I did the decorations—extra paint and gilding, and all that—out of my own pocket, doctor."

"You have zeal for the Service, then?"

"Not a bit of it. The Admiralty hold out no encouragement for men to be zealous. But I have zeal for my own comfort, and you won't catch me in a box-heater (ironclad), or a torpedo-boat either, if I can help it."

In the captain's private cabin was a large sealed box of private despatches. This, on being opened, was found to contain letters for war-ships both at the Azores and Bermuda. So the vessel's course was changed to a more southerly direction, and on she sped, with stun'sails set.

Well might Leeward be proud of the appearance of his ship's decks. Brass-work shone like burnished gold; hard wood glittered like boatman beetles. Never a rope's-end was left uncoiled; the decks themselves, scrubbed early every morning, were as white as piano-keys, and so were even the capstan bars; while the sailors themselves, with their brown, hardy faces, were dressed in white trousers and jackets of blue.

It was not a temperance ship, yet, although the man who did the day's cooking for each mess of sixteen men had a plentiful allowance of rum, no one was ever reported by the master-at-arms as being even a trifle the worse of drink. On fine evenings Captain Leeward encouraged games. Ship's quoits was a favourite pastime, so was the running high-leap; hop-step-and-jump; and leap-frog, once begun, would be kept up all round the deck till the men were ready to drop. Of course, with the swaying of the ship, the men had many a tumble, but this only added to the general mirth and merriment.

Don't imagine, dear reader, that the gun-room officers took no part in these sports. They couldn't keep out of them, and Paddy and little Scottie might have been seen vaulting over each other, time about, as if their very lives depended on it.

Dr. Grant must have his little joke at times, and one day he announced to the officers of the gun-room mess that he was in a mood to offer a first, second, and third prize for the winners at standing high-leap.

Next forenoon the sports came off. Well, the ship that day was rolling rather, so that it was a difficult thing to stand at all.

However, everyone had the same chance, so the game came off. Creggan made a fairly good third, but Paddy and Bobbie tied for first.

"It's you and me, old stupidnumerary," cried Scottie. "You first. *Ignis via*—fire away!"

The rod was lowered several pegs, and the "stupid-numerary" cleared it easily.

So did Bobbie.

Up another peg, again the same, and so on till some inches over four feet.

Now, as Paddy was about to leap, the ship gave a bit of a bob, and the poor "stupidnumerary" kicked off the rod and fell on the softest part of his body.

"Hurrah!" cried Bobbie. "Scotland's going to clear it!"

He waited a few seconds till the *Osprey* was on an even keel, then sprang over it like a bird.

He had won, and the cheering was deafening, even Hurricane Bob the Newfoundland and Oscar joined in and made the welkin ring, while Bobbie pretended to clap his wings and crow.

Then all hands, including the victorious trio, drew aft to be present at the distribution of the prizes.

"Midshipman Robertson—First Prize."

Bobby sprang forward with alacrity and received—a mustard leaf.

"What is this for?" he said, with a droll look.

"Damp it," said the doctor, "and put it on your face to make you blush. I'm sure nothing else can."

"Midshipman O'Callaghan—Second Prize."

Up came the supernumerary and received—an ounce of Epsom salts.

"But, doctor, dear," cried Paddy, "what am I to do with them, at all, at all?"

"Swallow them, lad, to draw the blood from your head.

"Third Prize—a box of rhubarb pills."

Creggan laughed.

"Pills," said Dr. Grant, "and medicine of nearly every sort, are the best things in the world for the inside—of a rat's hole."

Creggan thanked him, and retired.

That evening the captain gave a dinner-party, invited to which were Creggan, Grant, and the second lieutenant.

It was a pretty little dinner. The captain's cook was really a *chef*, and the steward a smart young fellow from Austria, whom he had picked up at a London hotel, and who now acted also in the capacity of valet and took the greatest interest in all his master said and did. They say that no man is ever a hero to his valet, but it is the exception that proves the rule.

Antonio Brisha was that exception.

Both Hurricane Bob and Oscar were among the invited guests to the dinner-party.

Now there was only one drawback to Hurricane Bob's presence either outside or inside the captain's quarters. He was so black that the steward, who, when the ship was rolling a bit had to keep his eye on the dish he was carrying so as to balance it, could not see him in the gloaming, and more than once he had tumbled right over the honest dog, while the dish was smashed and the joint of meat continued the journey on its own account.

On such occasions Antonio used to say "Bother!" only he said it more so.

But on this particular evening everything passed off delightfully. When told they must behave, "Oh, certainly, sir", the dogs seemed to reply, and Hurricane Bob at once jumped up and on to the captain's beautiful sofa—the room was furnished like a lady's boudoir.

But Oscar, with his bonnie face and long sable coat, was not going to lie on the deck any more than his companion. So he not only leapt upon the sofa, but from thence on to the top of the piano, there lying down on the loose sheets of music with his chin upon his fore-paws, so that he commanded a bird's-eye view of the table and everything thereon—the snow-white cloth, the bright silver, the sparkling cruets and crystal, the flowers, and the fairy-lights.

"Oh, sir," cried Creggan half-rising, "shall I turn him out?"

"Not a bit of it. Let poor Oscar lie there, he has more good qualities than many a Christian."

Oscar moved not. But he shook his bushy tail by way of thanks.

During this delightful little dinner-party, the conversation was quite untrammelled by anything like conventionality—free and easy, as a sailor's dinner should be. No one attempted to restrain himself from laughing, if there was a good thing said; and, as is the case wherever sailors meet, the conversation changed from one tack to another, often going right about, like a ship in a sea-way, if any new subject suggested itself.

"Yes, Captain Leeward," said Grant, "I believe I will have another small slice of that most delicious beef. Ah, sir," he added, "I fear we won't live like this all the cruise. Fighting cocks aren't in it, sir."

The captain laughed as he helped his doctor.

"Ever been nearly starved, sir?"

"I can't really say I have. You?"

"Oh yes," replied the Doctor, "more than once. But on one occasion, while slaver-hunting on the East Coast of Africa in the little P— —, our mess ran into debt. The commander was honest to a fault, and determined we should live on ship's provisions—salt junk, pork, peas, &c., with rancid butter and barrelled eggs—ugh!—till we cleared off our debt. But this wasn't the worst, for our ship's stores had run short, and it would be months before we could get another supply, so we were put six upon four."

Creggan looked inquiringly.

"I mean, Creggan," said Mr. Grant, "that six men—the number in our mess—had to live on the allowance of four, and share it as well as they could.

"We had plenty of biscuits, however, but so full of dust and weevils were they, and so black with the attentions the huge cockroaches had paid them, that before we could eat them they had to be fried in bacon fat.

"There was no growling or snarling, however, we were all very young, and formed as jolly a little mess as anyone could wish to be member of.

"I was caterer. It was a red-letter day, or two even, if, while on shore at say Mozambique, I could fall in with a sucking-pig."

"You requisitioned it?" said the captain.

"That's it. I used to say, Piggie, I arrest you in the Queen's name. Piggie spoke out, but I used to hand it to my marine, and he stopped the squealing.

"Huge yams roasted in the engine-room ashes, we thought a dish fit to set before a king. One yam, with pepper, salt, butter, and fried biscuit, would make a midnight supper for four of us. Then we could sleep.

"Sometimes on shore I stumbled across an Arab who had a few ostrich's eggs for sale, and again we were in clover."

"Are they very large, Grant?" said Creggan.

"Well, one broken and made into a kind of mash was all that six of us could eat for breakfast, flanked, of course, by a morsel of salt pork. After such a breakfast as this we would go singing on deck. We did manage to shoot some gulls now and then, and when skinned they didn't taste so very fishy.

"One day we caught a young shark; he made some trouble on deck, but gave up the ghost at last, and submitted to be cut up and shared with all the crew.

"Flying-fish wouldn't come near us, but a bonito was sometimes hooked, and when inshore we got bucketfuls of rock-oysters. So we didn't do so badly upon the whole, except when far out in the Indian Ocean making a long passage from one island to another.

"We took a Bishop of Central Africa[3] and a Doctor of Divinity down with us to the Cape—a three weeks' voyage from Zanzibar. It was then we suffered most, for even the skipper's "prog" ran short, and as we couldn't have the Church suffer, we used to give them some of our scanty allowance, in return for which Captain Mill never failed to send us a bottle of wine—we had no rum. We mulled that bottle of port at eventide, steeped weevily biscuits in it, then drank and yarned and sang.

[3] Bishop Tozer.

"While eating our miserable dinner our chief conversation turned upon the 'spreads' we had enjoyed at English hotels, and the 'feeds' we meant to have when we once more reached

'The home of the brave and the free'."

"Well," said Captain Leeward, "your yarn, doctor, reminds me, that when I was a mite of a middle, only thirteen years of age, and that is longer ago than I like to believe, I was serving in the old flagship *Princess Royal*, on the China station, the ward-room mess, which contained some sprigs of nobility, got terribly into debt.

"This was a serious matter for the chief engineer, a plain-going old fellow, who had a wife and healthy family at home in England, and for the staff-commander, or master also. But the latter undertook to cater for a time, so as to free the mess from debt. He was to cater on the most economical principles. I may tell you, however, that between the chief engineer and master there was almost a blood feud. But the former, although objecting to expenses, dearly loved a good luncheon, and this was the meanest meal of the day.

"The chief would come below, give one glance over the table, then sink into his chair as sulky as a badger. Then didn't the wags around the mess-table tease him anyhow."

At this point of the yarn there was a smart knock at the ward-room door, the midshipman, or rather the midshipmite, of the watch entered, and, saluting the captain, told him that there was a clear light far away on the weather bow, and so low in the water was it, that the first lieutenant thought it must be in a boat, and that as the light was being waved about as if to attract attention, the men must be in distress.

"Is there much wind?"

"No, sir; we're not doing more than two knots an hour."

"Well, bear up towards the mysterious light, anyhow, and let me know again when you get alongside."

"Ay ay, sir," said Bobbie, backing astern and shutting the door carefully after him.

"Now, sir," said Grant, "perhaps you'll finish your yarn."

"Oh, certainly."

CHAPTER XVIII
ST. ELMO'S FIRE

"I was saying," he went on, "when Mr. Robertson came in, that knowing the chief engineer's weakness, they chaffed him unmercifully.

"'Dalison,'[1] one would say, 'allow me to send you some liver?'

[1] Not the chief's real name.

"'No, thank 'ee,' gruffly from the chief, as he leant back in his chair and frowned.

"'May I help you to some tripe, Dalison?' This from another tormentor.

"'No, thank 'ee.'

"'A morsel of kidney or heart, Dalison?'

"'No, thank 'ee.'

"Then he would bang his fist on the table, shouting, 'None of your hoffals (offals) for me! Stooard, bring in a lump o' bread and the blue cheese!'"

After the rippling laughter ceased, the captain, cracking a walnut, continued:

"Chaff was much more common in the service in those days than it is now, and if a brother officer had any peculiarity, he was sure to catch it hot.

"Dr. R—— was a grumpy old surgeon that I was shipmate with. He was not only grumpy, but surly and uncongenial towards his fellows. He was generally a little late for breakfast, and on his entering the ward-room detested being talked to.

"Here was food for game, and as soon as he came in, every officer all round the table had a kind word and inquiry for him.

"'Oh, good-morning, doctor.'

"'How have you slept, doctor?'

"'How do you feel on the whole, this morning?'

"'I trust I see you well?'

"At first he merely growled and grunted, but at last getting fully exasperated he would suddenly turn round and roar out:

"'Oh, good-morning! Good-morning! Good-morning! Hang the whole lot of you!'"

"Capital!" cried Grant. "Give us just one more doctor's yarn, Captain Leeward."

"Well, then, this next one hinges upon an admiral as well as a doctor. This gallant officer was always fancying himself ill, though there was never anything of the slightest importance the matter with him, and was never happy unless his fleet-surgeon, a dear little Irishman, paid him a daily visit and ordered medicine.

"A certain pill used to be prescribed, and was found to be most efficacious.

"But one day the admiral, or 'Ral', as he was called for short, gave a great dinner-party, and many mighty magnates, gentlemen and ladies as well, came off shore. Among the guests was, of course, the Irish fleet-surgeon.

"During the dinner the admiral somewhat inopportunely called out:

"Oh, doctor, those pills you gave me last are by far the best ever I've had. You must let me have the prescription when we pay off. What are they composed of?'

"Now, the good doctor did not half-relish the notion of 'shop' being brought on the tapis at so fashionable a dinner-party, so he answered with emphasis:

"'What are they made of? Why, bread! Bread, sir; nothing else!'

"There was a momentary silence around the table, and everyone looked aghast to see how the reply would be taken. But the admiral was a gentleman in the truest sense of the word, and always most considerate for the feelings of others. He saw that he had touched on a very unpleasant theme, so he smiled kindly, and passed it off by saying in his quiet way:

"'Well, well, well, such is Faith!'

"But the pills were really rhubarb after all."

So with pleasant chat a whole hour passed away, and then once more the midshipmite Bobbie knocked at the door.

"It is a boat, sir. Five poor men in it. Two lying apparently dead under the thwarts. The first lieutenant has hauled the fore-yard aback and is sending some men over the side."

The *Osprey*, I may say here, had already visited the lovely fairy isles called The Azores, and was now well out into the Atlantic, steering about west-sou'-west.

The captain's room was soon emptied now, all going on deck. The night was very clear and starry, with a bright scimitar of a moon slowly sinking in the west.

Yes, Bobbie was right. Two men were dead, and the other three could scarcely speak, owing to sheer exhaustion.

"We'll hear their story to-morrow. Dr. Grant, I'll leave them in your charge."

"I shall see to them, sir," said Grant.

Then he shouted "Sentry!"

"Ay ay, sir."

"Pass the word for the sick-bay man."

In another quarter of an hour the poor fellows, English merchantmen, were snug and warm in hammocks. Grant ordered some beef-tea, with a modicum of brandy, and they soon fell sound asleep.

But so weak were they next day that the doctor forbade their talking, and it was three whole days before they were strong enough to tell their story.

A TERRIBLE TALE OF THE SEA

There was no false pride about Captain Leeward of H.M. paddle-frigate *Osprey*. Some commanding officers that I have known would have had one of these unfortunate castaways to tell his story in the sick-bay. But instead of this the captain told the doctor to bring him in to his quarters.

He was a brown-faced, hardy, bearded sailor, but his cheeks were hollow now from his want of food and terrible suffering.

One hand was tied up in a sling.

He bowed and scraped as he came in, and if ever a sailor looked shy he did.

He gave just one glance around him, and then looked at Leeward's pleasant smiling face. The glance reassured him.

"Why, jigger me," he said, hitching up his trousers with one hand, "jigger me, sir, if ever I cast anchor in such a pretty saloon as this afore. Easy chairs, sofa, piano, fiddle and all, to say nothing about flowers and fairy-lights. Cap'n Leeward, sir, I ain't in a dream, am I? Mebbe the doctor here will 'blige by sticking a pin in me, up to the blessed head, if I am."

"Never a dream, Mr. Goodwin. Well, if you will bring yourself to an anchor, we'd like to hear your story. Have a little wine, sir?"

"Purser's wine is the only sort as suits me, sir."

"Steward, the rum!"

A tumbler and wine-glass were placed before the good sailor. The latter he pushed aside. Then, while the castaway held the tumbler with all the four fingers turned towards the captain, the steward filled it fully four inches. This is what is called "a bo's'n's nip".

"A little water, my lad?"

"No, sir, no; not for me. This rum is too good to be drowned."

He quaffed it, sighed, and put down the empty tumbler.

"Ah, sir!" he said, "now that very word 'drowned' makes me shiver. I've been, on and off, boy and man, at sea for well-nigh twenty years. Just entered as a boy, a tow-headed lad of Liverpool. Nothing to do till I growed a bit 'cepting to empty cook's ashes and pail, look after the dogs and ship's cat, feed the monkeys, and get kicked about all over the deck by anybody who wanted to stretch his legs a bit.

"But I grew into an able seaman at last. After'n which I gets to be second mate o' a Newcastle collier. Then fust mate. Then I up and studies for my certificate. You wouldn't think it, mebbe, of a rough chap like me, but I passed with flying colours, and steered homewards, wi' stunsails 'low and aloft, jolly happy now.

"I meets some maties, and two more overhauled me. So what could I do but go with 'em to wet my certificate.

"Sakes alive, cap'n! but I'd blush like a wirgin even now, if I weren't so brown and weather-beaten that ye wouldn't notice it.

"For, sir, I awoke next morning with a two-horse headache, and a tongue like kippered salmon. Clothes all on too, boots and all. I'd turned in all standing, but couldn't remember who'd brought me into port.

"Never mind, sir. 'Twere a lesson to me I ain't going to forget. Thankee, sir, I will have just another nip.

"But I s'pect, cap'n, I'm a kind o' hinderin' you I always do take longer time to tune my fiddle than to play my tune.

"Well, sir, it ain't more'n six weeks since I sailed from Glasgow, in what I might call the sailing steamer-barque *Ossian*. Our orders were to visit Azores, Madeira, St. Helena, Ascension, on our way to the Cape and Madagascar, and our supercargo, a business Scot, was to deal everywhere, for cash or goods, for we were laden up with 'notions' as the Yank calls 'em.

"Well, cap'n, our ship was as nice a craft as ever I stepped on board of, and the crew, too, was on the whole fairish; only too many blessed foreigners among them to please me. Most o' these'll work, ay, and sing too, in fair weather and fair wind, but they ain't no hand, sir, at reefin' topsails in a dirty night, wi' green seas a-tumbling in, and mebbe the yard-arms 'most a-touching the water every time the ship leans over.

"And we had dirty weather all along; sometimes 'twould be blowin' so hard we wouldn't be doin' more'n two knots against wind and sea, full steam up.

"We dawdled about the islands a bit, and the fine weather sort o' come at last, cause we was told to sail all we could and save the coals.

"We weighed at last, and had made a good offing into the Atlantic, 'cause it had occurred to Brown, the supercargo, that he could do a bit of honest biz at Bermuda, and the man was all in the interest of his owners.

"Some two or three hundred miles to the west here, we got into a circular storm and suffered severely. Our foremast was torn out of her, and two men slipped overboard in clearing away the wreck.

"Thankee, cap'n; but mind ye, this makes my third nip. Howsomedever, it's as mild as cocoa-nut milk.

"When we got clear away from that baby tornado, we was pretty nearly all wreck, gentleman. Bulwarks anyhow, mainyard even fallen (a rare accident), and our very winch half-throwed up on its end.

"But worse were to come, cap'n.

"First and foremost the weather got finer, but there was a strange kind o' a haze in the sky that I didn't like. That shortened the sunbeams considerable, and brought night and darkness aboard of us before they was due; and the moon couldn't well be 'xpected to shine through clouds that the sun hadn't been able to tackle. We managed to step jury-mast and bend new sails. But the wind was nothin' to signify now, and I made bold to tell the skipper that he ought to clue and get up steam.

"'There's no hurry, Jim,' he answered; 'even if we be becalmed a bit, it's cheaper than burning tons o' coal."

"Well, gentlemen, becalmed we was just after tea-time.

"I went on deck arter this, and such a night I'd never seen afore. Never a puff o' wind, sails hangin' idle, and the waves, as much as we could see of them, just like glycerine. I expected to see dead fish floating about on their sides.

"The bo's'n was walkin' with me in the ship's waist; but none of us had very cheery yarns to spin, we just stuck to our pipes and spoke but little.

"I could feel the bo's'n's arm tremble a little, though, as more than once a long quavering cry came over the surface of that hazy, oily ocean, dyin' away in a kind o' wail, like some poor creature in faintin' agony.

"Yes, I believe 'twere on'y a bird, sir; and there do be a shark that cries thus on windless nights near to the echoless ocean—the Sea of Weeds, or Sargasso. And 'twere there we were at this time. Every now and then we could observe long dark strips of the slimy stuff layin' along the rippleless waves' sides, dark and fearful, and looking for all the world like dead serpents.

"I'se a kind o' partial to pottery (poetry), cap'n, and lines from Coleridge's *Ancient Mariner* would keep risin' up in my mind, and didn't seem out o' place either on a night like that. 'Cause you see that, here and there, there was phosphorescence in the sea, and a shark had once or twice appeared on the surface, his sly eyes flashing, his fins dropping fire, and we could see him as he dived below getting smaller and smaller, till like a little wriggling worm of flame. Even little strips of weed that floated here and there looked like water-serpents.

"'The moving moon went up the sky,
  And nowhere did abide:
Softly she was going up,
  And a star or two beside.

But where the ship's huge shadow lay,
The charmed water burned alway,
  A still and awful red.

"'Beyond the shadow of the ship
  I watched the water snakes;
They moved in tracks of shining white,

> And when they reared—the elfish light
> Fell off in hoary flakes.'

"But, cap'n, when ye looked horizon-way—and the horizon weren't far off,—at one moment only the moon haze was there, next moment the summer lightning played along fitful but incessant. Then you could see great banks of ugly rock-and-castle clouds in front, a sight that made us think another baby tornado was a-brewin'.

"I was drawin' away at my pipe, and not saying a deal, when all of a sudden the bo's'n seized me by the arm.

"He was all of a shake now, and his eyes was eyes of terror, as he pointed aloft with outstretched arm.

"'Look! oh, look!'

"Yes, sure enough, cap'n, on the mizen topgallant mast-head, burned a strange tapering light as tall as a man's arm.

"We both stood mute with fear. It burned brightly for a minute, then flickered and went out. Only to reappear, however, in a few seconds, this time more blue than white. Then, flickering once more, it fled, and we saw it not again.

"Neither spoke for long seconds. We looked into each others' faces inquiringly-like.

"'That,' said the bo's'n, 'is St. Helmo's (St. Elmo's) fire, and this bloomin' ship is doomed.'

"I said nothing. I merely walked below, and passin' thro' the saloon entered the skipper's cabin and touched him gentle-like on the shoulder. Two candles was burnin' in jimbles, and a book he had been reading lay on the white coverlet. Sound asleep as a baby he were, but sailor-like he opened his eyes the moment I touched him.

"'Well, Goodwin, anything up?'

"'Nothin' much, sir. Only St. Helmo's fire been a burnin' on the mizen truck.'

"'That's nothing, lad. How's the ship's head?'

"'Why,' says I, 'you might as well ask how her stern is. Both are anyhow. Not a capful o' wind. She is (again I was quoting pottery)—

> "'As idle as a painted ship
> Upon a painted ocean'.

"'And,' I adds, 'we may as well get the fires up, for we're precious near the Sea of Sargasso. If we gets swallowed up there with mebbe a broken screw it may be a two years' job, if ever we sees blue water again in this world.'

"'Well, well, lad. If the winds doesn't blow get steam up. Meanwhile, go and whistle for the wind. I'm tired!'

"I left the cabin slowly, only just stopping to have a tot o' rum, for there was a kind o' hincubus a-weighing me down. But little did I know of the horror to come."

CHAPTER XIX
THE BURNING SHIP

"At twelve o'clock," continued Goodwin, "I went below to call old Deadlight, our first mate.

"When he came up, I stopped a few minutes to talk to him and tell him what we'd seen, and the captain's orders in case of getting too near the Sargasso Sea.

"I was just slueing round to go below, when I couldn't help thinking I felt smoke, like.

"At first the mate wouldn't have it. It was my imagination, he said. I'd been thinking too much about St. Elmo's fire, and all that rot. I'd better go and turn in, I should be better in the morning. He were just agoin' on like this and laughin' low to hisself, when up the fore-hatch comes the bo's'n.

"'Beggin' your pardon, sir,' he said, 'but I think the cargo is a-fire on the port side.'

"Deadlight and I hurried below now. Yes, sure enough, there was smoke coming up from the hold through the crevices of the hatchway.

"The cap'n was called, and was on deck afore you could have said 'binnacle'.

"He and the mate were very cool. So was all hands; and, cap'n, I always think it is a blessing when the ship and precious lives are in danger not to have any ladies on board, or longshore passenger swells. They beat creation with the fuss they make.

"I was precious sorry now that I hadn't got steam up instead of waitin' for the wind, for then we could have turned it into the hold and soon put out the fire.

"All hands were called and the pumps were manned.

"We cut a hole in the fore-hatch of the hold, and poured tons of water down. But even there where we stood our soles burned with heat, and we walked cautiously lest we should fall through the under-charred deck and be devoured by the fire below.

"I guess, cap'n, that the water we poured in just sunk through a portion o' the cargo, like, and lay at the bottom.

"It was an anxious time,—you bet your last rupee on that, sir!—but all hands worked like grim death in cholera times, and we hadn't time to funk.

"Hours and hours, taking turn and turn about. Provisions and rum were got to the upper deck, and water too, for it was evident that the skipper feared the worst. At the same time the boats were hoisted to the davits and hung over the sea, all ready to let go. And they were provisioned, every one of the three o' them, for ten days.

"Nothing was forgotten, gentlemen, that seamanship could suggest.

"To our dismay we found that the fire was now working farther aft, so we determined to clear the after-hold of cargo.

"A working-party was at once organized, but, cap'n, when the hatch was opened, such a stream of sparks and such stiflin' clouds of smoke rolled up, that glad was we when we got that hatch back in position.

"Fires was now well lit, though, and steam was turned into the hold.

"This seemed to do good at first, and we worked with redoubled vigour, singing merry sea-songs as we did so. But while so engaged, suddenly not only did volumes of smoke roll up, but tongues of flame ten feet high, that soon would have fired the middle-deck had we not succeeded in battening it down.

"Our object was to keep the fire confined to the hold, until we should succeed, if possible, in reaching some of the islands of the Azores, there to beach her and escape in our boats.

"It was not to be, although the boys worked like African slaves.

"We scuppered the decks now in the cabin, and down through the hole made thus, cap'n, we put the nozzle of the hose.

"And so we worked away all that fearful night and long into next forenoon. We didn't think much o' rest, gentlemen, nor food either. We just choked down a bit o' junk now and then, or a morsel o' biscuit, and kept it down with a peg o' rum. But, bless you, sir, our eyes was burnin', our faces hangin' in bags of blisters, and our mouths so dry by this time that there was no good trying to sing, for we were hardly fit to talk.

"Soon, now, the deck all along became so hot that the men had to leave in relays to put their shoes on.

"The end came so suddenly that we was thunderstruck. Somewhere near the fore-hatch the deck blew up with the force of the steam.

"Ah, what a sight! The clouds of smoke risin' as high as the foretop, and the tongues of red flame following and licking them up!

"About the same time the fire spread up out of the scuppered hole, and the saloon was all in a blaze 'fore ye could have said 'marling-spike'. It was all over now.

"But, next minute, and just as we was preparin' to lower the boats, a white squall came thunderin' over the sea, took the *Ossian* aback, and for five minutes at least we stood holding on to the riggin' or stays, while she went ploughin' astern. We 'xpected, cap'n, to see her go under, stern foremost, every minute. Mebbe I was a bit white, cap'n. I don't know, but my pals was."

"It was really a fearful situation," said Captain Leeward.

"Yes, sir, and gettin' worse as the time went on, for so long as the squall lasted the smoke and fire and sparks flew over us. But it stopped at last, and the breeze came round the other way.

"Then we worked like devils, cap'n, to get her afore it, and when we did it weren't quite so bad.

"Well, you know, gentlemen, a squall often brings on dirty weather. So did this. Seemed to me it was a choice o' deaths—to stay on board and sink with the burnin' ship, or lower the boats to go to Davy Jones in them. There was more hope in the last idea, so we lowered the boats one by one. I insisted on the skipper goin' in the gig—she was a good boat,—and then came the lowerin' o' the last, and that was the one, sir, that God's mercy enabled us to fetch you in.

"The lowerin' o' a boat, as you know, sir, is a ticklish thing in a heavy sea-way. Somehow our boat didn't take the water on an even keel, but stern first, but we got her righted and scrambled in at last. Night were a-comin' on now, cap'n, fast and dark, and a dirty night it were bound to be.

"We had a compass in each boat, but not a rag of a sail, just the oars; and so wild was the sea that, what with keepin' her head on to the big coombing waves that else would have sunk us, precious little progress was made, I can assure you.

"We saw that burning ship an hour after we'd left her. Then she suddenly disappeared, and at the same moment the roar of an explosion, louder 'n thunder, rolled over the sea, and for the time being the waves hadn't a chance o' bein' heard.

"About the beginning of the middle watch the wind began to go down, and the sea too. 'I think, boys,' I said to my pals, 'we can have a bite and a sup, now.' But, mercy on us, sir! when I bent down to scramble for the provisions—none was there! The tack must have slipped overboard as we lowered the boat stern first.

"There was a bottle o' rum, that was all. I poured out just a little, in the shell of an old silver watch my poor mother had given me, and the men was thankful.

"But they was mostly exhausted, and I was feared they'd sleep. So, getting hold of some lanyard, I made 'em make the oars fast to the rowlocks, with freedom to move and no more.

"In an hour's time the storm had passed away, and the night was clear. I put just two to the oars, leaving two men to sleep and to relieve their pals when they began to nod. Good thing I'd tied the oars, cap'n, for by an' by one poor beggar fell off the thwart and I kicked up a sleeping chap to take his place.

"Well, now that the sea was quiet, steerin' was of no account like. I just told 'em to go on and keep their weather eye on a certain star I pointed out.

"Then I curled up and slept like a stone. It was daybreak when I awoke. There was a glittering blood-red path across the waters where the crimson sun was shinin'. The sea was lumpy now, but the day promised fine."

"Where were the other boats?"

"Not one, sir, to be seen near or far, and we've never seen or overhauled them since. This was a terrible trial for us, as we had no food. No, nor water. On'y the rum, that could only excite us and make us by and by more wretched and unhappy.

"I put it to the vote, cap'n. Should we drink the rum or leave it till it was more wanted? Right bravely came the answer, ringing from for'ard:

"'We won't touch or taste it, till we ain't able to sit up.'

"All that day we rowed as well as we could, watchin' sea, watchin' sky, for a sight of a boat of our own, for sight of a sail. But the sun went down like a great blood orange, and weary and faint now, we hardly cared to row.

"There was neither moon nor stars that night, and so I just lashed the helm so as to keep her driftin' a kind of in her course.

"We stepped a little mast for'ard, and hung up our lantern. We blessed God that we had this, anyhow.

"Then we tumbled down to sleep, and long and sound that sleep must have been, for it was the short gray gloamin' o' mornin' when we pulled ourselves together again.

"And what think you was the first thing my hot eyes caught sight of?

"Why, cap'n, as sure as,—thanks to you!—I'm now a livin' man, it was our own biggest boat—a kind o' pinnace. She was stove in at the bows, and bottom up."

"How could it have happened?" said Captain Leeward, sympathetically.

"She must have fouled the other boat, sir, and without doubt both of the crews went to Davy Jones together. The skipper had been in the big boat. Poor chap! he leaves a young wife and three pretty kids.

"Our hearts sunk down, down after this. No one cared to speak much above his breath, and I noticed more'n once that day, cap'n, the tears quietly streamin' over the cheeks of a young sailor. Our fate, we feared, would be worse by far than that of our other brave shipmates.

"I told out a watch-shell of rum all round at eight bells, and we were a little heartened after this.

"But now, cap'n, the wind began to rise and moan over the sea once more, and though it was right for us, if it increased we couldn't keep her long afloat. Well, what does we do, sir, but tie two jackets together to make a sail, and bent them on two oars.

"The poor fellows were half-dead now, and couldn't have rowed two hours longer. After a rest and a kind of dreamy doze, we found the wind still higher, and the seas breakin' on board of us all the time.

"Nothing for it now but bail her out. We had two pannikins and our sou'-westers, and wi' these we just managed to keep her afloat till the second dog-watch.

"Another little tot o' rum at eight, and when the sea and most o' the wind went down we bailed her out once more, and then just tumbled down in the bottom, wet, shivery, wretched.

"When day dawned, and there was still no sail nor land in sight, we kind o' gave up in despair. The young sailor,—Tom Ball were his name,—sort of went dotty, cap'n, and tried to eat the flesh oft the ball of his thumb. I gave him four watch-shells of rum, and he sunk like a wet swab down between the thwarts. Bill Jones took off his own coat and covered him up.

"We suffered more from thirst than hunger, though, and Tom had drunk salt water, which sent him nearly mad, you see. So none o' the others touched it.

"I dozed again several times that day, and always my dreams, cap'n, was the self-same. I was wanderin' among beautiful woods, near my own old home in Berkshire, birds was singin' in the trees, there was wild flowers all along the banks of a stream, and again and again I stooped to drink, then all became dark and dreadful and I awoke with a shriek.

"You don't mind me quotin' pottery, cap'n, do you? For I really is main fond of it.

> "'All in a hot and copper sky,
>   The bloody sun, at noon,
> Right up above the mast did stand.
>   No bigger than the moon.
>
> "'Water, water everywhere,
>   And all the boards did shrink:
> Water, water everywhere,
>   Nor any drop to drink.'

"And again, sir, I may say:

> "'There passed a weary time. Each throat
>   Was parched, and glazed each eye;
> A weary time, a weary time,
>   How glazed each weary eye!'

"How that night wore along I cannot tell you, cap'n. No one rowed, no one steered.

"Next day our sufferings were fearful. Oh, cap'n, may you never know what it is to be afloat in a foodless boat on the bosom of a deserted ocean.

> "'And every tongue, through utter drought,
>   Was withered at the root;
> We could not speak, no more than if
>   We had been choked with soot.'

"I served out more rum towards evening.

"Having swallowed it, Mearns, an able-bodied seaman, leant forward towards me and said hoarsely, with a mad gleam in his bloodshot eyes:

"'Mate, we must cast lots who shall die, or shall we chance it and kill the young un?"

"I knew this man would soon be a raving maniac, so I gave him four more shells of the rum; then he slept.

"Another sunset.

"Another weary night begun.

"I prayed then, cap'n, as I'd never prayed before, that God in his mercy would let us pass from life before we woke.

"Then once more I dozed, once more I dreamt, and again the green summer woods all a-wavin' in the sunshine, the bird-song and the purlin' brook.

"But I had not slept long ere I was aroused. It was the young Tom Ball shriekin' in a strange high-pitched voice—for his throat was as dry as emery paper.

"'Mate, mate, mate!'

"'Yes, yes, here am I, boy.'

"'A ship, sir,—away down yonder!"

"I rubbed my eyes for a time, then saw your lights through a kind of haze.

"'The lantern—quick!' I cried.

"It was handed me, and with my hand all a-shakin' I brought out my match-box.

"O God, cap'n, there was but one lucifer there! On this our lives depended, and I felt that, if I did not succeed in lightin' that lamp, I myself should go mad and throw myself into the sea, to be devoured by the shark that, all throughout this weary time, had followed in our wake. I stood the hurricane-lantern under the stern-sheets; then I put one hand holdin' the empty box inside, lest a breath of air should blow out our only hope.

"Then I struck the match. A flare at first, then only a tiny blaze of blue. I turned it round, and its light grew brighter and whiter.

"The lantern was lit, and Bill Jones seized it from me, just as I fell down in the bottom of the boat in a dead faint.

"Young Tom Ball crept aft to me, while Bill kept waving the lantern on high.

"I was all doubled up, with my chin on my breast, and but for that young fellow Tom I should have died. But he laid me flat out, and rubbed my chest with rum, and when I sighed—a sad, sobbing kind of sigh it were, so he says—he got me to swallow a mouthful, and just as we got alongside your ship, cap'n, I was able to sit up.

"And I knew we was saved, though I didn't know then that the two hands lying asleep, like, in the bottom of the boat, was dead."

CHAPTER XX
GUN-ROOM FUN

If the reader—who I sincerely hope is going to be a sailor, for there is no life like that on the ocean wave—will take a glance at a map of the world and ferret out Venezuela, he will note that by sailing south-west by west in almost a bee-line for about 4700 miles, he would strike this land of beauty, and land of flowers and forests.

After leaving Azores, if his ship called there, he would find himself in a long and lonesome sea indeed, and after some weeks the Caribbean Islands would heave in sight, and our young sailor would know then he was far, far away from home.

Our own land—God bless it, and wouldn't you and I fight for it just?—is but like the cloud of fog that hangs over a city, compared to the loveliness of many of these fairy isles. The blue sky is fringed with the tall palm-trees that shoot from the soil, the islands themselves as you approach them appear to hang on the horizon, and so azure is the ocean, so cerulean the sky, you scarce can tell in fine weather where they meet and kiss.

The water around one's yacht or ship is sometimes so clear, so pellucid, that you see the bottom full ten fathoms beneath, where corals lie deep, where gorgeous and magnificently coloured shell-fish move slowly about, where marine gardens—more lovely far than any on earth,—planted and attended to by mermaids one would think, dazzle the eyes and delight the senses, and where on clear yellow patches of sand you may see flat fishes float, their sides so bedecked with patches of bright crimson, orange, and blue, that you cannot help thinking there must be a fish's fancy-dress ball on.

Then between you and the bottom float medusæ or jelly-fishes—bigger and more transparent than even those in Skye, for the limbs of these seem to be rainbow-tinted, or studded with gems of purest ray serene, diamonds, rubies, and amethysts. Yet all the creatures in that submarine garden wide and wild are not beautiful. Perhaps you are lying in a boat, gazing down through your water-telescope entranced, and half believing you will presently see a mermaid come out of a little cave combing her bonnie yellow hair, when, instead of the tiny mermaid, some patches of black-brown weeds are visibly stirred, and an awful head with fore-fins or fore-feet and claws, you cannot tell which, is protruded. Oh that deformed, scaly, warty head and these awful eyes, bearing some faint resemblance to a nightmarish caricature of man or fiend! If you are a nervous lad you will think and dream about this slimy apparition for weeks.

Well, all around Bermuda the rocks and sea-gardens are almost quite as lovely. Had the *Osprey* been going straight to Venezuela it would have been out of her course to stop here, but she had despatches to leave.

Two of the *Ossian's* shipwrecked crew were left there, but the mate begged to be allowed to remain and the captain had no objections. Goodwin was a naval reserve man, and even a lieutenant in that service.

This mate of a merchantman was in some ways a singular being, for although I think that the English he spoke was often rude, he could talk the language purely when he chose. Moreover, he was a student of gunnery, and could have worked a gun with any officer afloat. He was made an honorary member of the warrant officers' mess, and having no particular duties to perform, he spent most of his time making models of the newest guns and machinery of great iron-clads. Having got together, with the aid of the gunner and carpenter, some nice models, he announced in the gun-room that he was willing to give lessons to the midshipmen therein which would be of use to them when war's pennant floated red and bloody over the main. And many availed themselves of the kind offer, chief among them being Creggan himself and the Ugly Duckling—more about the latter presently. But even some of the ward-room officers, and now and then the captain himself, would look on as this ultra-enthusiast in naval warfare described the play of a battle of giant iron-clads, and the use of the terrible guns.

"Ah, boys," he would say, "there was much romance attached to the glorious days of Nelson, when hostile fleets lay in rows, mebbe two deep, one to support t'other like. When it was ship to ship, and hammer and tongs till one blazed, blew up, and sank, or when the skipper of a Britisher shouted through his trumpet to the master at the wheel: 'Lay us aboard that frog-eating Frenchman!' When the master steered so close to the foe that guns met muzzle to muzzle, and high o'er the din o' battle rang out the order: 'Away, boarders! Give the beggars Rule Britannia, lads!' The days when our brave blue-jackets used to swarm over the sides of the enemy's ship, or creep in through the ports, pistol in hand, cutlass in mouth perhaps, and lay the Frenchees dead at their guns.

"Yes, boys, these were the dashin' days of old, and somehow I sighs w'en I think they're gone.

"But the future sea-fights, young gents, are goin' to be fought with cool heads on sturdy shoulders. Excitement or rashness will mean annihilation; manoeuvring will be prominent, ay, and pre-eminent."

Here Goodwin would pause perhaps, look funnily down at his models and smile.

"You may think it a droll remark o' me to make, lads, but I do believe that, given two hostile battleships, encountering each other, then that skipper who is a good whist player, and has a long head that can see a bit into futurity as it were, or guesses before-hand what t'other chap will do when he, the whist man, plays his next card, will win the game o' war.

"This will kind o' knock some o' the romance out o' naval warfare. But not so much as we may think. Moral courage, mind you, boys, is of a far higher sort of quality than physical. And altho' the poet asks—

> "'And how can man die better,
> Than facing fearful odds,
> For the ashes of his fathers
> And the temples of his gods?'

one might answer him thus: He may die more truly courageously, more bravely too, if calm, if he meets his fate on a sinking iron-clad man-o'-war."

After their visit to Bermuda, and a delightful ramble through the beautiful island, Creggan was glad enough to find himself steering south and away via Puerto Rico, and bearing up for Venezuela. For the sea had already cast a glad glamour over the young man's life and soul.

Whenever he had time he wrote long delightful letters to his mother, to Daddy the hermit, to Archie, and to the Nugents, as well as to the manse. Perhaps his best and dearest of letters were those received by Matty. For Creggan couldn't help loving the child, and often he used to dream of her when far away at sea. Somehow she always appeared to him sitting in the stern of the skiff, her bonnie yellow hair toyed with by the breeze, and her eyes glistening with joy and happiness.

It was not pleasant, however, to be awakened from such a delightful dream at the dark hour of midnight to go on deck to keep watch on an angry sea.

It is needless to say that Creggan's letters were received at home with joy, read over and over again, and even laid aside for future perusal.

Goodwin was frequently invited to spend an evening in the gun-room mess, and these were red-letter nights for the middies, for this warlike mate of a merchantman could even make the sallow-faced young clerk smile. As for the Ugly Duckling, he smiled aloud till the beams rung and the plates on the table wanted to skip like lambs.

This midshipman's mess was always a merry one. Guns may change their form in the service, and ships as well, but our bold blue-jackets, and our daft, fun-loving and gallant middies, will never change as long as Britain's flag is unfurled,

"To brave the battle and the breeze".

Creggan, though somewhat older than midshipman Robertson, the plain-faced lad whose sense of humour nevertheless carried his mess-mates by storm, liked the droll boy very much, and they were together on shore whenever there was a chance. Along with them usually went the gentle Sidney Wickens.

Poor Sidney—he is dead and gone now—enjoyed a joke but never played one, but his smile was very pleasant, and at times even sad. He had, however, a quiet, quaint way of putting things that often made his mess-mates laugh. His fad during this cruise, as well as in the flag-ship at Sheerness, was the collection of beautiful gold rings. He often asked one or two of the warrant officers to look at these of an evening. And if the bo's'n, for instance, particularly fancied and admired one, Sidney would quietly hand it over his shoulder, saying, "Here, will you accept it, and wear it for my sake?"

Gun-room officers are fond of chaff, and unsparing in the use of it, no matter how it gives offence or how it is taken. But they always like best when the banter is returned. There is the banterer and the banteree, and woe betide the latter if he gets angry!

I believe Sidney—he was always called by his Christian name in a kindly, brotherly way, and somehow no one ever chaffed him—Sidney, I was going to say, was often sorry for the Ugly Duckling. But nothing could possibly upset the Ugly Duckling himself. Not even Bobbie's chaff. So good-natured was this droll duckling, that his extreme and quaint ugliness was really never observable. And his manner was as soft and gentle as that of a young girl, except when his soul was just bursting with fun and merriment, then he used to take to the rigging with Admiral Jacko to expand his extra steam, and allay his feelings.

A question whether Admiral Jacko or Duckie was the uglier, at times arose in the mess, even in the lad's presence. One day midshipmite Bobbie had the cheek to ask the Duckling to sit side by side with the Admiral during dinner, so that the right conclusion might be arrived at, and our friend did so readily and good-naturedly.

The Ugly Duckling is, you will readily believe when I tell you, a sketch from the life, and now that my memory brings him once more up before my mind's eye, I believe I am right in asserting that poor Mr. Duckling's face was more droll than ugly. Somewhat difficult to describe too. Forehead receded somewhat; nose nowhere, or hardly anywhere; eyes half-shut and full of fun; plenty of cheek, moral and physical; a longish, protruding upper lip; and an immense square jaw. His ears stuck out too, like lug-sails.

"Mind, Mr. Ugly Duckling," Bobbie told him one day at mess, "you must never get lost on the coast of Benin."

"Why, Scottie?"

"Why? How can you ask? Forgotten all your history? The king of Benin, you know, always nails his captives by the ears to a tree, and your ears you know, *mon ami*, are wonderfully suggestive!"

That day when the Duckling sat beside Admiral Jacko there was a good deal of amusement. The Admiral, I may tell you, was a very large and by no means handsome species of ape, and though he could not use a knife and fork, he ate most contentedly from the plate that M'Carthy the steward always placed before him, and he even used a table-napkin. On this particular day he more than once put his head cheek-by-jowl with the Duckling's, and the merriment increased.

The Admiral was exceedingly fond of the Ugly Duckling.

"Oh, look, mess-mates, look, now that their heads are together!" This from Bobbie. "Why, I declare that Jacko takes the cake!"

"For ugliness?"

"No; for beauty, boys!"

But Admiral Jacko had another very dear friend, namely, the ship's cat, a beautiful, half-bred brindled Persian.

After every meal Jacko used to collect tit-bits and stuff them into his jowl till his cheek stuck out, then he went at once in search of pussy and fed him. The action was almost human. Indeed it might have been called more so, for the "lower animals", as we are all too fond of calling them, often exhibit more kindness to each other than mankind does to any of them.

There was something quite out of the common about Jacko in many ways. He really had less mischief in his mental composition than monkeys generally. Hurricane Bob and Oscar used to be washed regularly once a week. The gun-room steward, superintended by Creggan himself, used to perform this operation. After the rubbing and rinsing with warm water and soap, they were always deluged with pailfuls of clear, soft water, and after they were dried down with half a dozen towels—the dogs' own property—they were combed and brushed.

Then ensued a wild scamper round and round the *Osprey's* decks, that made everyone laugh who saw it.

Admiral Jacko used to squat on top of the capstan while the doggies were being washed, and from the long, doleful face he wore, it was evident he pitied them. But as soon as the scamper up and down the decks after belaying-pins that the men threw to them was over, both dogs went and lay down on the quarter-deck in the sunshine. And now Jacko considered that his duties had commenced. He would leap solemnly down from the top of the capstan, Creggan would hand him the comb, then off he went to his friends the dogs. No peasant woman in Normandy could have combed her boy's hair more carefully than did Jacko go over Hurricane Bob's coat first, and then honest Oscar's, with finger-nails and brush. Well, if he did catch an errant flea it was executed on the spot; but the earnestness with which Jacko did the work, and the exceeding gravity of his face while at it, would have drawn laughter from a California mule.

I myself have never yet seen a more active middy on board a British man-o'-war than the Ugly Duckling was. No part of the ship's rigging was inaccessible to him. He would climb to the main-truck and wave his cap to those below.

One day, however, he attempted a feat that, although he had often performed it in harbour, was undoubtedly dangerous at sea, even on the calmest day. The sea all around that forenoon was as still and quiet as the grave, and the *Osprey* was on an even keel. They were now nearing the north coast of South America, and though steam was up, and the ship churning up a long wake of froth that trailed for miles in the rear, it made no other motion save vibration. Well, Jacko and the Ugly Duckling had been having fine fun that forenoon, much to the delight of those below. Up aloft they went, to top after top, and down again to deck by a back-stay. Hand over hand up that back-stay again, and so on, seeming to have no tire in them. But at last, to the horror, it must be said, of the officers on the quarter-deck, the Ugly Duckling slowly drew himself up to the top of the gilded truck, and then slowly and cautiously stood up.

There was no laughing now among those below, all were mute with fears for the poor boy's fate. This daring middy balanced himself first on one foot and then on the other, and then—will it be believed?—he took from his jacket pocket a tiny ebony fife, at playing which he was a great adept, and commenced to pipe *The Girl I left behind me*.

He never finished the tune, however.

Something had suddenly unnerved him, and well he knew that to fall deckwards would be death. He was seen, therefore, to suddenly crouch, and putting his hands in swimming fashion above his head, to spring into the air. He came down like a flash, and sunk far into the water, many yards on the port side of the ship.

"Away, life-boat's crew!"

Never, perhaps, was that life-boat launched more speedily. A life-buoy, too, had been thrown overboard.

The Ugly Duckling was too good a swimmer, however, to need such assistance, only he kept close to it, as he did not wish it to be lost.

Now the great danger was the sharks, cruel tigers of the seas, that in these hot latitudes swarm.

But the boat picked the middy up just at the very moment that two monster sharks sprang at the life-buoy and hauled it down.

The Ugly Duckling had stuck to his fife all the time, and now much to the amusement of the life-boat's crew commenced once more to play *The Girl I left behind me*, and continued to play till the boat got alongside. Then up ran the still dripping Duckling, and on gaining the quarter-deck first saluted it and then saluted Captain Leeward.

"Come to report myself, sir," he said, "for leaving the ship without leave."

"And I ought to punish you, sir," said the captain, trying in vain to suppress a smile; "but I will forgive you if you promise not to stand on the truck again."

"I promise, sir, readily; for, sir, it wouldn't be half good enough to be swallowed by a shark, fife and all."

And down below dived this queer middy to change his dripping garments.

CHAPTER XXI
JACKO STEALS THE CAPTAIN'S PUDDING

It would take a good many chapters to tell my readers all the tricks that this favourite of the gun-room mess played.

The surgeon, Dr. Grant, and he were excellent friends, and were often together; and sometimes if one of his mess-mates was a bit off colour, the Ugly Duckling would prescribe or pretend to prescribe for him, and his prescriptions were at times droll, to say the least.

One day, for instance, the white-faced young clerk was ailing. He frequently was.

"No use you going to Dr. Grant," said the Duckling; "he'll only give you black-strap and make you worse. Here, out with your note-book and I'll dictate a prescription. Are you ready?"

"Yes, Duckie."

"Well then, heave round: '*Recipe*'. Got that down? It's Latin, you know, so have a care, but all the rest is English. Place a saucepan on the galley fire, and when it is heated to redness pour therein seven ounces of spirits of wine."

"Yes."

"When it comes to the boil place therein the tail of a toad—"

"But toads have got no tails."

"Well, a frog's tail will do."

"And frogs have no tails, Duckie. You're a bit off your natural history."

"Well," cried the Duckling, "a garden worm will do. That's all tail. Got 'im down?"

"Yes."

"Next, place in your cauldron a hair of the dog that bit you."

"Yes."

"And next—mind, this is very important, and will greatly aid the efficacy of the medicine—five drops of the sweat of a murderer's right hand."

The white-faced young clerk glared up aghast.

"Wh—wh—why," he faltered, "there is no murderer on board!"

"Well then, kill somebody yourself!" shouted the Ugly Duckling. "Ta-ta! I'm off to give the doctor a dancing lesson on the main-deck."

Well, that was precisely what he was doing five minutes after.

Dr. Grant was a splendid dancer of Highland flings and reels, &c., but, good-looking fellow though he was, he would have told you himself that he always felt a fool at an English ball or hop, and he hated being a wall-flower.

So the Ugly Duckling had offered to teach him, and had you come forward on the fighting-deck during practising-time, you would have seen a sight to amuse you. There was the chief bo's'n, a capital violinist, seated astraddle on one of the big guns, and playing some sweet, sad waltz, and yonder the little Duckling and the great Scotch doctor floating round and round the deck, with an awkwardness, however, that caused all the onlookers to shout with merriment.

The doctor didn't laugh a bit. It was a very serious matter for him indeed. His happiness was at stake; so he stuck to it, and tripped on the not very light fantastic toe.

His assiduity was finally rewarded, however, and he became one of the best dancers on board, and on shore was quite a favourite with the ladies.

At first the great monkey had been simply called Jacko, or Able-seaman Jacko. But the Duckling determined to raise him to the rank of admiral. First and foremost, however, he took no small pains in teaching his simian friend to walk erect. This he soon learned. Then to salute, &c.

After he was perfect in these accomplishments Jacko's promotion came. Well, you know, reader, it isn't the first time one of a ship's crew has risen from powder-monkey to admiral.

Then why shouldn't Jacko? Why not indeed?

The Duckling took up some nice ship's serge and buttons and gold-lace from the paymaster, and then he made friends with the ship's tailor. In less than a week after this, behold Jacko rigged out in the full-dress of a rear-admiral, cocked-hat, sword, and all.

No ward-room officer except Dr. Grant was "in the know", and the doctor good-naturedly gave the Duckling the use of the sick-bay for training purposes, and for the practice of their evolutions.

I verily believe, from the aptitude to learn which Jacko evinced, that the droll rascal was not a little proud of his splendid uniform and epaulettes.

Anyhow, his education was soon complete. So one evening, as the captain, all alone in his quarters, was bending over a chart—the ship being then not far from land,—Bobbie, the wee Scotch midshipmite, who was a great favourite with Captain Leeward, knocked smartly at his door and quickly entered.

"An admiral come off to see you, sir!" he squeaked. "Shall I show him in?"

"Most certainly, Mr. Robertson. But—"

And the captain rose in some agitation, and pushed back his chair.

The state of his feelings may be better conceived than printed when in marched Admiral Jacko.

Jacko took off his cocked hat, and bowed.

"Ah—ha—ah—ha," the monkey said, for all the world like a nervous man beginning a speech, and held out his little black hand as if to shake.

Bobbie stuffed his mouth with his handkerchief. It would have been rude to laugh before his captain, but when the latter threw himself down in his chair in an apparent state of convulsions, then the midshipmite laughed too, and even the captain's steward could not refrain from joining the chorus.

Five minutes after this the ship seemed shaken from stem to stern by the wild hilarity of the ward-room officers. They had been at their dessert when Bobbie introduced the Admiral.

The best of it all was, that Jacko himself looked as grave as an Oxford don. Never a smile was on his face. Not even the ghost of one.

But the new admiral was given a chair and a plate, and, behaving himself with all decorum, enjoyed a hearty feast of nuts and raisins. After this, accompanied by Bobbie, he bowed and took his leave. He had taken good care, however, to stuff one of his cheeks with nuts before he got down off his chair, till it stuck out like—so the doctor phrased it—a very bad case of inflammation of the parotid gland.

Admiral Jacko, it must be admitted, was a very funny fellow, but I fear I could not certify that he was strictly honest. Real rear-admirals would never, for instance, do what Admiral Jacko did once. He was on the fighting-deck one day, and noticed the captain's steward pass into the saloon with a nice little plum-pudding.

Jacko, in full uniform, walked past the door several times and had a sniff, the sentry smiling and presenting arms to him. But presently an officer entered to inform the captain that a strange man-o'-war was in sight, and leaving his luncheon he went on deck to have a look at her. This was the Rear-admiral's chance. He rushed in and as quickly came out again, hugging the brown and savoury pudding in his arms.

The sentry didn't present arms to him this time, only he determined not to tell upon poor Jacko.

"Bring in the pudding, steward," said Captain Leeward.

"Oh, sir, I brought it!"

"Then where is it?"

"That's what I should like to know, sir!"

He clapped his hand to his head, and for a moment looked confused.

"Oh, sir," he cried next minute, "I'd lay my life if you'd let me, sir, that Admiral Jacko has collared it! Shall I run and hunt him up and recover it?"

"No, no, steward; it wouldn't be much worth by this time."

And, sure enough, there was Admiral Jacko in the main-top discussing that delicious "plum-duff", with half-shut eyes and all the airs and graces of an epicure. After he had eaten all he could swallow, he stuffed both cheeks, pitched the remains down on the head of an able seaman, then slid down a stay to find and feed the cat.

On the whole, then, I think it must be admitted that the *Osprey* was rather a happy ship.

When they neared the coast of Venezuela they had the good luck to fall in with the flag-ship of the station. Captain Leeward delivered his despatches and letters for officers and crew, and then to his surprise found that the admiral had a cablegram for him. It was to the effect that he, Captain Leeward, was to join the South American fleet for a few months. This was on account of a cloud that was gathering in Venezuela concerning disputed British possessions on the borders. At that time the cloud was no bigger than a man's hand, but it might spread till it covered all the sky, and darken even our relations with the United States of America, whose president was apparently spoiling for a fight with Britain.

The fleet was to hold itself in readiness to land blue-jackets and marines at any moment.

So they all went cruising together.

The poor Irish "stupidnumerary" was transferred for service to a tiny gun-vessel, and very sorry indeed he was to part with his mess-mates. For, bar chaff, they had all been as happy together as a summer's day is long.

For months the fleet hovered around the coast, only putting out to sea now and then if a storm threatened to blow them on to a lee-shore. But there was much intercourse between the various ships, and at the towns they anchored near, the inhabitants were most hospitable. The flag-ship often gave a dinner or a dance on the upper deck, which was tented over in its after part, and gay with flags and flowers and perfumed foliage.

What a happy, jolly life is that of a young naval officer on occasions like these, and how quickly, while waltzing with some lovely young girl to dreamy music, does he forget all the dangers of the ocean that he has come through!

He just lives for the present. And oh! that present glides far, far too quickly away, yet it is something to look back to with pleasure when once more he is out upon the lone blue sea!

CHAPTER XXII
IN THE WILDS OF VENEZUELA

Although the *Osprey's* visit to Venezuela may have but little interest for the reader, still it would be unfair to drag him away from that land without first inviting him on shore to have a look at some of its wild and lovely scenery.

A young fellow—a Spaniard, though he talked capital English—came off one forenoon. He was received by Creggan and the Duckling at the gangway, and after talking for a short time on deck they invited him below.

This Spaniard was a gentleman in every sense of the word, and possessed of all that old Castalian courtesy and urbanity which you see so little of in these matter-of-fact days. He owned, too, that he was independent, if not indeed rich.

"Oh, señor," he said to Creggan, "think you that your captain would permit you to spend a few weeks on shore with me? And your dear friend here? I will do all I can to make you happy."

"I do not doubt that for a moment," said Creggan, "and if we can succeed in getting leave we are at your command."

"Oh, I rejoice!" cried young Miguel.

"I myself," he added, "am bound up in botany, in sport, and in natural history. Ah! we will enjoy our little selves, see if we don't!"

Leave was asked for and granted that very day. The *Osprey* was going down the coast and would leave them here, returning again in three weeks' time.

"Ah!" said dark-eyed young Miguel, "that does mean six, my capitan. You look good, and good you must be."

The captain smiled.

"Oh, señor, Venezuela is a vast country!"

"Well, well, Miguel, I'll let the young fellows oft for five or six weeks. I think they will be safe with you, and it will do them both good."

"Oh, safe, sir, as the everlasting mountains. And I have two houses—one is my yacht, and the other my dwelling on shore on the banks of the great Orinoco. You have no such rivers in Britain, I believe, señor capitan?"

"Well, no," replied Leeward, smiling. "You see, we are somewhat cramped for space, and a river broader than any of our two counties we should find somewhat inconvenient, to say the least."

"A thousand thanks for the leave, sir!" cried Creggan impulsively.

Then he added:

"Pardon me, sir, but you are so different from Commander Flint."

Well, Creggan and the Ugly Duckling had as many good-byes and hand-shakings given them as if they had been going off for a whole year to fight for their Queen and country.

The Duckling's parting from Admiral Jacko was quite affecting, as far as feeling on the part of this strange but clever ape went. Perhaps from his excessive and droll ugliness Jacko looked upon the middy as a brother. Be that as it may, he hung with his arms around his neck and his cheek against the Duckling's, and the expression of his face was so sad that the gun-room officers would not have been at all surprised had he burst into tears.

"Take care of my brother Jacko, boys!"

These were the Ugly Duckling's last words as he seated himself in Miguel's boat, and the sturdy semi-Spanish sailors bent bravely to their work. Out there, where the *Osprey* lay at anchor near to a small but beautiful island, there was a kind of "jabble" of small waves, caused by cross seas and currents. But after bearing in towards the green-fringed shore for about three miles, the men singing as they rowed to the sweet, soft notes of a guitar touched by the fingers of Miguel himself, they rounded another island, and were soon lost to view from the deck of the *Osprey*.

The water was now more smooth, though the outward current ran high. The tide in fact was ebbing. When it flows here it flows fast and furiously, and there are times when the battle betwixt sea and river is so furious, that no boat could float in the turmoil of breaking waters.

The Orinoco is undoubtedly a grand river, though certainly not so wide as Captain Leeward would lead one to infer. It is a grand stream, and a wildly romantic one too—higher up, I mean, for, like the river Nile, it forms a delta. This is about one hundred and thirty miles from the wide Atlantic, and here it divides itself into a great number of mouths, most of them navigable.

The principal mouth or main-stream is called the Boca de Navios, and it was up this great stream that our heroes went with Miguel next morning, in his pretty little steam-yacht, of which the young fellow was so justly proud.

So light was this craft and so little water did she draw, that she could go anywhere, and being strong even in a buffeting sea-way, could have done anything. She was not, however, quite so light as the Yankee's boat that was warranted to sail wherever there was a heavy dew.

I am writing from memory only, so I cannot give the exact tonnage of the *Orinoco Queen*, but fifty tons is near enough. Her beam was broad, though. Her little cabin or cuddy quite a lady's boudoir, adorned and perfumed with the rarest tropical flowers, through which at night peeped coyly the glow of fairy-lights. The one great lamp that swung from the skylight had a crimson shade, and thus the cabin looked like a scene from dream-land.

At night Miguel played his guitar, and sang wild and martial ballads of the romantic Spain of years gone by, or soft lullaby-like love ditties. The music of these latter seemed to breathe o'er the strings. You could have told it was a serenade, and in imagination you might have seen a beautiful girl-face appear one moment at an open lattice-window above, and next, from a white and shapely hand extended, you might imagine a flower drop down, to be rapturously caught and pressed to the lips of the serenader. Spain, deprived of its romance, were nothing now.

Hammocks were hung on deck, and surrounded, as far as Miguel's guests were concerned, by mosquito curtains. But the captain, Miguel himself, slept on a grass mat.

The crew of the *Orinoco Queen* consisted of five men and a boy, two of the men being engineers. This little river craft, however, had a main and fore mast, on which were carried, alow and aloft only, fore-and-aft sails. The men were lanky and brown, dark in hair and eyes, with bare necks and chests, and legs all exposed below the knees. But they were as lithe and active as panthers.

From the very first Creggan and the Duckling knew that they were going to have a real good time of it. Miguel believed in taking life easy. With half-shut eyes, while the yacht steamed slowly up the river, he would lie or recline on a grass hammock on deck, a small perfumed cigar between his lips, making little else save interjectional remarks for an hour at a time.

Miguel had no middle-mind, if I may so express it; that is, he was either dreamy happy in a kind of lethargy, or as active as a pole-cat on the war-path.

In this respect he resembled the monster caymans, or huge alligators with which the yellow-white waters of the river swarmed. Terrible monsters indeed these are! You can see their great heads protruding over the moon-lit water, if you are keeping the middle watch. So lazy look they, that scarcely could you believe that anything could excite them, or wake them into activity. But let a man fall overboard, or—awful accident!—a boat capsize, and they cleave the water, quick as seals, and Heaven have mercy on the mariners, for the caymans have none!

In five days' time, taking it very easy, and often-times landing on wooded islands, or at the mouths of rivers—tributaries to the "Mother of Waters",—they reached Ciudad Bolivar.

Both the Ugly Duckling and Creggan were fond of the beautiful in nature, and everything they saw on the pretty arboreal islands which they touched at was new and strange. Many of these were inhabited, and the languid natives, who lived in thatch huts of wattle and clay, existing for the most part on fish, I think, were exceedingly kind to them. They brought them light wine, fruit, eggs, fish, and goat's milk.

Sometimes on a day of racing clouds and sunshine, Miguel would cast anchor at the mouth of a tributary river, and in his boat would start up stream with his guests.

Such rivers were wondrously beautiful. The overhanging trees, laden down with green foliage till the tips of the branches touched the water, were cloud-lands of a beauty that was rich and rare. For not only were their leaves a sight to see, but the climbing flowers that often bound them into great crimson, blue, or orange garlands, dazzled the eyes with their loveliness.

I said the branches bent downwards, yes, and formed cool sylvan arbours, in which the boat could lie for luncheon.

Miguel—kind-hearted he was and thoughtful—had forgotten nothing that could minister to the comfort of his guests, and serve to make this visit to Venezuela an ever-memorable one.

The mosquitoes of these regions are very lively little persons, and very fond of British blood, but a tincture that Miguel gave to the boys with which to rub face and hands, kept them well at bay.

After luncheon Miguel would sing and play for an hour.

Meanwhile the great snakes that lay sometimes all their length on the branches above, or hung head down therefrom, were no source of comfort either to Creggan or his friend. They could not keep from looking at them at first, fearful lest they might drop into the boat; and these serpents are deadly monsters.

"Do not look, my friends," said Miguel; "they may fascinate you."

"Is that story about fascination not all a myth?" said Creggan.

Miguel leaned forward and lit another cigarette before he replied: "Not so, Creggan. I have heard many stories of the power these monsters possess over the minds of men.

"But," he added, "one I do remember personally. I and a friend from Trinidad were hunting the panther in a piece of forest-land far away north of here, and among the Llanos[1].

[1] Tracks of uplands, covered with wild grass, trees, &c., and with cañons between.

"We came to a snake-infested jungle, but being very tired we determined to camp there for the night. We tied our donkeys to leafless cocoanut-trees, that looked at a distance like masts of ships. Then we swung our grass hammocks ready, and cooked supper.

"We were only on the borders of the ugly jungle. Yet it contained game-birds, and in pursuit of these Antoine and I entered its gloom. We got several, and were returning to our camp, I being about ten yards ahead of my companion. Suddenly—it makes me shudder even now—I heard my friend utter that strange quavering low scream that issues from a man in nightmare.

"*Oo—oo—hoo—oo!*

"I turned quickly. There stood poor Antoine, a huge snake depending from a tree not a yard from his face, and evidently about to strike.

ANTOINE WAS IN A STATE OF MESMERIC FASCINATION, AND PALE AS DEATH

ANTOINE WAS IN A STATE OF MESMERIC FASCINATION, AND PALE AS DEATH

"Antoine was in a state of mesmeric fascination—visage pale as death, staring upturned eyes, arms straight down by his side, and clenched hands.

"I fired at once, and the snake fell with shattered head, but writhing, leaping, and dancing body.

"A snake, my friends, never looks more hideous than when, headless, he twists and coils in the thraldom of death.

"My friend Antoine had fainted, but though he soon revived I noted something strange in his manner. It put me in mind of the childish hysterical nervousness of speech and movement a wine-bibber sometimes exhibits.

"But I marked also, that whenever that day he saw a huge snake hanging on a tree, he would stop and gaze at it with dilated eyes, and even after passing on he would turn again and again to look once more into the ever-open glassy eyes of the serpent.

"My friends, the worst was to come. I may tell you first, that the nights at this time were brightly moonlit. Well, we supped and turned into our hammocks, but after I had slept for hours I awoke suddenly with a strange kind of fear and coldness at my heart.

"I naturally glanced towards Antoine's hammock. It was too loose and puckered to have anyone in it.

"My friend had fled!

"I turned out at once and roused my men, and together we hurried down through a bit of savannah to the jungle. I was hoping against hope. But to all our shouting no response was given, except from the throats of wild beasts. We returned to camp now disheartened, to await the coming of daylight.

"At last, dear friends, the sun's crimson rays darted through the deep orange hue on the horizon, and after a hasty breakfast we hastened back to the jungle.

"We had not entered far, when, O Dios! my friends, the sight that met our gaze seemed to turn our hearts to ice. I shall never, never forget it.

"Antoine lay on his back; his face and hands were purple and swollen; on his brow were two vivid spots of vermilion; while his open glassy eyes were staring unmeaningly heavenwards through the trees.

"Dead? Yes, my friend was dead, and coiled around his neck was a large and fearful snake!"

As Miguel finished his little story, Creggan gazed upwards at the overhanging boughs and the ever-present snakes. But his host hastened to reassure him.

"Do not fear," he cried, "do not dread. Snakes are never vicious. They are good and kindly creatures, and at no time will they strike unless attacked, or in defence of their homes and their progeny."

I—the author—have had in my time a larger experience of snakes than I ever at any time desired, and I can quite believe the story that Miguel told his guests that day. Nevertheless, Creggan was never very sorry when the boat was once more out in the open stream.

The bird and insect life in these lonely dreamy woods it would be impossible for me to describe. Suffice it to say, that they were beautiful beyond compare. And yet the birds—that looked like flying flowers—had but little song. Their beauty of colour is granted them by God that they may resemble the orchids, and so deceive their reptile foes. If they sang much their presence would be revealed.

CHAPTER XXIII
DOLCE FAR NIENTE

Few authors bother themselves, or their friends either, with maps. But I am an exception. Wherever my bark may be, in whatever part of the globe, on whatever sea, I like to know my bearings and view my position on the chart. It is the same if I journey inland.

Then, when writing my tales, I like my boy and girl readers to be with me, and each of them to keep his or her weather eye lifting, as I do mine. Indeed, as to my latitude and longitude in any portion of this small world, I am as particular and as "pernicketty" as any old maid is over her cat, or her cup of brown tea.

So—if thou lovest me, lad or lass,—just take your atlas and turn to the northern parts of South America, and you shall speedily find Venezuela, and the great Orinoco river also. Cast your eyes inland, along this mighty stream, and you will strike Ciudad Bolivar (Angostura) on the south bank and Soledad on the other.

It was for Soledad that Miguel made tracks first, and here he and his guests went on shore and dined at the poseda or hotel. It was a brisk time here at this business season. For to Soledad come now many a well-laden wain, and many a string of hardy, loaded mules, bringing with them the produce of the northern interior to ship over across stream for Ciudad Bolivar itself.

Tobacco, cereals, horns, hoofs, and hides, with cotton, corn, and rice, great cheeses, poor ill-used pigs, and quacking ducks with fowls in bundles and baskets.

Our heroes were lucky to arrive at such a time, and the landlady, though busy, set aside her best rooms and cooked her best dishes to please the "boy" Miguel, as she fondly called him. The boy had brought his guitar with him, and rejoiced the hearts of many lads and lasses from up country, who had come down with their fathers' wains to buy their dresses and bonnie things, and so go back again happy to the solitude of upland and forest.

Heigho! I fear Miguel was a sad flirt. He wasn't going to play the guitar all the evening, I can assure you. No, he must needs hand the instrument to a friend, while he mingled in the glad, the mad, the merry fandango. Well, those beautifully graceful girl dancers, with their innocent sweetness of face and dark languishing eyes, were enough to make a less susceptive young fellow than Miguel flirt. I cannot say whether Creggan flirted or not—I shouldn't like to say he didn't, but I know he danced, though it was hot work.

Poor Duckling! He was sitting half-hidden in a bank of flowers that adorned one end of the hall.

"I'm too ugly," he told Creggan, "to get a partner. I'll be a wall-flower for one night."

But—think of it—a sweetly pretty girl, after waltzing past through several dances, eyed him many times and oft. I'm sure from what followed that she pitied the poor sailor-boy in his sad loneliness. For presently, fanning herself prettily, she sat near to him.

She peeped shyly over the top of her fan a few times, then summoned courage to say:

"You no can dance—valse?"

He smiled drolly.

"Oh yes, dear, I can dance well. But—but—I think I am too ugly to find a partner."

"No, señor; no, no. A good heart is yours. I see it in your eye. Come, dance with me."

And she waltzed with him almost continually till the poseda closed.

Kind-hearted was she not?

Well, after a few days spent here the yacht was taken over to Ciudad Bolivar, in the neighbourhood of which was Miguel's house. Here dwelt this rich roving lad's mother, and he was the only son. The father had been a man who for many years held very high rank in the country, but the excitement of business and politics killed him at last.

I wish I had time and space to linger over the happy life those young sailors spent for over a fortnight at Miguel's mansion. His little sister—strange to say, she was blue-eyed—took quite a fancy to the Ugly Duckling. It might have been a case of Beauty and the Beast! Some ill-natured beings would not have hesitated to say so, but Natina saw only the boy's mind, and his kindly ways and manners.

She was only twelve. But in her innocence and naïveté she told him once that if he returned in a few years she would love him still more, and that then the *padre* should join their hands, and they would and should live happy ever after.

Creggan had never seen the Duckling blush before, but he did so now. Still, he held out his brown sailor hand and clasped Natina's wee white one:

"I'll come back, Natina, and marry you."

"Ah!" thought true-hearted Duckie, "shall I ever get here again? Do sailors e'er return?"

However, he ratified the agreement in the most natural way possible, and this precocious little lady henceforward considered herself of no small account, being engaged, you know.

Duckie, as his mess-mates often called him, mostly for fun but partly for fondness, measured her finger and promised to send her a ring. I may as well add here that he did, and that the correspondence kept up between them was, on her part anyhow, of a somewhat gushing description.

The temptation to remain longer at this beautiful house, with its terraced lawns, its tropical gardens, in which were fountains through the spray of which rare and beautiful birds dashed backwards and forwards all day long, and with the grand old forest stretching away behind to the far-off Llanos, was very great indeed, but time pressed, and there was yet very much to be seen in this land of delight. As to the parting between Natina and Duckie, I must tell you that Natina cried a good deal in a quiet way, wiping her eyes with her bonnie black hair, and that, woman-like, one of the last things she said was:

"Señor Duckie will not forget his Natina's little ring?"

Ships from all nations call at Ciudad Bolivar, although the population cannot be over seventy thousand, judging from memory. Then, though the streets are narrow in the business parts, Ciudad Bolivar looks charming as seen on a bright moonlight night—as seen from the river, I mean. The stream here makes an inward bend, forming a kind of bay, and is escarped by bold rocks, on which wave a few trees. Then the houses and mansions rise up and up the hill in rows or crescents, till they reach the top, where stands the lofty cathedral.

Creggan and his friend brought from Ciudad Bolivar many strange curios, and at the first chance that offered he sent these home to his mother, and many to Matty, for sailors when far away at sea never forget the dear ones at home.

After dropping down to the mouth of the river Orinoco, young Señor Miguel stood out to sea some distance to be clear of shoals. Then the wind being fair, though light, fires were banked on the little yacht, and slowly along the coast northwards they held a course.

All around here the sea is very lovely indeed—beyond compare.

When at Miguel's mansion our heroes had been startled by a shock of earthquake, accompanied by terrible thunder and lightning, more vivid than they had ever seen before. Miguel made light of it next day. He said it was only a baby-quake, and couldn't have rocked a cradle or basinette.

Anyhow, it seemed to have brought fine weather, and now the sky above and the sea below were both an azure blue, the wavelets sparkling like diamond dust, and now and then breaking into tiny caps of snow-white spray, as the gentle wind toyed with and fanned them.

Skip-jacks now and then darted from wave to wave; blue-black flying-fish, too, flew high into the sunshine, apparently singing *I would I were a bird*.

Sometimes these got on board at night, leaping high towards the lanterns. When Creggan saw them there, he picked them up and threw them safely back into the sea.

"Why should we," he said, "who have so many of the good things of this world, cruelly take the lives of those gems of the ocean wave?"

Shoals of porpoises were common enough, and occasionally a sea-cow with splendid eyes would raise her beautiful sleek, dark head above the water, and gaze long and curiously at the white-sailed passing yacht.

Sometimes Miguel laid to his vessel and lowered a boat, that he and his guests might enjoy a few hours' fishing. And it was fishing, too. The fish seemed as keen to be caught as they were in Duntulm Bay when Creggan, our hero, was a little boy, and this brought back to him sunny memories of days never to be forgotten, so that he often closed his eyes in the bright sunshine that he might think once more of the past, and long to be back again in Skye, the Island of Wings.

A week after this we find our heroes in the yacht anchored in the Caño Colorado—Caño meaning a creek; but in this case, at all events, it really is no creek, but the long quiet mouth of El rio del Guarapiche, a river that, rising afar among the wild hills and forests of the west and north, sweeps briskly on for many a league, forming here and there a cataract, and here and there a broad brown pool, where fishes love to bask in the sweet sunshine or leap gladly up to catch the passing flies.

It is all youth and sunshine and joy with the river at first. Beautiful wild flowers nod over its banks and use it as a mirror, bright-winged birds dip in it as they go skimming through the air, and cloudlands of trees bend down to kiss the gurgling stream. But after many more miles, it goes roaring through dark wild cañons, and is overhung by frowning rocks which narrow and deepen it. The river passes through jungle also, where nightly the wild beasts fight and roar. Then, getting broader now — its happy youth all gone, — less transparent old age seems to gather over its once glad waters, till, weary at last, it glides calmly, softly, into the great Atlantic Ocean.

Miguel landed at the Caño. The young fellow appeared to have friends everywhere, and to be everywhere as welcome as early primroses.

The owner of a property that lay up a creeklet, and had thereon a pretty wooden bungalow, was most happy to see Miguel and his friends. Of course they must stay to dinner, and that meal was one that Creggan could not despise. Delightful curry, most delicious fish, plantains, sweet potatoes, and the rarest of fruit.

And so with talk and song the evening passed away. Then down the creek in the starlight they dropped, and just about

"The wee short 'oor ayont the twal"

everybody was fast asleep — except the sentry — on board the yacht.

On next day towards Maturin.

In no hurry, however. 'Twas best to lounge and dawdle thus, enjoying the *dolce far niente* by the river's green wooded banks, or out amid-stream in the sparkling sunshine.

On shore many times and oft, however, to enjoy the scenery. Once a huge and insolent cayman attempted to seize a boatman where he sat. They were just then nearing the yacht. Almost instantly after the crack of a heavy rifle in the bows of the *Queen* sounded the death-knell of that terrible cayman. Even before the sound had ceased to reverberate from rock to rock, he was lashing the water with his tail like some fabled monster of a bygone age, and dyeing the water with his blood.

Once they landed on the north bank of the river, and after dragging the light boat a long way through a rough country, they launched her on a lovely lake of cerulean blue, that, extending far on every side, looked like some vast inland sea.

Miguel had brought along to-day an extra good luncheon. The water teemed with fish, so sport was excellent. They landed in a little cove,

"O'erhung with wild woods, thickening green",

and there in cool umbrageous shade they dined. Then romantic Miguel, who never went anywhere without his sweet-and-sad guitar, played and sang.

They returned not until the moon was shining high and clear over the mirrored lake. Some hands from the yacht met them in the landing-cove, and the boat was again dragged riverwards.

Not without adventure, however.

Creggan always took with him from his ship a Highland plaid, to be worn at night if belated. He was wrapped in that—happily for him—on this particular evening.

The boat was still being dragged along a terribly rough cattle-track, and Creggan was a little way behind. Suddenly from out the jungle came a roar that seemed to shake the earth, and next moment a huge dark beast sprang high in the moonlit air, and our hero was thrown violently to the ground.

The American lion, his yellow eyes glaring, his red mouth spitting spume, tore at the Highland plaid. But the beast's last hour had come, for with an activity but little less than his own, Miguel attacked him. It was a clear-shining dagger that shone aloft. It descended with a dull thud, and was lifted again wet with red blood. In less than ten seconds the wild beast was despatched.

His skin was taken as a trophy by the men, and presented, after being cured, to Creggan himself. That skin is now lying as a rug in the drawing-room of Creggan's mother's house at Torquay.

Half-way up the river Guarapiche lies the town or city of Maturin. Spanish, of course, with quaintly-tiled or thatched houses, laid out in terraces, streets, and squares.

The people are peaceable enough, though sometimes quarrels ensue in gambling or drinking dens, knives are drawn, and red blood spurts all over glasses, decanters, and counter.

There are many Europeans here, and, I think, they stand by Scotch or Italian. The latter may occasionally draw a stiletto, but Sandie doesn't. Sandie usually owns a fist as hard and big as the butt-end of an elephant rifle, and if a row begins, he finds that fist wondrous handy.

I believe that Miguel never thought anything about the cruelty of cock-fighting and bull-baiting; and at his invitation our young heroes went to see both. They were disgusted with the former, and even more so with the latter. The poor horses are often gored even to death, and on that night our

Creggan and his friends saw one unhappy animal rushing wildly around the arena with—will it be believed?—a portion of his entrails gushing from his side. The only incident of this one-sided bull-fight which the Ugly Duckling really enjoyed, was when a bull picked a fallen matador airily up by the trews—the fellow was on his face—and flung him over into the crowd.

The twisting of the tails of the bulls is very cruel and shocking. The matadors want Britishers to believe that they throw the bull over by sheer strength of arm. Nothing of the sort. The nobler animal throws himself over to avoid the excruciating agony of the twist.

These matadors are, as far as I could ever judge, cowardly fellows, as all cruel men are. I asked one once to have a boxing round or two with me, for love. He excused himself prettily in Spanish, and I think he did well, because there was no hospital anywhere near to carry him to after the engagement.

Well, the time was getting on, flying fast indeed, but to return without seeing the strange, wild, and dreary scenery of the Llanos would have been out of the question.

The yacht was left in charge of its somewhat ragged crew, and the three friends with servants and plenty of arms for sport—well provisioned too—started at last, and after a long, stiff climb found themselves, full three hundred feet above the sea-level, on a wide and open plain.

It extended—oh, such a distance far away to the horizon! The sea itself seemed less extensive than these

"High plains......
And vast savannahs, where the wandering eye,
Unfixed, is in a verdant ocean lost".

CHAPTER XXIV
ON THE LONESOME LLANOS

The vast and lonesome uplands, called Llanos, on which our heroes now found themselves, are the pampas of the far southern districts of South America.

There is a weirdness about them, especially in the silence of the night, that strikes one with awe. But sometimes, indeed, day is more silent than night, for then the stillness is unbroken by howl of wild beasts or scream of birds of prey. So quiet is it then on some portions of the Llanos, that you can hear the sound of the human voice in ordinary conversation full two hundred yards away, while if you wander long here, so great is the strain on one's nerves that the slightest sound will make one start—a tiny snake rustling among the grass, a breaking reed, or lizard nibbling at a stalk of couch.

Humboldt, the great traveller, is not, I fear, much read nowadays, but he speaks about these solitary regions as follows:—

"Here in the Llanos, all around us, the plains seemed to rise to heaven; and this vast and silent desert appeared to our eyes like a sea that is covered with sea-weed, or the algae of the deep ocean. According to the inequality of the vapour floating on the atmosphere, and the alternate temperature of the breezes contending against each other, was the appearance of the horizon; in some places clearly and sharply defined, in others wavy, crooked, and, as it were, striped.

"The earth there seemed to mingle with heaven. Through the dry mist we sometimes perceived palm-trees in the distance. Stripped of their leaves and green feathery summits, these stems, rising out of the low-lying fog, resembled the masts of ships, which one descries on the horizon at sea."

Miguel's little party was accompanied by donkeys; some of these had panniers, on which the luggage or baggage was carried, as well as the general commissariat. But while two of Miguel's sailors trotted on foot, he himself with Creggan and his friends bestrode strong and agile donkeys.

As guides, they had two hardy Llaneros or plainsmen. These fellows are wilder far than your Mexican cow-boy,—who, by the way, is just as often as not a braggart and a coward. But your true Llanero, with his brown skin, his tattered clothes and cow-hide boots, and the ever-ready lasso across his chest, a knife or pistol in his belt, is as daring as a puma or panther itself. He knows no fear, and takes no hurt wherever he sleeps, or however hard his toil and poor his fare.

No need for a traveller to fear these men. Treat them fairly and squarely, and they will do their duty, ay, and fight to grim death for the man they have undertaken to watch and guide.

Our brave youngsters were marching southwards and west, and would so march for days, until, after crossing many a creek and cañon, and many a river that goes roaring, brown and awful, through gorges among the hills and woods, they should strike the River Tigre itself.

One of the rivers they crossed is wildly beautiful—the Mapiriti. They spent two nights and days near to its green banks, and in a bonny wooded and bosky glen. But they had shooting and fishing also.

Night alone was dreary—and dangerous too. To protect the donkeys from the attacks of wild beasts, they had to cut down branches and throw up a kind of laager, for after supper was cooked and eaten, and the fires burning low warned them that it was time to sleep, the cries and roaring of beasts of prey began, and the brutes came all too close to camp to be agreeable. But the sentries—two there were—had orders to fire if they heard but a bush stirring. The quick sharp ring of the rifles generally ensured peace for a time.

Miguel slept on some bundles of grass, with a pillow of the same material. Nor wild beasts, snakes, nor mosquitoes ever seemed to annoy him.

But the Ugly Duckling and Creggan had each a hammock, hung gipsy-fashion from crossed sticks a few feet above the ground.

After Creggan had said his prayers and lain down, he used to promise himself that he would lie awake for some time and think of his far-off Highland home. But he never succeeded in doing so with any degree of satisfaction. The fatigue of travel, the pure, fresh, and bracing air, to say nothing of a good supper, all tended to induce slumber, and soon indeed was he in the land of forgetfulness, seldom opening his eyes till breakfast was steaming and simmering over the fire.

I must draw in my horns, as the snail said to the blackbird; for it was not my intention to give an elaborate account of this great land of Llanos, of broad bright rivers studded with islands like emerald gems, of cayman-haunted creeks, of green savannahs, of waving palms, of deep dark forests surrounding many a lonesome gloomy leaden lake, and of mountains towering to the moon. No; see Venezuela for yourselves, boys. If you do, you can say afterwards that you have lived, should you never visit any other foreign land save itself.

Suffice it to say that, laden with the spoils of the chase, the *Queen* one beautiful forenoon brought our heroes safely back to the mouth of the great river Orinoco, and that their arrival was a scene of rejoicing.

Poor Admiral Jacko was worn and thin, for sadly had he missed his Ugly Duckling, and now sprang into his arms with a fond and plaintive cry, and in his own strange language told him a weary, weary tale.

It was delightful to get home again to the ship after all, and that night, after they had dined with the captain, Miguel being also a guest, our wanderers slept more soundly than they had done for many and many a day.

CHAPTER XXV
PROMOTION

I may tell my would-be or will-be sailor-boys, that time flies fast enough when one is serving in a pleasant and happy ship on a foreign shore. Just a little weariness and longing there may be for the first month or two, then one settles down.

You do not cease to think of home, however. As regards love of home, absence really makes the heart grow fonder. You think of it often and often when keeping your lonesome middle-watch, as you gaze upwards at the star-studded sky, or outwards far across the darkling sea, and you dream of it while rocked in your hammock or tiny cabin-cot; and somehow these dreams are nearly always pleasant. Then again, a dear delight it is to receive letters from home. The next greatest pleasure is in writing them.

Writing letters home, as far as the Royal Navy is concerned, is an occupation one should engage in at all odd moments. The letters should be ready to go at any time, for you never know when a chance may occur. A homeward-bound ship may be sighted and lie to, then aft and forward rings the cry, "Letters for home!"

If the midshipman of the watch or a bo's'n draws aside the gun-room curtain, and shouts "Any letters for England, gentlemen?" and you have not got yours ready, owing to a spirit of procrastination that lately dominated you,—well, you will be ready to bite the tip off your tongue. You will feel just real mad with yourself.

But so many incidents and adventures, to say nothing of duty's strict routine, go to make up a sailor's life, whether young or not, that it is wonderful how speedily pass the months, ay, and the years too, until the "Ordered home" arrives.

Then indeed is there excitement. But once the jib-boom is pointing straight ahead towards our own beloved land, time no longer flies, it abjures the swift, darting flight of the swallow and lags along at the pace of a slug.

Well now, two whole years have passed away since Creggan and his friend made that memorable though all too brief tour in Venezuela with the kindly young landsman Miguel, and it would be difficult indeed to cram the story of all their ups and downs into even a dozen chapters. I have no such intention. In fact, though I tell this story from the life, it is impossible for me to remember all they did or didn't do in that time.

I will just inform you, that at the end of two years they were once more back again at the mouth of the great white rolling Orinoco, and, as history repeats itself, Miguel once more came on board, looking not a bit changed, and once more Creggan and the Ugly Duckling went with him up stream to his mother's beautiful mansion.

This time they intended going no farther, but they were accompanied by dear, kind little Sidney Wickens, and also by their two staunch friends, Hurricane Bob and Oscar.

Now, I must tell you something. Sidney was a genial but quiet young fellow, whose very manner appeared to invite the confidence of his fellows, and when, one evening, nobody but he and Duckie sat together in their little mess-room—this was shortly after their first visit to Venezuela,—the latter had suddenly begun to laugh.

"Oh," cried Sidney, "give us a chance to join you, old man. A good laugh is invaluable, from a health point of view."

"Well, I'll tell you, though I wouldn't tell everybody."

"No? Well, let me hear."

"Then," said the Duckling, "you wouldn't think that anyone so awfully ugly as I am would have a little sweetheart."

"My dear fellow," said Sidney soothingly, "I'll tell you the truth. As to beauty you are not an Adonis, but your manner is so good-natured and pleasant and humorsome and all that, one never thinks about your features. Besides, as a rule girls hate pretty faces on men; that is, sensible girls do."

"Well, but my sweetheart is only a child."

"Tell me."

The Ugly Duckling did, from the beginning of the story down to the parting and the promised engagement-ring.

Sidney was much interested.

Then getting up he said quietly, "I'll be back in a minute."

He drew aside, the curtain and disappeared. Down to his big sea-chest in the cockpit he dived, and soon returned singing low to himself, with his jewel-case in one hand. He placed it on the table, and opened his show of sparkling gems.

"Give me that bit of cardboard," he said, "with the size of Natina's finger in it. Ah!" he cried jubilantly a moment after, "this one will just fit. A trifle large, but her sweet wee finger will grow to it. See how it sparkles! Isn't it just too awfully lovely for anything?"

"But, dear Wickens, I—I—"

"Come now, none of that. If you won't have it, why, I'll keep it and give it to the pretty Natina myself, and so cut you out."

"I shall have it," cried his companion laughing as he stretched out his hand, "But, how can I thank you?"

"By not saying a word. If you thank me I'll shy a bit of biscuit at you. So there!"

Well, on this second visit the Ugly Duckling would not go up stream without Sidney, and they all spent a most happy week.

Of course Natina was greatly delighted with the ring, and just as pretty and affectionate as ever, only she divided her affections most impartially between the dogs and the Duckling.

Miguel gave a party and a dance or play every night. His guests stopped at the mansion, and when good-byes were said at last they were very sincere indeed, and, as far as innocent little Natty was concerned, accompanied by tears.

The *Osprey* had got her anchor up, and started now on a very long cruise indeed—all the way to New Zealand and Australia.

I always think the study of a really good map of the world is quite a delight. It gives one such a thorough insight as to the bearings of his own little land, to the seas and vast continents in other parts of the globe. Geography, I believe, should always be taught and learned in the easiest and most pleasant way possible.

Now, I suppose that if I were to tell you that Cape Horn was the southernmost point of land in South America, and that the ship was now going to coast down and round this stormy cape, you would naturally think her course would lie south all the way.

Not at all. Oblige me by looking at your map.

And now let us sail along in the jolly old frigate.

We leave, then, the mouth of the mighty Orinoco, and instead of steering south it is pretty nearly all easting until we reach Trinidad, the most southerly of all the West India islands, then our course is about south-east and by east till we cross the burning equator and round Cape St. Roque, then about south till we look in at Rio Janeiro.

Rio Janeiro stands next to Edinburgh as the most romantic in situation and surroundings in the world. The city itself perhaps looks best at a distance—well, Scot though I be, I must confess that there are some parts of Old Edinburgh itself that at best will hardly bear close inspection. Rio simply means a river, and Rio Janeiro is the city of romance.

We take a course now with a bit of westerly in it, and in time reach another Rio—the Rio de la Plata. Yonder on our starboard beam lies the great and painfully-neglected Argentine Republic.

Coasting still to the south we skirt the shores of Patagonia.

Somehow we associate everything big and large with this long stretch of wild country. Land of giants, land of the llama and swiftly-bounding guanaco. Land of the lasso, too, and stalwart men on fleet horses that can use it. Not a bad lot of fellows at all, if you take them the right way.

But here we are at the entrance to the Straits of Magellan. No, we are not going through this voyage. We pass between the coast and the lonely Falkland Islands. These islands of the far south are somewhat akin in climate to our Orkneys, healthy and bracing, though the country is subject to terrible storms. It has hills and dells and glens, with many a dark tarn and rippling stream, crowded with fish that are by no means shy. The islands number about eighty in all. The summer is very pleasant. If you and I go there to spend a few months, reader, we'll have excellent sport, and no letters or morning papers to worry over. The Falklands are almost treeless, but that does not signify much so long as one is happy and can eat a good breakfast.

Well, here is Staten Island. Rather different is this Argentine isle from the Staten of New York.

Ugh! how bitterly the north-western winds are howling around its rocks. And see, yonder—summer though it be—its dark gloomy cliffs, home of the penguin and many a strange bird besides, are capped with snow; so, too, are its mountains.

Occasionally now a sea-elephant looks up to stare at us, and now and then a shoal of the ubiquitous porpoises go dancing and cooing past, or a solitary whale ploughs across our hawse but deigns not even to look at us. He or she is intent only on her own business. Perhaps she has a calf alongside her sucking like an overgrown puppy—great, sweet innocent,—and she is taking it north to warmer water.

My conscience!—as they say in the north of bonnie Scotland,—how ships that can only sail have to rough it while rounding the Cape! Snow and fog, icebergs, and sometimes howling winds from the west-north-west!

> "And now there came both mist and snow,
>   And it grew wondrous cold;
> And ice, mast-high, came floating by,
>   As green as emerald."

Yes, green enough as to its sides sometimes, but all clad in deep, deep snow above.

And we now walk the icy decks carefully, blowing occasionally on our half-frozen though mitted fingers. The ear-lappets of our sou'-westers are pulled down, our faces being either blue or white according to the strength of the circulation.

Small pieces of ice rattle along our quarters and bump us, but we care not for that; we do but pray that in the darkness of night we may not foul the fore-foot of some fearful berg. Should we do so, backward our barque would reel and stagger, to sink all too soon in the deepest, blackest sea, that rolls anywhere around this terrestrial ball.

To our starboard, though we cannot see it, lies the terrible island of Tierra del Fuego, literally the Land of Fire. Land of the canoe islanders, the most implacable savages to be met with anywhere. Who is going to take his life in his hand and spend a year in exploring this wild country? Will you come with me, boy-readers? Why, we should make a name to ourselves, if not fortunes. We should come back, if the savages didn't roast and eat us, with a book. We should add much to the geography and the anthropology of the world, and discover—coals.

But our ship is clear away from the black stormy sea at last, and clear of the ice.

So we sail merrily on across a wide and trackless ocean on a beam wind for weeks and weeks, till, hurrah! we are past Bounty Island and reach bonnie Dunedin itself. And here let me tell you, that if there be a single drop of Scottish blood in your veins, you are sure of a Highland welcome.

The cruise described in this chapter is just as near to the life as I can make it, and pretty much what our bold crew of the *Osprey* found it. And the paddle-frigate soon after this came across the new flag-ship for the Australian station. Captain Leeward himself boarded her, accompanied by a lieutenant, leaving the other officers to wait impatiently for his return.

"I wonder," said the Ugly Duckling to Dr. Grant, "if we shall be ordered home."

"Not the ghost of a chance of that, mother's brave and beautiful boy," replied Grant; "but we'll have letters, and lots of further despatches sending us off wild-goose chasing all over the world."

"Well, I like it," said Creggan.

"So do I," said Sidney Wickens.

Creggan was twenty-one now, and a handsome sailor he looked in his jacket of blue, with his budding moustache of darkest down, his bright face, and happy smile that nothing could banish.

When Captain Leeward returned, they soon found that Grant was right in his surmise. There was no "Ordered home", but plenty of despatches for many parts of the world.

There were letters from home. It is needless to say that these were hailed with delight.

But there was something else as well, namely, an order addressed to sub-lieutenants Creggan Ogg M'Vayne and Sidney Wickens to repair forthwith on board the flag-ship and pay their respects to the admiral.

"Something good, I'll be bound!" said Grant. "Ah, you're lucky lads! The Lords Commissioners seldom think of us poor slaving surgeons. Heigho!"

The admiral received them on his quarter-deck with great affability. Then he asked them in to his own quarters and bade them be seated.

"I have good news for you both," he said, "and, not to go about the bush, you are both promoted to be lieutenants.

"And," he added, "you can go home in the $D--$, which will sail from Port Phillip a month hence, and take up your commissions."

Both the young fellows smiled joyously and thanked him.

"Well, sir," said Creggan, "is it absolutely necessary that I should go home? Could you not grant me leave to remain in the dear old *Osprey*, mess in the gun-room, and see all that is to be seen until the paddler is ordered home?"

The admiral laughed right heartily.

"Well," he said, "it is the drollest application ever I heard. What about you, Mr. Wickens?"

"Oh please, admiral, I'll go home."

"Then I grant you leave to stay, Mr. M'Vayne. But I have still better news to give you.

"Commander Flint," he added with that pleasant smile of his, "under whom you served, and whose life you saved in a particularly gallant way, has been moving heaven and earth, and Whitehall as well, to obtain for you the Victoria Cross for conspicuous bravery in presence of the foe. And I think I can assure you he will be successful, so you may look forward, Mr. M'Vayne, to having that grand decoration conferred on you by the hands of our dear Queen herself."

Creggan felt himself growing red and white by turns. He could only blurt out a few words which I dare say were very stupid. But the admiral laid a kindly hand on his shoulder.

"Go on board your own ship now, Lieutenant M'Vayne, and say no more. But you must both come and dine with me to-night. Till then, adieu."

Every man-Jack felt sad when Sidney Wickens sailed for home. He had endeared himself to all. And his mess-mates never saw him more. He was buried, I think, at sea, in the bosom of the blue Levant.

CHAPTER XXVI
ADVENTURE IN A PAPUAN LAKE-VILLAGE

And now, if you will take one further wee glance at that prettily-coloured map of yours, you shall find Australia easily enough. But look at its northern shores, and you will be able to see a great gap there called the Gulf of Carpentaria, and on its eastern shore and point is Cape York, separated from the large island called New Guinea by the Straits of Torres. There! I am teaching you geography in a more pleasant way than you have it dished up at school.

Well, this vast island has never been really or thoroughly explored, for two reasons principally, because the inhabitants—a mixture of Papuans and aboriginal Australians—are never quite civil to white men, and because the climate is moist among the forests or tropical verdure that lies low along the shores, and fever, therefore, always ready to make a victim of the adventurer. But inland, if one gets safely through the regions of damp and forest fogs, will be found many a beautiful hill and dell, quite a mountain-land, exceeding in romantic grandeur some parts of Scotland itself.

It was in 1889 that brave Sir W. M'Gregor explored the island—to some considerable extent. New Guinea, he found, is almost everywhere clothed with rich and highly diversified flora. His party, after passing successively through the dominions of tropical plants, such as the cocoa-nut, sago, banana, mango, taro, and sugar-cane, and of such temperate or sub-tropical growth as the cedar, oak, fig, acacia, pine, and tree-fern, were gladdened in the higher slopes by the sight of the wild strawberry, forget-me-not, daisy, buttercup, and other familiar British plants; while towards the summit these were succeeded by a true Alpine flora, in which Himalayan, Bohean, New Zealand, and sub-Antarctic forms were all numerously represented.

And this was the strange wild island to which the *Osprey* was now to steer. On what business bent I never could say for certain. But I rather think it was to spy out the land; our own half that is, for we kindly and considerately permit the Germans and Dutch to do what they like with the other half. Neither make good colonists; the Dutch are too slow, the Germans too frightened at natives.

These savages are either quite peaceable and industrious, or wild and fierce, with a strong liking for "man-meat" or "long-pig". These terrible wretches like pork, but will lick the backs of their black hands, and declare to you, that there is nothing in the world to beat roast missionary, as a *piece de resistance*, or cold side-dish. The fiercest tribes live among the mountains.

The *Osprey*, with fine weather nearly all the way, reached Cape York, lying in for a few days at the port of Albany.

Then she stood right away north to Port Moresby, where is a British government-station—not of great consequence, it must be admitted. Here the anchor was let go, and boats came off from shore. Our people shook brown, sun-tanned hands with their countrymen, and a hearty welcome was accorded to all.

The blue-jackets were permitted to land in relays, on pain, however, of punishment if they interfered in any way with the Papuan natives. For really Jack's ways with niggers—as he calls all black or even brown people—are sometimes rather free and easy, to say the least of it.

Now, Captain Leeward was fully alive to the quiet pluck and bravery that Creggan and his friend the Ugly Duckling had ever exhibited in the presence of danger, and would have trusted them to go anywhere and do anything. And they were always so willing and cheerful, that it was a pleasure to the captain to let them go exploring whenever so minded. He knew they would not be foolishly rash.

Well, when Creggan and his friend landed, they determined to have a good look around, and even to make a dive into the splendid tropical forest behind the settlement.

They took Goodwin the mate with them for a bodyguard, with one sailor, bold Jack Hing—poor fellow, he was afterwards drowned on the China station. For a handful of coppers they obtained the guidance of a "boy". This "boy", however, was fully forty years of age, judging from appearance. But he seemed kindly disposed, showed a splendid set of teeth when he smiled, and looked generally jolly.

Both Hurricane Bob and Oscar went on this picnic, and how they did scamper around and enjoy themselves, to be sure! But I must add that they sadly frightened the black ladies and children, as the Ugly Duckling grandly called them. They ran shrieking away as soon as Bob's voice sounded along the beach, and hid themselves in the cool darkness of their leaf-and-bamboo huts.

This tribe seemed very industrious. They were allowed but little rum. It is that which turns the ordinary savage into a wild raving maniac, and causes him to run "amok" with knife, or spear, or nulla, slaying every man, woman, or child he meets till he himself is slain.

The people here made pretty baskets, and worked in clay also, even young children assisting. Then Creggan found near to the shore many cultivated fields surrounded by wattling and hedges. In these grew paddy, sweet potatoes, and the lordly yam.

The men, too, went out fishing. There are two species of boats here. One I might describe as a kind of Papuan gondola of large dimensions. About fifteen tons or over. These boats are low in the centre, but sweep upwards at the stern and bows, rather prettily too. Then there is the ordinary dug-out, which is simply a tree-trunk formed into boat-shape by axe and adze, the inside finished off with fire to harden it, after which thwarts are nailed, or rather pegged across. But your dug-out would turn turtle if not fitted on each side with long out-riggers. This dug-out is common also in most parts of savage Africa.

Creggan's guide on this occasion was a very good specimen of his tribe. When you see one grown man you know what the rest are like. The guide, then, was as black as—as—I was going to say soot, but that is really a black that has a rusty tinge in it. As black, then, as the inside of an empty tar-barrel with the bung in.

Well, Ephraim—as Creggan called him, though why I am sure I could not tell you—had, to begin with, such a mop of frizzly hair, that had you turned him upside down it might have been used to sweep the decks with. This hair was black, but intermixed with silvery threads. Both brows and nose were rather prominent. His nostrils were wide, and moved about with every word he said. He was most spirited too, emphasizing every voluble sentence with strange gestures and shrugging of shoulders.

Most of the men seen had their hair and beards stained with reddish clay, but not so Ephraim. He was proud of his gray hairs. His mouth was quite the same as the real African nigger; wide enough to have engulfed an ordinary-sized turnip, and the lips were very bulgy and thick. Armlets, bangles, and ear-rings of brass are common to both sexes.

Little children went about entirely naked. Ephraim's whole suit of wearing apparel could not have cost much anywhere. He had a bit of manilla rope round the waist, to which his sheathed knife was fixed, and to which also was attached what looked like a dirty towel. This was tied to the rope in front, passed between the limbs, and was tied to the rope again at the back. But there was nothing repulsive about this man. He looked bold, erect, and honest; nor would his glance have quailed before the Queen.

His wife, for he had one, was positively prepossessing; and I am really glad to testify to this, for the pictures of Papuans placed before our schoolboys are terrible caricatures.

Ephraim's wife was certainly undressed from the waist upwards, with the exception of bangles and a necklace of teeth, and pretty shells, pink and snow-white. From the waist to the knees she wore a skirt of grass cloth, surmounted by a shorter one of fringed cocoa-nut fibre. She smiled affably and innocently when Creggan spoke to her, showing teeth as white as those of a six-months-old Newfoundland dog, and she glanced upwards at the handsome lieutenant with eyes that were certainly beautiful.

There was something truly good in Treekee's heart, I'm sure, for seeing the dogs pant, she brought a calabash of water, and lying down beside them in the shade of a tree-fern, made them drink from the half of a cocoanut-shell.

Honest Bob licked Treekee's black face to show his gratitude.

That day our heroes had a long tour through the forest with Ephraim and his wife. They had come armed, but did not find much to shoot, so they contented themselves by making a collection of splendid butterflies and beautifully-coloured beetles.

Ephraim got them back by three o'clock. He then proposed that they should be rowed over in dug-outs to visit a lake-village. Their own boat was hauled up safely under the banana-trees. So away they went.

It was certainly the strangest little town that Creggan had ever visited. It consisted of about sixty huts in all, each of which was elevated above the water on strong poles or scaffolding, fully nine feet above the surface.

The walls of these huts were of bamboo, that is, the framework. Over this slabs of pith were placed. The roofs were of grass and plantain leaves, and each was supplied with a shutter, generally open all day to admit light and air, and get rid of smoke. Into one of the largest of these huts our heroes crawled by a withy ladder, while Ephraim returned, promising to be back an hour before sunset.

Well, Creggan was quite astonished at the amount of room inside this lake-dwelling, although the walls from platform to eaves were only about five feet high.

The floor was of pith over bamboo, and spread with a charmingly-worked grass carpet. A fire could be lit, when needed for cooking purposes, on a red-clay hearth at one end. But at present it was out, so the room was delightfully cool.

Their welcome was a hearty one, and as Creggan had brought beads and ribbons and tobacco as gifts, the owner—a fine-looking specimen,—his young wife, and two toddling children were all delighted.

But Creggan, or rather Goodwin, had brought also a bountiful repast. There was quite enough for all.

The chief—if chief he was—nodded significantly to his wife, muttering something that our young fellows could not understand. She immediately arose and put both children to bed in a corner. They didn't require any undressing, for the dear wee black totties, as Ugly Duckling called them, wore nothing save a string of kangaroo teeth.

Then the good lady brought knives and spears, and other implements of savage warfare, and laid them down on the mat on which Creggan and his friends were squatting.

This was an act of good faith, and said plainly enough:

"Lo! you are safe in my hut. Behold I place all my weapons at your feet."

But this chief could talk fairly good English, and he spun some terrible yarns, about the fierce men who dwelt among the wild mountains. He entreated them not to venture there, else they would return "plenty dead, and much bloody".

This was not encouraging, so Creggan thought over a plan he had formed for visiting the hills, and finally gave it up, for a time at all events.

"Plenty bad mountain men. Plenty white men dey makee fat, den roast and gobble up. Brains smashee out wi' one club. Oh, mountain men plenty mooch big fellows!"

"But for all that," said Creggan to his friend, "I should like to go some day."

"Yes," replied the Duckling; "but I wouldn't like to be fed up and killed and cooked—eh, would you?"

"Roast duckling and green peas," said Creggan maliciously. "Come, sing these folks a song, old chap, and you sha'n't be cooked. There!"

The Duckling did as told, and the chief and his wife seemed charmed. Even the children sat up on one end in the corner, and rolled their white eyes in ecstasy.

So the time passed away very cheerfully indeed. But lo! just before the hour for the dug-outs to arrive a squall came on, the water or spray dashed high over the roof of the hut, and when Creggan peeped out it was all a-smother as far as he could see.

They hoped against hope that the weather would moderate, but squall succeeded squall, and soon darkness fell over land and water. It was evident, therefore, that our heroes were prisoners for one night.

Well, your true sailor always tries to make the best of every adventure. They had plenty to eat of their own, and lighting the fire the kindly Papuan lady cooked and placed fish before them on palm-leaf plates.

Then they had delicious fruit—bananas such as you never see in our land, guavas that tasted like strawberries smothered in cream, glorious rosy mangoes, and cocoanut-milk to drink.

They were happy.

More songs were sung, more stories told, and then, with the utmost confidence, our sailor-lads laid themselves back on their mats, using their jackets for pillows, and were soon sound and fast asleep.

Daylight was shimmering in through the crevices of door and shutter when Creggan awoke. The room was hot, so, seeing him wipe the perspiration from his brow, the chief, after nodding a kindly good-morning, opened the gable door.

The water was deeply blue, not a cloud was to be seen in the cerulean sky, and the wind was hushed. Beyond was the beautiful cloudland of forest trees and waving palms, and away on the horizon the everlasting hills.

CHAPTER XXVII
A TERRIBLE TRAGEDY

The others were still asleep.

"No wake," said the chief. "No wake, poor boys. Plenty soon I catchee breakfast. Den my vife she cook. Ah! man-meat no good. Arrack no good. God heself he send de cocoa-nut and de fish. Missional man he tell me foh true."

Then down squatted this strange black man in his doorway, with his legs dangling over, outside. He had a short rod and line, and really the fish required but little coaxing, for he soon hauled up seven or eight big beauties.

These were sprinkled with salt and various kinds of pepper, placed on hot stones over the fire, and covered with fragrant wet leaves. They were soon done to a turn. So were yams and sweet potatoes. Then Creggan asked a blessing, and all declared that they had never eaten a more delightful breakfast in their lives.

By and by a strange kind of chant was heard coming nearer and nearer to the village, and presently the plash of paddles.

Lo! the dug-outs had arrived. So, bidding their kind host and hostess adieu, after filling the children's hands with sweets, they lowered themselves into the canoes and were quickly paddled on shore.

They reached their own ship that forenoon in safety, much delighted with all they had seen and heard, and now, business being transacted, steam was got up, and the *Osprey* went heading away for far northern China seas.

The letters from home which last mail had brought Creggan were very delightful reading, especially those from Daddy the hermit, from his mother, and little Matty Nugent. Nugent's own letter brought him sad enough news, however, to the effect that poor M'Ian the minister had been borne to his long home by his loving parishioners, and that all that countryside of Skye was plunged in grief.

Mrs. M'Ian and her children, Rory and Maggie, had gone to reside in Perth for the better education of the latter. Maggie, or Sister Maggie, wrote a sad little letter to Creggan—it was really blurred with tears, and grief was en evidence throughout every page of it.

The voyage to Chinese and Japanese waters was a very long but somewhat uneventful one. It took them westward through Torres Straits first, then across the bright and beautiful Sea of Arafura, all dotted with little green-fringed islands hung like emeralds on the horizon. Next, across the Sea of Banda, and so away and away past Molucca and Gilolo, till they skirted the Philippine Isles, Formosa, and Loo-choo, then they were indeed in Chinese waters.

But no storm or tempest had marred the pleasure of this almost idyllic voyage, and they reached Shanghai in safety.

Here they met several man-of-war ships, more than they expected to, and everybody had a real good time of it. Some of these ships of war were sent from the East India station hurriedly, their object being to protect British interests in these waters, and north beyond Corea, in the Sea of Japan.

Well, Japan seems, to look at it on a map, only a little, little island compared to that vast tract of land called China, that teems with its hundreds of millions. True, but Japan is civilized. Japan has a splendid army of fire-eating soldiers, and a navy fit to go anywhere and do anything, while China is still wrapped in the mists of heathendom, and ruled by a government as blind as it is ignorant. Foreigners are hated by the Chinese. Hated and hooted wherever they go. The country is two thousand years behind the age, and not even while I write is it yet opened up to commerce.

Well, Captain Leeward learned now for the first time that war-clouds were banking up in the eastern horizon, that the war-wind would blow from the east, and that soon the storm would burst in all its fury over Corea and the self-conceited Chinese.

No one knew the day or the hour when the first angry shot should go shrieking through the air.

It was a season of breathless suspense, like that which thrills the mariner's heart with its very silence, before the down-come of an awful hurricane at sea; when the stillness is a stillness that can be felt, when the very birds are silent and float listlessly on the smooth oily billows, or perch on the fins of some basking shark.

But a vessel was now sent round to Bombay, and here despatches awaited her which she was to carry back with her to the British fleet in Chinese waters.

We were, it must be remembered, quite neutral in this great and bloody war, but I think that the heart of every true-born Scot or Englishman went out towards the brave Japanese, and followed them with intense interest throughout all their glorious career.

I have no desire at this part of my story to be dry and technical. I am never so. I am built, I trust, on the keel of common sense, but I would rather laugh and be merry any day than talk politics, and would rather spin a good sailor's yarn than preach.

But still it will do the reader no harm to know somewhat of the provocation, that the brave Japanese received, before they let slip the dogs of war. I shall let the historian speak, however. The bone of contention really was the great Peninsula of Corea.

"The first complication in Corea," says the historian, "which threatened the peace of the three countries of the far east, happened in July, 1882. Kim-Ok-Kim and other Coreans had been over to Japan. Surprised and pleased at the wonders they had seen, they came back partisans of progress and enthusiastic supporters of Japanese influence. Their ideas were not favourably received by the ex-regent, or Tai-Wen-Kun, who was a hater of everything foreign, and he began to intrigue with the Min, a peaceful faction in Corea.

"It was then decided to drive the Japanese out of the country by violence. The soldiers were infuriated by having their rations diminished, and then malicious reports about the Japanese were spread about the capital. A furious mob began to hunt to death all the defenceless Japanese that could be found.

"A Japanese officer, who had been drilling the Corean troops, and seven others, were murdered in one day, the Legation was attacked and burned, and the minister with twenty-eight Japanese had to fight their way through the streets of Seoul (the capital), and through the country to the sea, where they embarked in a junk, and were picked up by the British gun-boat *Flying Fish*, which took them to Nagasaki.

"The Japanese government at once took measures to obtain redress for the outrage; troops were got ready for any emergency, and the minister was sent back to Seoul with a military force. The Chinese also sent troops to Corea. The Corean government had then to apologize to Japan, pay a large indemnity, and give pensions to the widows and relations of the slain.

"Moreover, Japanese soldiers were now stationed permanently at Seoul to protect the Legation."

China did not quite like this, and she sent a still larger detachment of her hen-hearted soldiers; a soldiery that cannot fight half so well as Newhaven fishwives, an opium-eating, deteriorated race, which but to look at makes one think that the end of the world cannot be far away, or that if these creatures called the Chinese are really descended from the ape—with apologies to the monkey tribe,—they are speedily "throwing back", as breeders say, to their ancestry.

Well, for two years longer things went smoothly enough in Corea, though the Min or old fogey party had all the best places.

In December, 1884, a great party was given to celebrate the opening of the post-office at Seoul. This was more than the Chinese could stand, an attack was made, the party was broken up, and there was a massacre of ministers. The old-fashioned Coreans, dominated by the Chinese, wouldn't have progress at any price. There were now the same murderous riots and scenes in Corea, though on a larger scale, that had taken place two years before, and not only were the Japs attacked by a Corean mob, but by Chinese soldiers also.

A convention was afterwards signed between China and Japan, and it was thought that peace would be permanent, but lo! in 1894, Kim-Ok-Kim, the leader in the awful massacres of 1884, was murdered. The facts are these. After the defeat of his party he had fled to Japan, but now he was prevailed upon to visit Shanghai by a Corean, whose front name was Hung. Perhaps he would have been better hung. But he received great provocation from his highness Kim, for the latter gave him a bogus cheque, for money owing, to the tune of five thousand dollars. Hung returned furious and made his way to Kim's bedroom, where he found the man who had fooled him lying down. He shot him twice, and on Kim springing up and rushing into the corridor, his assassin followed and completed the job. He then fled.

Both these men were Coreans, but till now, at all events, Corea was considered but a portion of China, subject to its rule and sway in every way.

Things went on from bad to worse. Two men nagging at each other usually come to blows, and it is the same with nations.

Japan proposed reforms in Corea, China refused to honour these. Corea was shilly-shallying. Corea was like the fat party who sits between two stools, and ultimately falls with legs in the air. Japan was discontented. The memory of the murders rankled in her mind, and she cared not how soon she drew the sword and went straight for stale old China—China the multitudinous, China the effete.

Then came an attack on the king's palace at Seoul.

While hostilities had really broken out war was not yet officially declared. But that lurid cloud hovering over Corea and the seas around, was soon to burst now, and terrible would be the results.

Next comes a brisk little naval action. Chinese men-of-war had been despatched to Corea, and three of the fastest Jap cruisers had at the same time left Sasebo. I don't want the reader to worry over the names of these, for though to my ear they are musical enough they are difficult to remember.

It was not very long before the Japanese cruisers met the two battle-ships of China, near to the island of Phung. (N.B.—So far as the Chinamen were concerned, Phunk would have been a better name for it.)

Now, although the Chinese knew of the doings in Corea and the attack on the king's palace at Seoul, the Japanese had been at sea for several days and didn't. They were, therefore, much surprised to note that the China captains did not return their salute, and that they had really cleared for action.

"Oh, if that's their game," said the commander-in-chief of the three cruisers, "it is one that we can bear a hand in!"

Now, I don't go in for cock-fighting—dog-fighting is worse, and bull-fighting is terribly cruel; but I must confess that the story of a neat little fight at sea makes my eyes sparkle, and I rub my hands with delight.

I sha'n't say much about this battle, however, but the Japs tried to get the Chinamen more into open water. They meant business. The former didn't like it. I suppose they thought the nearer to the land they were the better. Feather-bed sailors, you see. So they opened fire in a nasty, shabby kind of way.

Then at them went the Japs, hammer and tongs. Oh, it was just too awfully lovely for anything, as the Yankees express it. How the guns roared! How viciously the fire spat out through the clouds of white smoke! How I wish I could have seen it!

Well, boys, in a very short time the *Kuang-yi* (China) was *hors de combat*, and had to run ashore, and the other battle-ship put up helm and fled to Wei-hai-Wei, so riddled with shot that she looked like a pepper-box, while down from her scupper-holes trickled the blood of her wounded and slain.

But the Chinese—who are nothing if not distorters of the truth—spread the report, or rather tried to, that on the whole they had the best of it

It makes one laugh to read the Chinese report of the battle, especially that yarn about killing the Jap admiral. He was on the bridge, says John, when he was shot, and he leapt so high in the air that he turned three somersaults before descending, dead. Well, I have seen many a Chinaman turn somersaults, but Japanese are not so cowardly active and tricky.

But this brisk little action did not terminate here, for it ended in a fearful tragedy, thus. While the Jap cruisers were chasing the Chinamen, two other ships hove in sight. One was a Chinese gun-boat, acting as tender to the British S.S. *Kowshing*. This steamer had been chartered by the Chinese to carry troops to Corea, and had on board about twelve hundred Chinese officers and men, with guns, ammunition, &c. The gun-boat was at once captured, and the *Kowshing* overhauled.

The European officers declared their willingness to return, but the Chinese soldiers rushed to arms. Fools!

The commander of the Jap cruiser, *Naniwa*, ordered the Europeans to leave. They were not allowed to by the Chinese. Then after a reasonable time the Jap cruiser ranged alongside.

Oh, it was horrible! This great ship-load of helpless men was to be sacrificed to the goddess of war.

Hear the roar of the great guns and the swish of the awful torpedo!

An awful explosion follows on board the *Kowshing*, and the vessel is enveloped in black smoke and coal dust. The European officers spring overboard to swim for their lives, amidst a rain of Chinese bullets. Again and again the guns of the *Naniwa* roll their thunders over the sea, and in twenty minutes' time the *Kowshing* sinks.

No less than a thousand went down in that doomed ship. Nor can we altogether blame the Japs, but I do blame that British greed of gain that leads us to carry the troops of foreign nations, and defiantly run blockades. No one can pity such merchantmen when they come to grief.

The sinking of this ship probably went far to decide the future fate of China in Corea, for had these twelve hundred picked men, under the command of a skilful German general, landed in Corea, it would have gone hard with the Japs at Asar.

War was at length formally declared, and soon it raged fast and furious. But in almost every engagement the Chinese, though double, sometimes even triple in numbers, had to give way before the brave and well-drilled Japs.

I have now to relate an adventure of a somewhat extraordinary kind, and very sad in its way, which is more intimately connected with our story than any narrative of the China-Japanese war could be.

CHAPTER XXVIII
"THE BATTLE RAGES LOUD AND LONG"

I do not really know how far the old-fashioned, out of-date paddler *Osprey* could have gone in for protecting British interests. In an engagement, even with a cowardly Chinaman, she would very soon have been paddle-less, and a good shell would have blown her two decks into one.

I grant all this, but the bonnie white flag with its red jack in the corner, that floats astern even on an unarmed man-o'-war officer's boat, is one to be respected, and one that has made many a tyrant tremble and pause thoughtfully, with, figuratively speaking, his hand at his pistol-pocket.

That flag is respected wherever it waves, in battle or in breeze. For behind it, though unseen, lies all the might and power of Britain. Moral suasion is often of more use than Gatling guns, and so here is the *Osprey*, while around her, many times and oft,

> "The battle rages loud and long,
> And the stormy winds do blow".

One morning early, while lying off a Chinese river, it was necessary to send letters to some British families—traders who, with their wives and children, desired to be taken to a place of safety, the Chinese having threatened their lives.

The messages sent were to assure them of protection. They were told to hold themselves in readiness, and that as soon as the weather moderated they would be taken off.

Creggan was sent with this boat—the pinnace,—the Ugly Duckling also, and Goodwin went as interpreter. A good show of marines was also to the fore, and these were to be left with our poor countrymen by the river's brink.

Though the breakers ran mountains high on the bar, there was a gap, and after a long pull and a strong pull Creggan and his merry men got inside. They then hugged the bank, and were at their destination by seven bells in the forenoon watch.

They had come in time, for the Foo-kies, as our blue-jackets used to call the Chinamen, were in swarms, and threatening to fire the houses of the "foreign devils".

I may state here that they afterwards did so, and that our countrymen had to fight for their lives in a laager, till rescued some days afterwards.

Having dispersed the cowardly mob at the bayonet point, and received assurance from the head-man that nothing should happen to the Europeans, Creggan made all haste to join his ship.

They rushed the boat down-stream therefore, and were soon at the gap. Here great caution was necessary, for a boiling sea was being driven in on a high wind to fight with the quick-rolling river.

Alas! they had not gone far, ere a heavy sea struck the port bow and dashed the boat round, broad-side on, to the waves. At the same time three men were washed away and speedily sank.

The breakers rushed over them now, and almost filled the pinnace. To make matters worse, night had all but fallen, despite the haste Creggan had made. Through the mist of that turmoil of breaking water they could just descry the lights of the *Osprey*, and as Creggan had got the boat's head round again, hope once more began to rise in his heart.

Alas for hope in this case! She was speedily struck by a huge wave, and this time turned keel uppermost.

The officers and one man managed to cling to the upset boat, but so terrible was the war 'twixt river and sea on this dread bar, that the boat was sometimes keel uppermost, and sometimes right side up but swamped.

How they struggled for life no one can ever understand who has not been in the same fearful situation.

The sailor suddenly let go hold, and with a wild shriek threw up his arms and disappeared.

Creggan gave all up for lost. All his young life and loves arose before his mind's eye now, and he prayed, as perhaps he had never prayed before, that God in his mercy might spare them. He soon found that he could hold on no longer, but at that moment a light flashed across his eyes, and a cheery hail resounded loud over the roar of the breakers.

He knew no more until he opened his eyes and gazed bewilderingly around.

A surgeon—Japanese—was bending over him, bathing tenderly a wound in his temple.

"This is not the *Osprey*?" Creggan managed to mutter.

"No; your ship had dragged her anchor, and when nearly on the rocks got up steam in time and saved herself by putting out to sea."

All this in perfect English.

"Pray, rest quiet," he continued; "you will be safe and sound to-morrow. This is our flag-ship, the *Matsushima*."

"One word, sir; are any saved but me?"

"Yes, sir; one officer—young, not handsome—and one brave brown man. He would not permit himself to be saved until you and your friend were hauled on board our boat."

How glad was Creggan next morning to meet Goodwin and the Duck. All were fresh, though the memory of the terrible accident lay heavy at their hearts.

The Japanese officers were more than civil, they were the quintessence of hospitality. They would do all they could for our *Osprey* heroes, but meanwhile they were guarding a fleet of thirty transports, under the command of Marshal Yamagata, who was proceeding to Corea to land 10,000 men, 4500 coolies, and nearly 4000 horses.

The Chinese fleet was somewhere else similarly engaged, and the bold Japs were hoping to meet them.

"Ah!" said the surgeon laughing, as he addressed Creggan, "depend upon it, we shall give them battle and blazes both. You shall see how our bold iron-clad navy can fight."

Both Creggan and his companions were delighted.

"If an engagement does take place," said the former, "I greatly fear that we will not be able to resist the temptation to work a gun or two."

"I was thinking," said the Jap doctor, "that as you belong to a neutral nation, I should requisition your services to assist me with the wounded down below."

"Too tame, doctor, too tame; I'm a Scot, sir."

"Oh!" cried the Jap doctor, "I have read your splendid history, and of all your terrible struggles against the Saxons of the south, five times your number. I loved your Bruce, your Wallace, ay, and even your bold Rob Roy."

"If I may speak a word," said Goodwin, "I am equally unwilling to do cockpit duty."

"Well, well, well!" cried the bright, busy little doctor. "I shall address our admiral, and you all shall fight!"

Not as long as he lives will Creggan forget that memorable morning of September 17th, 1894. Both he and his true-hearted friends were up betimes. Time enough at all events to witness the rich and beautiful sunrise. The fleet, in fine order, was off Hai-Yang, in the estuary of the Yalu river, and were now under steam for Tahi Island, when there came a hail from aloft which, though couched in Japanese, even Creggan could understand.

"The Chinese fleet in sight!"

This was at 11.30.

How that shout made the pulses of every man and officer in the flagship, and in every other ship, thrill with joy—

"That stern joy which warriors feel
In foemen worthy of their steel!"

Bustle and excitement followed. Yet not to any very great extent, for in war-time the Japs are like the Britons, "Ready, aye ready".

Now, as far as my knowledge of the battle goes, I think that the fleets were well matched, although the Chinese fleet numbered two ships more (twelve against ten). The Japs had it somewhat in tonnage if not in guns.

But, boys mine, do not let anyone persuade you that because the dashing days of old have passed away, with its ship-to-ship fights and boarding cutlass in hand, men of heart and pluck count for nothing.

Indeed, indeed they do. Give me an admiral as courageous as a lion, smart and clever, and possessed of an eye like a Scottish eagle, with bold captains under him ready to obey every signal, and blue-jackets of the British type on every ship, then I should not care if, in action, the enemy's vessels outnumbered ours. We should capture, sink, or burn them,

"For England, home, and beauty".

The Chinese were well supplied with torpedo boats, and could handle them too, but in manoeuvring they did not show half the skill exhibited by the now cool-headed and calculating Japs.

The battle was almost like a game of whist, owing to the Japanese admiral's far-sightedness. There were also gallant fellows enough to work the signals.

The Jap fleet was divided into a flying and a main squadron. Admiral Ito had one disadvantage to contend against from the first, and I trust we British will not forget the lesson. The ships in his two squadrons were not of the same speed, so that the swift fliers had to wait for the slow.

It would be impossible, without diagrams, to give a correct notion of the evolutions. However, I can refer boys interested in this noble naval battle to books on the China-Japanese war.

It was one o'clock before the two fleets approached on deadly warfare bent. The Chinese in a single line, its strongest ships in the centre, which Ting the Chinese admiral thought would have to bear the brunt of Ito's awful onset.

The flying squadron led the Japanese van, but soon separated and skirted the enemy's right in fine form.

The main squadron also deviated, the bold *Yoshino* leading and bearing the brunt of a terrible fire from the foe. But they outflanked the Chinese thus early, and the Chinese weaker ships, which had been placed at each end, were skilfully riddled, and the *Yang-Wei* was soon in flames.

Ito had meant to sweep right round the left flank of the enemy, and the flying squadron had already ported to do so. But seeing two new Chinamen and six torpedo boats coming up to join, the flying squadron attacked these and they fled.

And now the main squadron swept past the Chinese right, and soon had another of their ships on fire.

It will be seen how pitiable it is to have ships in action of unequal speed, when I tell you that the Japanese *Hiyei* had to lag behind. She was 2200 tons, but, exposed to the Chinese line, would soon have been sunk, had not her brave commander instead of passing along this fearful line of fire boldly dashed through the enemy's centre. Fortune favours the brave, and this vessel escaped even the torpedoes; but alas! when she rejoined her squadron she was in flames. She signalled to that effect, and a brave little ship, but slow, steamed to her assistance. Oh, the pluck of this bold wee *Akaji*! Mind, she was little over five hundred tons.[1] She was chased by a Chinaman double her size, her commander was killed, her steam-pipe destroyed, still she fought like a fiend, and when her main-mast was carried away she hoisted her flag upon the stump. But at last this brave wee Jap set her foe on fire, and the duel ended. The *Akaji* and *Hiyei*, however, were still in great danger, and other Chinamen took up the pursuit.

[1] The *Akaji* has not been reckoned in line of battle, nor the *Saikio Maru*.

Admiral Ito ordered the flying squadron to their assistance, and some terribly hot work ensued at 2.30 P.M. For the Jap called the *Saikio Maru*, was catching it very hot between two fires, while a torpedo boat crossing her bows launched at her two torpedoes, both missing their mark. Down crashed the flying squadron and turned the odds, so the three weaklings of the Jap fleet escaped and got out of battle and reach.

Then the two squadrons swept round the Chinamen in opposite directions. The two Japanese fleets have now closed upon the foe on both sides, and

> "The battle rages loud and long".

It was then that the two flag-ships *Matsushima* and the Chinese *Ting-Yuen* faced each other, and fought the most fearful naval duel of modern times.

CHAPTER XXIX
LIKE A BATTLE OF OLDEN TIMES

The fight between those two splendid battle-ships *Ting-Yuen* of 7430 tons and the *Matsushima* of 4300 tons, was a combat that puts us in mind of some of the battles of olden days, when chiefs met single-handed, and before their assembled armies decided the fate of the day.

It will be observed that the Chinese ship was fully three thousand tons heavier than the Japanese, and she carried more heavy guns too.

But the admiral of the latter had skill and daring and his vessel had far greater speed, for, while the Chinaman could only steam fourteen knots, the Jap could do over seventeen. She had also more quick-firing guns, and no living thing can stand a moment before these terrible weapons of modern naval warfare.

Creggan was stationed in one barbette—the port—and his friend in another, while Goodwin worked a gun not far from our hero.

I have never had a chance of interviewing my friend the Ugly Duckling as to his feelings during their terrible ship-to-ship engagement, but it is not long since I talked with Creggan himself. He describes the battle as a fearful tempest of fire and blood.

"What were your feelings, Creggan?" I asked.

"You mean," he answered, "when we ranged up to fight the Chinese flag-ship?"

"Yes," I said.

"Well," he replied, "I cannot very well tell you. For to begin with, the *Matsushima* had already received her baptism of blood, and I had shuddered to see men mangled out of all shape of humanity by bursting shells, and others borne below, leaving here a limb and there a ghastly arm behind, the blood spurting fountain-like over the faces and clothes of the bearers.

"It might be my turn next, and that of the brave men who crowded the barbette.

"Was I afraid?" he continued. "I confess I was. It was something more than fear that took possession of my soul. I felt a cold terror creeping round my heart, for I had no hopes of life. Such terror as this it must be that a doomed man experiences when walking towards the scaffold with trembling limbs and cold perspiring knees. But I had prayer to support me. I do not know if you will quite understand me, when I say that I could see far beyond the awful din and roar and smoke of battle, see an eye above bidding me be of good cheer, whether death should come or not.

"Every bullet has it billet. Yes, but a bursting projectile in modern warfare has not one billet, but a hundred. The destruction some of these shells cause cannot be grasped by anyone who has not seen it.

"But here is a curious thing. No sooner did the first great boom of one of our guns take place, and our huge shell go roaring away on its mission of destruction, than all fear and terror passed away. I was as exalted now, although calm, as if I had taken a great dose of morphia, such as Dr. Grant once gave me.

"The first shot came from the foe—I mean the first that told. We could see from where I stood the quick, spiteful puff of white smoke and its awful tongue of red fire, and almost at the same time nearly every man around me had fallen to the deck with the fearful concussion as the Chinese projectile struck us almost amidships.

"But now the battle raged fast and furious. Small though we were in comparison with the Chinaman, we circled around, and hardly did we fire a shot which did not tell.

"We soon had the intense satisfaction of seeing the *Ting-Yuen* in flames. A few more of our shots and a torpedo would have sunk her, had not her sister ship, the *Chen-Yuen*, come to her and stood by her.

"The Chinese flag-ship was now unable to work her guns, but if," said Creggan, "my memory serves me right, it was the last shell she fired which worked such fearful havoc on board our poor ship.

"This shell was not only terrible in itself, but, bursting near to a large heap of ammunition, it exploded it, tearing our decks almost to pieces, and killing or wounding about eighty of our crew.

"I myself escaped that time," he continued.

"Yes," I said, "but you have an empty sleeve."

"True, but it was a shell from another vessel that tore away my forearm after this.

"But poor honest Goodwin was rent in pieces. I marked his brave looks but a minute or two before this, next when I saw him he formed one in that awful heap of carnage, when arms, limbs, heads, and bodies were huddled together, with stanchions, broken pieces of conning-tower, all torn up like pasteboard, and the smoke of warfare rising slowly from the bleeding mass.

"Ah, well! so quick was the death, that honest Goodwin couldn't have known what hit him.

"Meanwhile the battle raged on, and it was just an hour after this when I had my own disaster. I felt no pain. There was a bright flash of light across my eyes, that was all; and I was advancing to assist in training my gun, when a comrade flung himself towards me. I was for the moment unaware that I was wounded, but fell fainting to the deck.

"When I recovered my senses, I was lying in the battery with a tourniquet around my arm. I was shortly after removed below, and saw no more of the fearful fight. But I was told that at half-past three we sank the *King-Yuen*, and after this our fleet, which in its two divisions, had circled right round the Chinese, causing them great confusion, hemmed them in.

"The flying squadron passed the *Chih-Yuen*, giving her fits, turned, swept back again, and finally under its terrible fire she heeled over and sank with all hands.

"I may say that the carnage in our tops was fearful. Blood spurting from the dead and dying, and rushing in a red stream adown the masts.

"Owing to their wonderful strength and fourteen-inch armour belts, the Chinese flag-ship and her sister, though utterly wrecked and riddled as to their upper works, continued to float and fight to the end.

"The Chinamen had certainly fought well, but shortly before sunset thought they had had enough of it and fled. Our flying squadron followed, peppering them as they went, but just as gloaming was descending on the now gray sea they were recalled, and thus ended the ever-memorable naval battle of the Yalu river."

This brilliant Japanese victory, reader, had a great effect on the campaign on land.

"Even without it," says the historian, "Japan's military superiority was so overwhelming and China's collapse so complete, that no single event could have altered the fortunes of the war. But the crushing defeat of the Chinese fleet, and the consequent command of the sea held by the Japanese, facilitated all their operations, and enabled them to land their armies when and where they chose, and to conceive bold plans of campaign, which would have been too hazardous without such a naval supremacy."

I must refer the reader who is interested in the subsequent triumphs of Japanese soldiers to books on history. And these are plentiful enough.

One day about six weeks after the fearful fight in which Creggan had lost his forearm, the British paddle-frigate *Osprey* hove in sight, and both our chief hero and the Duckling, who, by the way, had come through the fiery ordeal all safe and unscathed, were transferred once more to their floating home.

They were both very sorry indeed to bid adieu to the brave Japs. Every officer was a gentleman, and had treated them with the greatest kindness.

CHAPTER XXX
COURT-MARTIALED

It would be difficult indeed to say which of the animals was most glad to welcome our heroes on their return.

Hurricane Bob, after a rough canine salute, must go dashing round and round the deck, to the danger of the limbs if not the lives of the honest sailors, flashing his white teeth and his red flag of a tongue in a vain effort to allay his feelings.

Oscar was different, he had so much to say to his master, who was once again soothing and petting him, that he got great-hearted, and whined and scolded and cried by turns. Just like a dog, you know.

But Admiral Jacko confined his attentions almost solely to his master, and his joy was one of fondness, if not effusion. He crept into the Ugly Duckling's arms, and it was said that he really shed tears. But I do not quite believe that, for I am of opinion that man is, after all, the only animal who weeps, or rather woman is. Yes, I have often heard of crocodiles' tears, and what is better still, I have more than once examined the face of one of these saurian monsters who dwell in the marshy interior of Africa, and I have never seen the vestige of a tear about the ugly beast's cheeks.

Perhaps you may say I didn't go near enough.

No, catch me doing anything of the sort, because the crocodile would have played the game of "catch me quick". But I have stood at a respectful distance, and made my inspection through the telescope.

Well, I have never seen a monkey weep.

Having done her duty in Chinese waters, and heard that the Foo-kies had been well thrashed, as indeed they deserved to be, the good ship *Osprey* sailed once more for Bombay.

Thence she was sent down to Zanzibar with dispatches, and from that place to the Cape of Good Hope again.

On boarding the flag-ship in company with poor one-armed Creggan, his junior lieutenant, Captain Leeward was not sorry to find that at long, long last the "Ordered home" had arrived.

It was time; the commission had been a long one, and the sanitary condition of the ship was not everything that could be desired. This was principally owing to the millions of gigantic cockroaches that swarmed everywhere.

There were very many other creepie-creepies on board the *Osprey* as well as cockroaches. Of these latter there were two species, one the little sort, about three-quarters of an inch in length, the other, the true *Blatta orientalis*, two inches and a half from stem to stern, with feelers three inches long, of immense breadth of beam, spiked legs, and an outspread of wing when they flew of about three inches.

Well, there were many kinds of spiders, scorpions, earwigs, an occasional tarantula, whose bite may produce delirium and death, and whole colonies of little ants. But now and then a gigantic centiped would appear, and these are dreaded even more than are snakes.

So on the whole, the *Osprey* at the tail end of the commission offered a fine field for the study of natural history.

Homeward-bound! What joy it spreads over every heart on board a ship, from that of the boy who helps the cook, feeds the pets, and gets kicked about by all hands, to the captain himself, who, if he does not say much, cannot hide the pleasure that beams in his face and eyes.

There is a commander in the Royal Navy (retired), still alive while I write, who was present at the funeral of Britain's greatest hero, Admiral Nelson. This officer might well be called the father of the navy, for he is now in his hundredth year.

Well, had he come on board on Saturday night while the *Osprey* was making her long homeward-bound passage from the Cape to England, he would certainly have considered himself back once more in the dear days of old.

There certainly was not the same amount of tossing of cans, but the main-brace was spliced by the captain's orders, and away forward down below, around the galley and at the fo'c's'le head, many a song was heard, many a yarn spun, and many a heart beat high and warm with the thoughts of home and Merrie England.

It really appeared that the *Osprey* herself knew she was homeward bound.

She was the sauciest of the saucy, "for an old un", as Jack phrased it.

"The old jade!" someone would remark, as she curtseyed to a wave, flinging the spray far over the bows; "the old jade! I believe she is doing it on purpose. Whoa, lass, whoa!"

And some of the songs sung on that Saturday night were perhaps homely enough, but every one of them breathed of the brine and the billows. Two verses, for example—they were trolled by Chips the carpenter, the hoarse old bo's'n putting in a good bass, and some of Mother Carey's chickens piping a tenor as they dashed from blue wave to blue wave after itinerant white-bait—I give below:

JACK AND HIS NANCY.

"Scarce the foul hurricane was cleared,
　Scarce winds and waves had ceased to rattle,
Ere a bold enemy appeared,
　And, dauntless, we prepared for battle.
And now while some lov'd friend or wife
　Like lightning rush'd on ev'ry fancy,
To Providence I trusted life,
　Put up a prayer—and thought of Nancy.

"At last—'twas in the month of May,
　The crew, it being lovely weather,
At three A.M. discovered day
　And England's chalky cliffs together;
At seven up Channel how we bore!
　While hopes and fears rush'd on my fancy;
At twelve I gaily jumped on shore,
　And to my throbbing heart press'd Nancy."

Well, that is all very well in song, but nowadays at all events Jack doesn't get leave to jump on shore at twelve if his ship comes in at seven. Nor for a day or two, or even three. There is a clean bill of health to be got first, and any amount of little matters and morsels of red tape to be seen to.

But Nancy may come on board, and Jack isn't a bit shy at such times. Oh no, I never met a true sailor who was.

I have now to relate a very strange experience that befell Creggan and his friend the Ugly Duckling.

The ship had not long lain at anchor off the Hoe, when, after a deal of signalling from the admiral's office, Captain Leeward, with a strange smile on his face, came up to the place where the two young officers stood looking over the bulwarks at the crowd of shore-boats, and passing many a quaint and humorous remark.

Seeing the captain, they turned and saluted at once.

"I regret to inform you, gentlemen," said Captain Leeward, "that you are both prisoners. Don't be afraid; it will be a mere formality, I am sure. Meanwhile, I must do my duty. You are on parole, if you give me your word you will make no attempt to leave the ship."

"Oh, certainly, sir. But—may—may I ask you what we shall be tried for?"

The captain laughed now.

"Why," he answered, "only for assisting the Japs against an enemy with whom we are at peace. Keep up your hearts, boys. I sha'n't put a sentry over you, but just give up your sword, Lieutenant Creggan Ogg M'Vayne, and you, young sir, your dirk, to the officer of the watch."

I have no desire at this end of my story to describe the formalities—solemn enough in all conscience—of the court of inquiry.

That sword of Creggan's and the Ugly Duckling's dirk lay side by side on the green-baize-covered table, surrounded by officers in fullest uniform, and the two prisoners stood between marines with fixed bayonets, near one end of the table.

Neither of the young officers denied anything, and when asked what he had to say in his defence, Creggan replied:

"Nothing at all, except that I wear an empty sleeve in commemoration of the grandest naval battle of modern times. But I must add that I would do the same again, for it isn't in British human nature to stand by with finger in mouth while battle is raging round."

There was much grave conversation after the prisoners had been withdrawn, and finally they were ordered in.

"I dare say," whispered the Duckling to Creggan a minute before this, "it will be a shooting case. Heigh-ho! what will become of poor Jacko, and I'm sure my sister will break her heart!"

But to their joy, when they returned looking pale and anxious, the sword and dirk were handed back, and they were told that they left the court without a stain on their character.

There were positively tears in the eyes of both young fellows as the officers shook hands with them.

The admiral of the port invited both to dinner that evening. He was as anxious as anybody could be to hear a personal narrative of the great sea-fight.

I may mention here as well as elsewhere, that before Creggan went back to his mother's house at Torquay he received the Victoria Cross from the hands of Her Majesty herself, and for such an honour as this I believe the bold young fellow would have been content to go through far more than he had done.

CHAPTER XXXI
SAFELY HOME AT LAST

Yes, after all their tales and adventures, our heroes are once more safe on British ground. What says Dibdin?

"No more of winds and waves the sport,
Our vessel is arrived in port;
At anchor, see, she safely rides,
And gay red ropes adorn her sides.
The sails are furl'd, the sheets belay'd;
The flag that floats astern display'd,
Deserted are the useless shrouds,
The lasses row aboard by crowds.
Then come, my lads, let joy abound,
We're safely moor'd on English ground!"

It only remains for me to "muster by open list", as we say in the Royal Navy.

Let me say a word or two, then, about my *dramatis personæ*, and so clue up.

There are always a few surprises awaiting the sailor when he returns home after a long cruise. Jack looks forward to these with some anxiety, as the ship is getting nearer and still more near to the chalky cliffs of Old England. He thinks himself a very happy man indeed if these surprises turn out to be pleasant ones; which, alas! they are not always. Some dear one,— father, mother, wife, sister, or sweetheart, who ought to have come out in a shore-boat to meet him, is missing.

But there are friends alongside to bear him the sad tidings.

She is dead! He is dead!

And poor Jack had been so expectantly happy for days and weeks before this! He had entirely forgotten that there was any such thing as death in the world.

Look at his sadly bewildered face now.

"Courage, Jack, courage!" says some brave mess-mate with a tear in his eye. Jack returns the pressure of the hard yet friendly hand, but—goes down below to weep.

As soon as the *Osprey* was paid off, and he had bade farewell to his mess-mates, Creggan, accompanied by his dearest friend the Ugly Duckling, took train for Torquay.

He did not even telegraph to say he was coming. The two arm in arm, after paying off the hansom they had chartered, sauntered up the terraced garden and rang the great hall bell.

Ah! but Matty herself had been watching. A lovely girl she was now of sweet seventeen.

The meeting of the lovers, for lovers I now may call them, was heartfelt and cordial; but Creggan did not venture to kiss her.

Then she spied the empty sleeve, and, girl-like, burst into tears.

"Ah, never mind, dear!" said Creggan soothingly. "See what it has brought me—honour and glory, and the Victoria Cross."

"Oh, Creggan, Creggan," cried Matty, "the poor arm was worth a thousand Victoria Crosses!"

"Oh, it wasn't for that I got the Cross! But how do you come to be here, Matty?"

"Oh, I've been living here for months. Just keeping your dear mother company."

"And where is mother?"

"She has gone into the town. She will be home soon. You will have time to tell me quite a deal before she comes."

The Ugly Duckling, with Admiral Jacko in full uniform, had been standing at some little distance, but now Creggan beckoned him forward and introduced him.

"My dearest friend and shipmate, Matty."

The Duckling bowed, ship-shape and sailor-fashion; so did the Admiral.

Matty was laughing now right merrily.

"I'm sure," said his master, "Admiral Jacko would make a speech if he could. I must make one in his stead. Well, Miss Matty, I can't help saying what I think, you're just about the sweetest, all-tautest little craft I've seen since I left Venezuela, and if I were not engaged to be married, why—I'd—I'd run my friend aboard, cut him out, and marry you myself."

Matty bent down over Oscar to caress him, but at the same time to hide her blushes.

"Well, I'm going to take Jacko inside," said the Duckling. "I'm sure I shall find something for him to eat, and something to drink."

And away he marched, which was really very kind and thoughtful of him.

Then hand in hand down through the shrubbery and rose lawns went Creggan and Matty. Ah! —

"There's nothing half so sweet in life
As love's young dream".

Creggan felt almost too happy to speak. But he did speak at last, and from all I know he told the old, old, but ever new tale.

"Now tell me, Matty," he said after this, "how your father is. You have said my mother is well."

"Yes, and dear old father too. But he is much in London now."

"And Willie?"

"Oh, that is why Daddy is in London. Willie, you know, stood for the borough of Blankham, and was duly elected. Weren't we all so happy just? And I've been to the strangers' gallery myself, and saw Willie in his place. And really he looked by far the nicest there. I only wonder that—"

She paused.

"That what, Matty?"

"That when he rose to make a speech they coughed him down."

"Exceedingly rude!"

"Yes, but they did; and Willie got so red in the face, and I thought he was going to cry. But he just took up his hat and was going to leave, when a kind-faced gentleman with long white hair put a hand on his shoulder. I don't know what he said, but Willie went straight back to his seat and sat down again."

"But you haven't said a word about my Daddy the hermit, and I hope he lives."

"Not only does he live, Creggan, but he has left Skye and his lonely island, and has come to settle down close beside us here. He dines with us every night."

"How delightful!"

"The minister says he is clothed and in his right mind."

"Poor old Daddy, he always was in his right mind."

"Ah! but you should see how nicely he dresses now. You would take him for some reverend old professor. You will see him to-night."

"And Archie M'Lean?"

"Still in America, and I think will remain there for years. They say he is making money, and that he means to come back and marry Maggie."

"What, Maggie M'Ian?"

"Yes."

"Heigh-ho!" sighed Creggan. "I feel getting very old."

Matty laughed right merrily. "Poor old sailor!" she said roguishly. "But, oh, look, here comes Daddy himself!" And so it was.

Matty might well have said he looked like an old professor. His hair was long and gray, and he was dressed in broadcloth. Yet there was no sign of age about him as the glad smile of surprise brightened his face, and he hurried up with both hands extended to greet and welcome Creggan home.

"My own dear sailor boy!"

He could say no more just then, and like Matty took refuge in the caresses he bestowed on Oscar.

Yes, Oscar knew him well after all these years, for dogs never, never do forget the dear ones they love.

Need I add that the meeting betwixt Creggan and his mother was a happy one? Surely that is unnecessary.

The Ugly Duckling and Admiral Jacko were declared to be prisoners for three weeks.

"But my sister, madam!" was all the former urged against his imprisonment.

That objection was quickly set aside, for Creggan's mother sent for her, and she joined the jolly party at "The Pines".

Years have gone since then.

Creggan has retired, of course. One-armed sailors are not considered available for active service.

But it is only a few months since our hero led Matty to the altar, a bonnie, bonnie young bride indeed.

And the Ugly Duckling, who has also retired, having come into some money, is now master of a beautiful barque (clipper), and she is all his own.

He took the newly-wedded couple down the Mediterranean on a long honeymoon. This was all the more jolly because the hermit himself, with Oscar and Admiral Jacko, were of the party.

And so the story ends.

Oh no, not quite; I must let the Ugly Duckling have the very last word.

He and Creggan were sitting together on the quarter-deck while sailing down the blue Levant, and while the stars, so lustreful, shone above them and were reflected from the sea, it was in answer to a remark of Creggan's that he spoke.

"Yes, dear boy," he said, "I'm going out to Venezuela soon, and if Natina still loves me, she shall be my bride. For who but romantic Natina could think of giving her heart and hand to so ugly a duckling as poor me?"